Agenda: Ebola

by

BJ Creighton

Center for Disease Control Scientist Gunn Shoreham discovers the source of an Ebola epidemic in the Mideast is American bio-terrorism. Apparently the terrorists can spread the disease wherever they wish.

Table of Contents

Prologue

Scientific American article, "Time to worry about anthrax again," discusses Soviet and Russian bioweapon programs and how anthrax can be weaponized.

Wall Street Journal headline on 28 February, 2017: "World Health Organization: New drugs needed to fight pathogens." Item is from Reuters.

Washington Post headline on 18 February, 2017: "Bill Gates: Bioterrorism could kill more than nuclear war — but no one is ready to deal with it." Article by Avi Selk.

New Scientist headline on 21 January, 2017: "Incurable infection." News item about a strain of Klebseilla that is resistant to all antibiotics and killed a woman in Nevada.

CBS News headline on 13 October, 2014: "As calls for Ebola *czar* grow, where's the surgeon general?" Article by Rebecca Kaplan.

Chapter 1 – Day 1, Wednesday

Atlanta, Georgia. Last Spring.

"Honey, there's an Ebola case in Israel," Pauline Shoreham called from their bedroom, where CNN ran on the TV. "Don't you want to come watch the news?"

Gunn Shoreham sat in his home office in the next room. A photograph of a young girl and a vial of seashells she had bottled for her Grandpa were on his desk. Gunn's sleeping black laptop sat on the side table. He put his hand over the mouthpiece of the old phone and called back to his wife. "There can't be Ebola in Israel. Some dumb-ass reporter got something all wrong. They're all big liars, as our big boss would say." He put the phone back to his ear and swiveled in his chair so he could feel the cool air coming through the open window from his backyard and see the red hibiscus in the glow from his office lights. "Tell me again about your project, Mele Mele. Grammy said something and I didn't hear you."

"Grandpa!" Mele Mele used the voice usually only acquired by teenagers, the one that shows infinite disapproval and exasperation. "What did you say? You used a naughty word."

Only once had Gunn heard such distress in Mele Mele's voice, that was when her pet cat, Raoul, died. He wondered if she learned showing disapproval using the overly dramatic tone from his daughter. Jeanne Anne hadn't used it until her teen years. He rubbed his eyes and saw the cute ten year old scowling at him, sitting with her feet tucked under her in the peacock chair they both loved.

"Oh, darling you're right. That was a bad word."

"If Mommy heard me say that I'd be in my room for a week. And I can't even think how bad it would be if Daddy heard it." Mele Mele sounded like she was lecturing a group of her classmates.

"Someone on the television upset me, but I should never say things like that, Mele Mele." Gunn shrank in his chair. He still had trouble using her new Hawaiian name. She insisted on it. He hadn't goofed and reverted to *Amber* yet.

"I think you're awesome and Mommy says you only talk like that to the television. She thinks you're awesome too. Well, she really says, if there's no television, you're fit."

His son-in-law, Major John Dalton, had bought the rattan chair for Jeanne Anne, but Mele Mele had immediately adopted it. He visualized the view of Manoa Valley from Mele Mele's living room through the glass wall behind her seat. John's posting to Pearl Harbor had taken the family to Honolulu, about as far away as possible, at least within the U.S. Worse, the marine's temporary duty took him to Baghdad, or somewhere over there.

Gunn smelled the flowers outside his study. Mele Mele's house would also be full of hibiscus aroma. "Thank you for the kind words. I try, but I need to stop with all bad words, even to the television." He shouldn't use them at work, either. He didn't talk like this when Jeanne Anne was young and shouldn't talk like an off-the-record politician now. He must stop and must also distract Mele Mele from thinking about what he said. "What did you have for lunch, Little Monkey?"

"Pizza. Mommy brought home one of those sourdough pizzas."

Gunn visualized an Hawaiian pie. A pineapple and sausage pizza. They were popular in Atlanta. Did Hawaiians love them too?

"They're interviewing the doctor." Pauline called from the next room. "Don't you want to come listen?" Pauline did not mis-report facts, even after a long weeknight party with an open bar. An open bar that all partners and associates in her law firm were expected to use liberally.

"Mele Mele, your Grammy told me to watch something on TV. Your pizza sounds yummy but I have to go. I'll try to be very good. Give your mommy an extra hug and kiss from me, okay?"

They exchanged goodbyes. He pictured his granddaughter climbing the pandanus tree in her front yard. His graceful little tomboy always seemed part monkey. Or was it grand-tomboy. He patted the phone on its cradle and ambled into the bedroom to listen to the news.

Gunn made an exasperated expression at the TV. He was a doctor at the top rung of the government service ladder at the Center for Disease Control and Prevention, and the CDC's leading expert on hemorrhagic diseases. He knew more about the etiology of Ebolavirus than anyone, anywhere. The first human case in an outbreak could usually be traced to a chimp or bat. The later ones were mostly direct human to human transmission. Typically, direct contact with body fluids from an infected person or corpse, at home or in a hospital. The Israelis didn't have an Ebolavirus or a primate research lab. How could some Israeli have eaten or been in contact with an Ebola carrying monkey? She must have been in West Africa.

There are some half dozen families of hemorrhagic fever viruses and about a half dozen in the Ebola family. All the types that infect people have high mortality rates and most start with easy to misdiagnose, malaria-like symptoms. Ebola is the hemorrhagic virus that captured the public's attention, but there were several others, like Hantavirus in the Four Corners states of the Southwest, and many more that had never been known to infect people. Primates rarely survived for more than a few days with any Ebolavirus. The disease showed itself after an incubation period of a few days or weeks. A gruesome death followed within days for most sufferers. Many internal and external organs oozed blood. Despite two decades of study, containment and treatment, Gunn hated what Ebola did to its victims. And his job was to be sure it never came to America. Maybe. His new boss seemed to think their job was to contain information, not diseases, in the absurd belief the facts would create a panic.

The television blabbed, "... there's no reason for panic because hemorrhagic fevers aren't spread by casual contact. Nevertheless, we are interviewing the sick woman's relatives, friends and business contacts to locate the source of this disease. But again, let me emphasize that these viruses cannot be spread by any sort of casual contact." The doctor on the television wore a suit but no tie, as he spoke to a cackle of reporters. He droned on, apparently to prevent tourists from fleeing. Israel must still be profiting from the last dribble of Easter pilgrims.

Gunn blew some obscenities at the television. "He should point out that no hemorrhagic fever has been known to spread even by being in the same room as a sick person. He sure isn't likely to placate Americans and Europeans with wishy-washy crap like that."

Gunn looked at the crowd behind the doctor. He wondered if he'd see any of his medical acquaintances. No one looked familiar. Most hemorrhagic fevers have never infected people, so this might even be a new disease. Tel Aviv ebolavirus, if it was new. That would make it really interesting.

"Well, he's got the first part right," Gunn growled at the television. "She probably was in West Africa recently. Or maybe some stupid bastard misdiagnosed her or mis-reported the whole incident."

The CNN report continued, "Viewers are warned the film we are about to show contains graphic medical scenes of flesh eating viruses..." The screen warned of shocking footage to follow. Pauline left the room.

"The reporter's really fucked up. There are no flesh eating viruses —they're all bacteria."

CNN showed stock footage of an Ebola victim. The black-African corpse had bruises over most of the body and blood oozed from the mouth and nose. The eyes were open and bloody. The body appeared to be in an African hospital, probably from the West African epidemic that finally ended in 2016. Gunn muttered more obscenities at the tube.

When the victim footage ended, Pauline returned. "That doctor you heard? Before you came in he said the victim hadn't been out of Tel Aviv for months. He also said he's never seen or heard of anything like this before." Pauline spoke in a conversational tone. Gunn knew she adopted it to avoid inciting him. She wasn't patronizing him. She came up behind Gunn as he sat in a leather wing-back chair next to their bed and massaged his shoulders. She ran her slender fingers through his dark blond hair. "Your muscles are hard as baled cotton. Is something bothering you?"

"No, I'm fine. Just tired. 'Cause of your party and 'cause it's so damn late."

"This Ebola thing is under your hide, isn't it?" Her voice was seductive, belying her words. "Hmm, but you mean there can't be an Ebola case in Israel?"

"Yeah. Not for someone who's never left the country. Can't come from someone who's asymptomatic and that person would've been diagnosed by now. Only way for her to get Ebola is someone flies in, gives it to her, then returns to Africa right away for his bloody death." Stupid sons-a-bitches. Israelis didn't even send docs to West Africa for that humonguous outbreak because they were afraid of this fucker. "It's all a bunch of horse turds."

"Is John in any danger?" She rubbed his deltoids with her thumbs. More gently than a real masseuse.

Gunn smiled at her in the mirror beside the TV. "Not from Ebola. Probably not from any virus, but even an Ebola outbreak throughout the region and spreading into Baghdad, would only endanger people in contact with those already sick." Gunn kissed Pauline's fingers on his shoulder and rubbed them with his cheek.

He stood, gave his shapely wife a hug then sulked out of the bedroom and returned to their study where he logged onto a CDC news-feed. No mention of hemorrhagic fever in the last few hours. Because of the late hour, maybe the site hadn't been updated. He googled "Ebola Israel," Wow. 108,283,000 hits. The first several were breaking news reports of the story on the tube. None of the URLs looked authoritative so he tried googling "Ebola Israel CDC" and found only old stories in the first couple of pages. What if there's actually something to this. Nah. Can't be. It's all as crazy as a leavened matzoh.

Chapter 2 – Day 2, Thursday

Atlanta, Georgia

Gunn awakened and slowly rolled over and kissed Pauline on the cheek then edged from bed to avoid awakening her. He enjoyed the sound of perking coffee. The aroma wafted from the Cuisinart. He was dressed when his radio turned on and "Morning Edition" started. The lead story was the "Ebola" case in Tel Aviv. He did not omit his decade old ritual—a cup of coffee in bed for his pretty blonde wife. He did skip his usual bowl of old fashioned Quaker oatmeal, with its ten-minute preparation time, for Post Raisin Bran. He hurried to leave for the office, with a full cup of coffee in his electric travel mug.

First order of business: call Moshe Eisenberg and find out what's really happening. Then, he better get out a press release to fend off the probable calls from bosses, politicians and reporters. Especially bosses. They'll be asking all sorts of dumb questions.

A news item will intercept a few of the calls and save some of my time palavering with reporters and peons about this nonsense. And maybe I can dispel at least one myth about viruses. Whether the news report is accurate or not, this was a chance to spoon feed a tiny bit of biology education to the public.

I-85 traffic was lighter than usual. What a great way to start the day, coming into work 30 minutes early. Gunn smiled at the Bach filling his S-

Class Mercedes as he drove south in the middle lane at exactly the speed limit. He told himself to remain calm, even when the "Ebola Outbreak" embroiled him.

Ten minutes later Gunn walked into his office. The only items on his desk were the telephone and photos of Pauline, Jeanne Anne, and Mele Mele. He connected the computer to power and network cables and checked his email. He opened his calendar and waited for Adobe to start so he could read a pdf attachment. Dr. Toshiro Ikeya had scheduled a meeting with him for 8:00. Josh was never in that early, must be about the Ebola news. Better hurry.

Gunn dialed Dr. Moshe Eisenberg at the Israeli Ministry of Health in Tel Aviv. Instead of Moshe's usual cheery "Shalom" the gruff phone greeting said, "Shalom, higata lemisrado shel Dr. Eisenberg medaberet Pasha." A Hebrew greeting he didn't know or at least could no longer recognize.

Gunn figured, some gatekeeper to get past. "This is Dr. Gunn Shoreham calling Dr. Moshe Eisenberg. Dr. Eisenberg and I have worked together many times over the last three decades since we were in graduate and medical school together. We recently coauthored a paper on reverse transcription virus sequencing." Gunn spoke slowly and made a special effort to enunciate clearly. He hoped the guy spoke at least a little English. Moshe said they all do. At least that should get some action.

"Please wait here." Sounded Slavic.

Where does he expect me to go? He visualized Moshe's desk with three piles of unread journals and several trays of unopened mail. Snail mail was useless for Moshe and even email chancy. Moshe might answer it or might lose it. How can such a disorganized slob do the kind of quality lab work he does? Gunn visualized a Gorbachev look-alike on his way to get Moshe with his dark curls going every way, a sort-of dark-haired, fat Harpo Marx.

Moshe was built like a Georgia Bulldog tackle and had tried every diet known to man or medicine. Gunn had liked having him along whenever he visited a tough neighborhood in Boston during med school. Moshe, the white bread and pastrami dieter, had never met a blintz he didn't like.

Still on hold, Gunn clicked on the press release to look at it again and Word crashed, taking his document with it. "God damn fucking crummy computer," he yelled at his empty office. He hit the keyboard with his fist.

"Hi, Gunn. Glad to hear from a friend. You scared the shit out of Pasha. What'd you say to him?"

"Oh. Hi, Moshe. I told him that we were old friends." Gunn realized he sounded mad. "I'm sorry, Moshe. I didn't mean to yell at you. My computer crashed, a moment before you picked up the call. I tried to beat my document out of it."

Gunn calmed. They exchanged a few pleasantries and asked about the health of each other's families. "Mele Mele, that's Amber's new name, is doing pretty well considering John went on TDY." Shouldn't use an acronym with Moshe. "Her father's temporary duty has him at the American Embassy in Baghdad for the next month or two.

After a few seconds of small talk, Moshe said, "I've been here at the office for almost ten hours with nothing but a couple hand fulls of pistachios. I'm exhausted and probably not coherent. I was about to call you about the sick woman, the one the TV insists has Ebola, when you beat me to it. What do your news reports say?"

"The damn reports here are saying *Ebola*, too."

"Well, I'm not sure she has Ebola or that she hasn't been out of Tel Aviv in months," Moshe said. "It's still a complete mystery to us. The press and some opposition politicians have incited the Ebola diagnosis. I'm pretty damn sure she has a hemorrhagic fever and it looks like a strain of Ebolavirus. But, hell, who knows for sure. I keep telling the reporters and politicians it takes days for a conclusive diagnosis."

"Damn, this is fucking ridiculous for a zoonotic disease. When'd she dissect a monkey? Is it legal to eat them? Is that keeping kosher?" Gunn was Jewish by ancestry but apatheistic about religion and agnostic about diet. He walked around his office at the limit of his phone cord and looked out at the Atlanta morning. The stop-and-go freeway traffic hid in Atlanta's trees.

Israel might know it was a hemorrhagic fever, but the analysis to identify the specific strain, if it wasn't in the CDC library, was way off for anyone. This is bullshit. It has to be bad reporting. No way there's a human Ebola we haven't seen. Is there?

"I knew you'd call if I didn't beat you to it. I want your analysis so I FedEx-ed some tissue this afternoon. The samples should be in Atlanta tomorrow morning. I'm afraid that if I waited, Mossad or your Homeland Security would veto the transfer. The package is all legal. It's double sealed and clearly labeled as containing bio-hazardous materials, I haven't done anything to tie it to the case here or to the press reports. And I addressed it to you with no Specimen Submission Form."

"Good idea. I'll check on your package and make sure it gets through to me and get the analysis started right away."

"Thank you," Moshe said.

"Oh, shit. You reminded me when you mentioned Homeland Idiocy. There's some big project for those bastards. They are tying up lots of our resources." Gunn's image of Moshe in a rumpled, blue suit with a white shirt but no tie evaporated. It was slowly replaced by a tree full of baboons in TSA uniforms who slowly morphed into howler monkeys yelling, probably at him.

"Will you be able to look at our slides?"

"Yeah. Those Homeland Insecurity jerks think they can boss us around. It'll slow us down. I'll get on it as fast as I can. I may not have full time or resources to devote to your samples."

"Thanks for your help."

"Thank *you* for the samples, Moshe. I *will* get to them right away." Gunn scratched his chin and put a note on his calendar about the package. He had to learn about this bug before people started asking about it. Bosses, reporters, politicians. They would all be after him soon.

"Anyway, I got to go." Moshe groaned. "I'm already late for my next meeting."

"Looks like it'll be a bad day here too." Armed with a full cup of coffee, Gunn went to Dr. Toshiro Ikeya's office. Josh, as everyone called him, dressed in his trademark blue pinstripe suit. His profuse black hair perfectly combed so he looked every inch a doctor, as professional as Gunn but unlike most of the younger scientists. His office smelled of Old English furniture polish from his daily dusting.

Gunn sat on the dark wood and soft green leather-seated chair. He stroked the cushioned leather arms. Always felt nice.

"Gunn, did you hear the report about Ebola in Israel?" Josh

fumbled with something on his computer.

Gunn liked working for Josh, an old friend and coworker. "Yeah. I think it's a crock. Probably shitty reporting. Hate to admit that Donald Trumpet is right about The Press. But reporter error seems likely. I've started work on a press release about Ebola and hemorrhagic fever viruses so we can straighten out the Press and maybe teach them a little virology." Gunn's drawl might hide his sarcasm from some, but he had worked with Josh for so long there would be no misunderstanding.

Josh stopped typing and looked up. "In this case we better tread slowly. I spoke to one contact I have in Israel and he says this looks serious and they don't understand it. Amhach must have received some similar message because he called me to watch the news before I was up this morning." Dr. Billy Bob Amhach, Director of the Center for Disease Control and Prevention, was the incompetent political appointee. Appointed by the Tweet-in-Chief, or was it Twit-in-Chief? The one who didn't know the difference between a "liar" and a reporter whose emphasis did not match the ego-in-chief's desires.

Gunn noticed Josh spoke slightly mechanically, like a reporter. He looked at Josh. His dark brown eyes looked tired; there was no indication of sarcasm or humor. Josh wore a Harvard tie today, as he did about once a week. Did the wake-up call from Amhach mean that some around-the-clock monitor had alerted the director during the night? Maybe he was called by some peon in Washington who had to prepare a report for the TiC. "I spoke to Moshe Eisenberg in Tel Aviv. How much do you think there is to these reports?"

"My contact seems to think there may be some substance to them." Josh scrunched his mouth. "He's nowhere near as connected as Eisenberg. What did you find out from Moshe?"

"He said the symptoms all pointed to a HFV." Gunn pronounced the acronym for hemorrhagic fever virus *huff-vee*. He frowned slightly and nodded as he tried to accurately describe his call. "Moshe was aware of the obvious inconsistencies and said most of the Ebola reports came from the press or opposition politicians trying to embarrass the government."

"Sounds like here, doesn't it?" Josh growled, almost out loud. "Be sure to run anything that might get to the public past me. I don't want Amhach to have a cow."

Gunn knew that Josh held no admiration for Dr. Billy Bob Amhach. The new Director was Josh's boss. Amhach may have been a great family doctor, but his only qualification to head CDC seemed to be loud yelling and contributing to Donald's campaign fund.

Gunn took the request from Josh as an order and thought about the wording of his press release as he returned to his office where the phone was ringing.

He answered his phone to an acquaintance from a start-up biotech company in Virginia, Charles Maçon.

After introductions, Gunn explained the message he'd left. "I tried to reach you last week to let you know about an RFQ. I thought you'd probably bid on it and hoped the extra lead time might help on your proposal." The CDC regularly issued requests for quotation when it needed to purchase equipment. The advance notice was like giving vitamins to a baby—it might help and it almost certainly would do no harm.

"Thank you. You've always been a friend. I was out of town and got your message yesterday."

"How is life at Virein?"

"We're struggling, as usual. There are still only two of us. We're about as healthy as anybody at Providence."

"That's too bad. Wish you were doing better. The RFQ is for a protein synthesizer. It will be out in a couple of weeks." Gunn was far enough removed from the procurement that he felt legal discussing a future request for quotation. Once it was officially announced, he wouldn't be allowed to talk about it. He would not even be allowed communication with any potential bidders, not until the bidding closed.

"Thank you. I don't even know if there's enough left of Virein for us to bid on your machine. Used to be our main revenue stream, too."

"That's sad. I hear it will have a small business set-aside. I guess that still leaves lots of competition." Gunn shook his head. He imagined Charles Maçon in black jeans and a rumpled bulky red sweater. All this work for Homeland and Ebola has us swamped. We need more equipment.

"Enough of that cheery talk. I also called to thank you for your support on our synthesizer. I wanted to let you know we have a contract from DARPA that keeps us alive. We're back to filoviruses for them." The Defense Advanced Research Agency funds all sorts of way-out research and is best known for funding the networking technology that led to the Internet, often overstated as claiming that DARPA, or even Al Gore, had invented it. Charles spoke as though he were describing an upset victory by his favorite team. "They like our ProteinBlaster because it allows us to create such broad-spectrum vaccines. I'd be completely happy if we had a bit more money so I could hire some techs. But the work's lots of fun for the two of us."

They talked shop for a few more minutes before Gunn begged an impossible schedule. "By the way, will you be down for the bio-tech entrepreneurs meeting next week in Chapel Hill?" Gunn asked as he was about the hang up.

"Hoping to be there. It's on my calendar. As usual, depends on money and conflicts with the crap here."

"Hope you can and do make it. Nice to see a known face." Gunn hung up and thought about the earlier call.

Damn the wait. Got to have Moshe's package. Wish tomorrow would hurry up.

Chapter 3 – Day 9, Thursday

Atlanta, Georgia

Gunn sat in his burgundy wing-back chair, burnished its leather arm with his grip, and stewed about the "Ebola" lab work while CNN went through interminable, but muted, commercials. He wished for ad-free TV. Moshe's blood samples flunked the antibody test for Ebolavirus. Ninety-six negatives for hemorrhagic fever viruses including four filovirus families. Five days of testing and the polymerase chain reaction test had yet to find a match. What is this stuff?

The CDC in Atlanta had both a library of hemorrhagic fever viruses and a start on the RNA analysis of the virus. Reporters would be asking questions about the origin of the outbreak and whether it was a terrorist act. It wouldn't be long. A half-dozen cases, and in a developed country. The infection rate was faster than in West Africa. Perhaps a couple of dozen cases within a few weeks.

The RNA analysis would eventually identify the specific virus strain. The analysis would probably tell them where the victims had contracted the virus. Eventually. RNA analysis is almost identical to DNA analysis, but usually faster because RNA molecules tend to be smaller than DNA's. Ebolavirus is an RNA virus.

Eight days after Pauline had called Gunn for the initial "Ebola" story, he watched the late television news, unusual for him. Pure dumb luck that Pauline had caught the news of the case in Tel Aviv last week. Her firm's partners' huge donations to the President's campaign coffers, opened the door to a judgeship and hence the party. Gunn and Pauline came home so late, the news gave him an advance warning of the nascent epidemic. Thank God it had provided extra time to prepare for the virological and reportorial onslaught.

The Mideast was quiet tonight, only the usual car bombings and killings of soldiers and demonstrators. The internecine war that had been going on for thousands of years. Arabs versus Arabs. Arabs versus Jews. Troy VII fell 3200 years ago despite support from half the World's powers in history's most famous conflict, the Trojan War. Just one *war* in their never-ending series in the Eastern Mediterranean. Must have been six before that. Why else would it be Troy seven?

Only a little after seven in the morning in Tel Aviv. It would be hours before CNN had any of tomorrow's news about the Israeli hemorrhagic fever outbreak. He turned off the TV. With Moshe's help the Israelis would contain and identify the virus, probably before he did. Their head start and less interference from security gave them a substantial edge. He would confirm their diagnosis, whatever it was. Soon they would be able to complete sequencing the virus. They would produce a list of its 19,000 or so letter structure. Like the rungs of the DNA double helix ladder, the bases make up the rungs of an RNA virus's ladder. They precisely describe each variant Ebolavirus.

Gunn picked up the telephone to call his granddaughter. When his daughter answered the phone he said, "Hi, Jeanne Anne. I called to talk to Mele Mele. I've turned off the news. I won't swear at it. Promise."

"Dad, does Mom know you're calling younger women late at night?"

Gunn admired her accusatory tone. "You should have been an actress." They had a good laugh. Gunn admitted that talking to her and Mele Mele were the high points of the day.

"What do you hear from John. He okay?"

"He says he's perfectly safe in the old Green Zone, but I'll worry until he's back. Thank goodness it won't be so long this time. Oh, and he said to tell you how much he loves and misses your bread. Nothing like it he can find in Baghdad."

They exchanged some more family news before Jeanne Anne handed the phone to her daughter.

Mele Mele described the songs she learned in her ukulele lessons. After a performance of "Hawai'i Aloha" she described her science project with an actual working volcano. "I made a model of Mauna Loa that has a soda bottle in it. I'll put coke in the bottle. Then, when I describe it to the judges, I'll dump some Mentos in it and poof."

Gunn thought about filoviruses. The electron-microscope images made it look like a long pieces of string with a fancy knot at one end. He realized Mele Mele had described her project. "How does that work?"

"I told you, Grandpa," she said with the exasperated tone that all kids master. "You can see a zillion of them on the EepyBird.com website."

"Oh, yeah. My mind wandered. I forgot."

At the end of their talk, he again asked about the volcano model. Mele Mele showed her irritation as she repeated details about the Mentos and coke eruption. Gunn asked her to give special hugs and kisses to both her parents for him. "I'll give Mom a hug," Mele Mele said, "I can't give Dad one 'cause he's in Baghdad."

"Oh, yeah. I forgot. That damn deployment."

"Grandpa! That's a naughty word."

"Oh, dear. You're right. I wish your father were there with you. I'll try to remember." Gunn banged his head with the heel of his hand. At least this assignment should be much shorter than his last tour.

Where had the virus come from? The patient must have been lying or delirious. She'd died five days after the world first heard about her, four days ago, so no more history from her. She suffered the rapid, gory death that was typical of unsuccessfully treated hemorrhagic fevers. No surprise. She had not been diagnosed in time to save her. But where the hell did she get it?

The Tel Aviv Medical Center had tried to preserve her privacy and dignity, but a number of pictures of her face shortly before death had circulated. They showed blood drooling from her mouth and oozing from her eyes and nose and huge blood-filled blisters on her left cheek. The

RNA held the origin of the virus. Its story was written in her blood. Eventually, they would tease the message from the slides in CDC's refrigerated safe.

 #

Gunn had nightmares of a hemorrhagic fever in Honolulu. Blood oozing corpses doing the hula. Zombies surfing. They chased John, Jeanne Anne, Mele Mele and Raoul, their cat.

Morning Edition awakened him. He groaned at the thought of the day's sectarian violence reported by NPR and the night's viral violence reported by his subconscious. He felt more tired than when he went to bed seven hours earlier. Steve Inskeep's voice came from the radio to ensure that Gunn kept his appointment with misery. "Our next report from Soraya Sarhaddi Nelson will fill in details on the lead story about three new Ebola cases in Israel."

What lead story? What's going on? He looked at the clock radio. *Oh, God. I slept through the first round of news. Steve Inskeep made me dream about ghouls.*

Gunn tried to make up the time from oversleeping by dressing quickly. He sprinkled brown sugar and put a half-dozen pecan halves on his Quaker Oatmeal, sprinted through his morning rituals, and headed to Clifton Drive. Forty-five minutes later he logged onto his computer at work and telephoned Moshe Eisenberg. "Okay, tell me about these new cases of *Ebola*, as the radio and TV here have been calling them." Gunn scrolled through the new email that hadn't been filtered into Trash. He read only the subject and sender lines and deleted half of his inbox emails, ones that his spam filter missed.

"We haven't gotten a fix on the virus yet," Moshe said.

"Us neither. But from the electron micrographs it's a filovirus for sure."

"Six people in Jerusalem and now two in Haifa," Moshe said. "We still have no idea of the source. We've started family interviews, but haven't found any connections between these people. They're not even all Jews; one's a Palestinian."

Even for a cautious scientist who never blurted out answers to questions, Gunn answered slowly. "We've got to catch this damn bug. Right now it seems to be doubling every five days, not each month like the '14 epidemic." Gunn banged his knuckles on his forehead. "God that wipes out Tel Aviv in three months."

He nodded at his computer screen, marking time. "Oh, I see you sent me some email."

"Yes. It should explain it all too," Moshe said. "Have you made any progress on your RNA analysis?"

"Where'd you get the idea that we're doing an RNA analysis on the virus?" Gunn leaned back and vacantly stared at a copse of dieffenbachias in the pot next to his window.

"Gunn, I've known you for what, 30 years now? You think I don't know what you're doing? Gimme a break. I know you'll localize the strain of virus. I'll bet you're comparing it to all the hemorrhagic fever viruses in your collection. And, I'll bet you're sure your CDC collection is the World's largest."

Gunn took his cell phone from his attache case. He studied it and the view out his window. He thought about the spying games and espionage discussions they'd had at Harvard. "You know, I feel sick. You better call me at home." Gunn gave Moshe his cell phone number. "Please call in five minutes." With the cell phone in his pocket he headed for the ground floor. As he walked across the CDC lobby, the phone in his pocket announced "Call from … Eisenberg, Moshe." Gunn gave Moshe a call back number and asked him to use a public or alternate phone. "I've been getting in trouble from that political hack upstairs. Talk to you in a couple of minutes."

In a small room near the main entrance, outside CDC security, he answered the conference room phone. Tapping of a public phone in an interview room like this one seemed unlikely. Well, not really unlikely, but unlikely to be tied to him. No doubt the National Security Agency would have a recording of the call in Fort Meade, but not Amhach. He hoped. Sad that pay phones had virtually disappeared. At least this would be better than his cell phone.

Gunn picked up the phone on the first ring. "U.S. CDC," he said in a high-pitched tone.

"Hi" was all the greeting, but in a familiar voice.

"Of course you're right, but we don't have any positive results yet. Homeland Security's hindering the genetic analysis. They claim they have to prepare for the flu pandemic so they're tying up lots of our people and machines with some cockamamie avian and swine flu virus studies."

Moshe and Gunn devised a circumspect way to discuss the Ebola cases. The bird flu virus family interested epidemiologists and DNA analysts in both countries. It provided their code word for the hemorrhagic fever viruses. H5E1 would be their code word for ebolaviruses, H5D1 for the Dengue family of hemorrhagic fever viruses, H5L1 for the Lassas, and so on. As they finished the short conversation, Gunn said, "Do you want a Ready Team to come over?"

Moshe replied almost as slowly as Gunn. "I can't believe we'd ever officially admit we need help."

"Okay, so that's too big and obtrusive. I can put together a small, inconspicuous team. Would a two person team be acceptable and helpful?"

Gunn could see Moshe twirling his hair on his finger. "I think that would be better and yes, I think it would be helpful. As long as no politician hears about your people, and they shouldn't." There was a long pause. "Yeah, we should be okay."

"Glad to know Israeli politicians are as much a pain in the ass as ours. I don't want our presence to arouse suspicions either. Don't want to unsettle people any more than they are. Any ideas on how we can avoid notice?" Gunn took his Cross pen and a small notebook from his shirt pocket.

"There is a small avian flu meeting next week at The Technion. In Haifa You could use that as a cover. That would also make our coded phone conversations seem even more innocuous, in case anyone does monitor them."

"It's not *in case* it's *when*," Gunn muttered to himself. "You've got it." Gunn spoke in normal tone. "Sounds perfect. I'll put a travel request together as soon as I get back upstairs. Don't know who my partner will be." Gunn started a list in his shirt-pocket notebook of the paperwork hassles he would have for a trip outside the U.S.

"No one at the conference will expect Americans, but I don't think you will surprise anyone." Moshe's voice sounded confident.

"Yeah," Gunn said slowly. "Is it an international meeting? Do you expect many non-Israelis?"

"European. But you won't raise any red flags." Moshe confirmed Gunn's hope. "Some South Asians have been invited. You'll fit right in. Nobody'll notice you."

Gunn hesitated a moment. "Hope to see you in a day or two. Make sure no one else finds out we've been talking and thanks for taking the precautions this time. If those bastards on mahogany row find out about this, they'll demand my ass."

"See you soon. I just wonder when you'll learn not to antagonize the brass."

"Probably not until I retire."

#

Back in his office Gunn prepared the travel authorization request. Trips outside the Continental U.S. are closely scrutinized by auditors and hence by bosses and boss's bosses. He had to be sure all foreign travel costs were exact and fully justified. He checked air fares and timetables, the conference late-registration fee, and lodging. He mumbled to himself about the complexity of CDC's foreign travel regulations and international travel pricing. He lamented that senior scientists had to make their own travel arrangements, a cost saving measure dating back a few administrations. "How the hell is it cost effective to have a 150K-a-year scientist spend two hours making travel arrangements instead of having a damn $50,000-a-year agent do it in one hour?" He yelled at his computer while he waited for a Delta schedule to download. The Government pays tens of dollars more on my ticket, even though they think its tens less, and wastes $500 of my time. Stupid. And my wasted-time guess is probably optimistic.

In his travel-request memo Gunn pointed out, "Two of us will not arouse any suspicions among the Israeli bureaucrats or politicians. I expect their doctors will be open and informative with us. In Haifa we will be in a good position to visit the Israeli Ministry of Health without drawing any attention to our visit. Because the conference topic is a virus, the team could inconspicuously assist the CDC's monitoring of the hemorrhagic fever outbreak."

He suggested Dr. Ian Powell go with him. Ian was a young researcher who had shown a flair for fast lab work when he solved some similar genetic puzzles.

Gunn was uniquely aware of the political, religious and cultural barriers that sometimes prevent cooperation and he had the most comprehensive understanding of hemorrhagic fevers of anyone in the U.S. He scanned the form and added a note. "Dr. Powell will need a full cash advance because he returned from a colloquium in Rochester, Minnesota, only a few days ago."

Ian had put himself through medical school at the University of Georgia. In four struggling years he had run up huge debts. Adding to his financial burden were medical bills for his wife. Soon after their marriage she was diagnosed with APL, a rare but fairly curable form of acute leukemia. He couldn't be expected to have money, even to pay for incidentals on the trip.

At noon Gunn sent the request package to Josh Ikeya and to the Center's Director, Dr. Billy Bob Amhach, who had to approve all overseas travel.

When Gunn returned from lunch he found an email note from Amhach who thanked him for the alert on the conference at The Technion and informed him that Powell and Dr. William Hiccock would represent CDC. *What do you expect from a political hack. Damn Republican.* A new note from Ikeya, "Please come see me, Josh."

He went to Dr. Ikeya's office. It was sparsely decorated with family mementos. Might be cluttered by Gunn's standards, but no one else would think that. Josh Ikeya asked him to close the door and motioned for him to take the leather upholstered chair beside his table. "Dr. Amhach worries that you lack tact and are not very diplomatic. He won't let you represent us in an area that is as potentially explosive as the Mideast."

"This seems as important an analysis as any, Josh," Gunn said. "What do you recommend? How can we stay on top of it?" Gunn's body language and tone contradicted the insubordinate words of his question. Because Ikeya was a career CDC doctor, he would know that both Gunn and the CDC had a real need for information. And Ikeya was a team player and would be privy to Amhach's biases as well as Gunn's. Ikeya managed by wondering about, an MBWA advocate. Amhach was more of an MBHIH type—he hid in his hole. Gunn felt sure Amhach was intimidated by his CDC staff doctors, nearly all of whom had specialized research training that Amhach didn't understand, probably couldn't understand. Idiot.

"I know I'm asking a lot, but I hope you'll try to stay on top of everything. Give Ian and Wild Bill direction and make sure they're able to do a great job."

"You know I'll bust a hump for them. I'll do everything I can. It's sad we have to leave something this big in the hands of some dumb-ass politicians."

Ikeya avoided eye contact as he said, "Thank you, Gunn. I knew you'd help."

"Damn political hacks." Gunn shook his head.

Gunn looked back up at Ikeya. "I'll brief Ian and Wild Bill on the situation in Israel. I hope they get in enough doors to understand the outbreak. At least they'll get to know some of the people at the J. Silver Research Center and in the European H5N1 community." Gunn's tone of voice and body language confirmed his distaste for the situation.

He worried that he sounded negative. "I'm sorry, Josh. My low enthusiasm is because I don't think this'll work. I'll do what I can—you know that. I suspect the important senior people at Ministry of Health will find ways to avoid any junior people. They're very class conscious. The fact that Ian and Wild Bill are American may elevate them one notch on the class totem poles, but not much more. A visitor's status at home will never escape the Israelis. Can you imagine if some junior visitors came here and tried to see Amhach? We'd never say no, we'd stall and waste their time."

"You're right, Gunn. Do what you can, please. The political situation here may improve. I'm on your side." Now Josh was back to his normal tone. He made eye contact and moved his open right hand as though dealing cards with his palm up.

Gunn thought about management styles. When there were dolts at the top, installed by the administration only for political loyalty, even the most competent civil servants were in danger of losing their jobs for failure to toe the administration line. A practice directly contradicting the basic intent of the Civil Service System.

With science gone, what does the U.S. have? He'd expected the Center to return to good practice and hire for competence, when the administration in Washington changed, but the Great Recession had prevented CDC from hiring many of the bright and dedicated doctors. Political lethargy and bickering slowed the search for a competent replacement director, and now they had even more unqualified management.

Gunn moped back toward his office. When the stairwell doors closed behind him, he smashed the bare concrete wall. "Damn this is ridiculous," he bellowed. "Damn it," he mumbled. "I have to stop swearing for Mele Mele. No more *damns.*"

Gunn pounded his fists on his desk. "Gotta ID this crap Moshe sent." He looked at his computer screen. No email on Moshe's samples.

Gunn needed a break from the Idiot. He left after lunch for the drive to the Bio-tech Entrepreneurs Association meeting in Chapel Hill. Maybe he'd find some RNA analysis tools or machines that weren't busy.

Chapter 4 – 11 September, 1987

CM in Greenwich Village

Long before the Israeli outbreak, at a time when the Ebola hemorrhagic fever virus was barely known, CM worked in his study with the window open. He had borrowed two books from the New York City Library about cell structure and chemistry. When he couldn't understand one, he turned to the other. His fellowship required excellent grades in every microbiology course. Knowing the material before class helped him through college and should in grad school.

He heard the door close. Must be Françoise. He studied a diagram of a virus infecting a cell in both books, but his sister's whimper interrupted his concentration. He grabbed a bag of licorice from his desk drawer and followed the faint crying noise. She sat on their couch, head down. Her jeans were dirty, something she never let happen. "What's wrong?"

"Jason tried to force himself on me. I kept saying *no,* but he wouldn't stop. I don't know what got into that monster." Françoise's arms were scraped and she had dirt on her face.

"That big creep. Thinks he's God's gift to women."

"What's it take to get him to leave me alone?" Her eyes were teary.

"Don't know." He tore open the candy bag and held it out to her. "Maybe if I talk to him." The only thing that bully understands is being beat-up. He poured Françoise's hand half-full of candies and sat beside her.

"He taunts me about hiding behind you." She shook her head. "Thank you for the Twizzlers, Candy Man."

"Well, he loves his car more than any person. Maybe I can get through to him that way." CM had taken a class on bullying and knew that bullies often flew into their targets with a rage that terrified everyone—the target, would be rescuers, bystanders—everyone. Maybe he should adopt that tactic and pummel Jason. No. It would never work, would it? Jason is too big, strong and athletic for me. Or is he? Can he be the bully-ee?

CM picked up a brick in the alley behind their apartment, set it down and found a broken piece. He took a deep breath. Too bad I can't duplicate this stink in his car. The combination of garbage and exhaust permeated the alleys of the Bronx. The chunk felt rough and uncomfortable in his hand. It was heavy enough to smash a car or face, but light enough he could easily handle. He also put two hefty round rocks in his pocket and walked toward the café where Françoise worked. Sure enough Jason's red Ford convertible was there. He wondered how easy it would be to get new glass for that old car. The top was down but the windows were up. He walked over to the car with the brick in hand and hit the passenger window as hard as he could. The glass broke and crumbled onto the front seat.

In only a couple of seconds that seemed like minutes to CM, Jason ran out of the coffee shop. "What the fuck are you doing? Are you fucking crazy?"

"Yes. I am fucking crazy and if Françoise even sees you again, your car will be totaled. If anything happens to her, no matter who did it, you're a dead man." CM held the brick in his hand and eyed the big athlete. "Think the Pros want to talk to a rapist?" He briefly considered the jerk's too-tight jeans and tee-shirt, the focused on his ugly face.

He ran at Jason and swung the brick at the bully's face. Jason parried the blow and wrenched CM's arm behind his back so hard the brick fell. Jason spun CM around punched him in the face twice in rapid succession. One jab hit him in each eye. CM fell backward and fumbled for the rock in his pocket as Jason jabbed him once more, squarely on the nose. "That's for my fucking window."

"If Françoise has any, *any*, trouble from you, you won't have a fucking car to have windows."

#

Françoise put some makeup on her brother to hide the bruises that were starting to appear all around his face. "Jason's car is worth more to him than his face. No number of black eyes would bother him and I couldn't give him one, anyway." CM winced and closed his eyes. "I'm going to go after that fucking LTD of his. If he ever gets close to you, let me know. I'll fix the car so he knows I'm serious."

"If he catches you, he may really hurt you. Don't do it."

CM didn't know if Françoise was serious or not. CM had promised their father he'd protect her. "I'll do it at night. I can disguise myself with some of your stuff. Nobody'll be able to identify me, not even on security cameras. Or maybe I'll take some germs from our lab and you can feed them to him."

"It's not worth the risk." Françoise shook her head in dismay. "I know you promised Daddy you'd take care of me. If he'd known he was going to be killed he wouldn't have asked for the promise. It was only talk to him."

"I'll get some bacteria or virus or something that you can put in his food if he comes in again."

Chapter 5 – Day 10, Friday, Evening

Chapel Hill

Gunn always felt a little uncomfortable at the Bio-tech Entrepreneurs Association because all the entrepreneurs were about Jean Anne's age. Actually, mostly younger. More grunge than gray.

He knew that CDC contract information and insights would help some members land CDC research grants. It was one way he could help these struggling scientists. Many of their companies were surviving week to week, often barely able to meet payroll, or maybe not always meeting it. Some of these BtEA guys would probably become billionaires from their work. They were the ones people would read about and remember. Most of their companies would wither and die. Their principals would be forgotten, at least this part of their work would be forgotten.

And then there were the Charles Maçons of the entrepreneurial world. The ones who had good ideas but bad luck and never managed to really get their companies going. Gunn hope Charles would be able to speed up the RNA analyses he had to do. Charles had one of the few private labs with the equipment for the analysis.

With the exception of Gunn with his yellow name tag and some attorneys and accountants with green ones, everyone of these young people with their white tags would either be millionaires or working elsewhere within a few years. He smelled the testosterone and end-of-day office aroma that was typical of any late-day meeting. The air had a gritty taste, probably from all the dust stirred into the air by the milling people. Gunn searched the throng for friends.

A six foot two guy in a neat black polo shirt came up to Gunn. His shirt exhibited his musculature and his white name tag identified him as Dr. George Austin, President of ProteinGen. The scowl he wore contradicted his unusual floral scent. Though he must have showered before coming, his 'tude hadn't washed away. He looked about 25, probably a recent grad. "Do you know why we didn't win one of the SBIRs last fall?" His slight lisp made him sound like a snake. He spoke each of the letters in the initialism for the Small Business Innovation Research grants from federal agencies.

"I couldn't tell you, Dr. Austin." Gunn felt uncomfortable with no tie and in a group of scientists half his age, even in his dark blue suit. He'd left the tie in his Mercedes with his pistol and opened the top button on his pale yellow shirt. Gunn recalled seeing one of the BtEA founders walking around with scissors cutting off neckties, or at least threatening to do so. Ties were an uncommon sight at these meetings. Nothing he could do about the age difference, but Gunn fit in a little better wearing a jacket but no tie. "I am rarely involved in proposal evaluation. Did you request a debriefing?"

"Yeah, but they didn't really tell me anything." Austin moved so his face only a foot from Gunn's. "I'd like to find out the truth." He spoke slowly the hiss in his voice increased. He stared directly at Gunn's eyes.

"Sorry. I can't help you." Gunn tried to sound sympathetic. "Oh, I have to meet someone." Gunn pointed toward a man in a red and black sweatshirt coming in the door.

"You're no more damn use than the friggin debriefing." Austin was practically shouting, at least it felt like shouting with his face only a foot from Gunn's. "You haven't told me a thing I didn't already know."

"Sometimes you have to slither into a win. I see Dr. Maçon came in and I have some work to discuss with him. I do hope you have better luck next round. SBIRs *are* very competitive, and there is a *lot* of luck as well as skill and capability in winning one." Gunn pronounced the program name "sibber," as most government employees and other insiders do, and used it for the program and its grants and requests for proposal.

"I bet you can't even give me any advice." Austin's voice had moderated a little. "Can't you do anything to help a guy?"

"Be sure your proposal addresses every item in the request and to submit many proposals. Title a subsection for every buzzword you see. Each procurement's a snakes' nest. You have to try many times."

"That may help a little."

"Don't use a rifle, shotguns are needed for SBIRs."

Austin looked puzzled and about to start shouting again.

Gunn frowned. "Sometimes the group's interests change after the notice is written so the evaluator is looking for something other than what he specified in the RFP. That means it may help to maintain contact with the actual people soliciting proposals. I'm rarely one of them. Keep trying and good luck."

Gunn pushed through the crowd away from Austin toward Charles Maçon in his rumpled clothes. When Gunn reached Charles, he said, "Sometimes I feel completely out of place at these meetings, like a cough at an AMA meeting. A young doctor assaulted me. He was mad at the CDC, and probably at me, because he did not win a SBIR."

"Bummer." Charles Maçon usually attended the BtEA meetings in Chapel Hill a few times a year. "I'm dying of thirst from the damn drive into Reagan and the plane ride down. Mind if I get a beer."

Gunn nodded and they worked their way toward the bar. "At least the guys who always lose proposals go out of business. Let me buy you a drink. Looks like Bud is the choice of beer." He put an elbow on the bar and turned to face Maçon. "I'm sure I'm as dry as you after the drive up. Let me pay for both of us." Gunn turned toward the bartender and put an Abe in his tip jar. "A struggling entrepreneur shouldn't waste his money on me." Gunn motioned towards the taps to ask Charles if he preferred regular or Lite. The bartender said he only had one red wine, which he showed to Gunn. With a nod Gunn accepted the Vendage Merlot, a poor substitute for the Cabernet he'd requested.

"But you can't bury wine on *your* expense account." Charles had won Small Business Innovative Research grants from Gunn's Center for Disease Control and Prevention and from the National Institutes of Health. His work was more innovative than most people who responded to CDC SBIRs. He seemed to always find new ways to look at problems and he had the facilities to work on some dangerous pathogens.

"True. And I wouldn't try." Gunn looked at the Merlot. "I'm not sure this is wine, anyway. All you can say about it that it *is* dry, red and wet." Gunn unbuttoned his jacket. "If I buy for you there will never be an accusations of graft or bribery. It's safe. And I'll be sure to drink my fair share so you won't need to feel guilty."

"Thanks." Charles took a sip of his beer. "Money is a struggle now. I do appreciate it on Virein's behalf." He held his beer up in a toast "to cheap beer and wine" and tapped Gunn's tumbler. No clink from the plastic beer glasses. "I wish we were in a position to bid on the RFP. We're just too small now."

And there goes our last chance and getting private-sector help on analyzing our Ebola. "At least most BtEAers are managing, or so it seems. We do what we can for y'all. CDC recognizes your importance and assistance to us." Even if none of you can help with our Ebola characterization.

    #

After a night in Chapel Hill and the long drive back to Atlanta Gunn rested Sunday by baking sourdough bread, his specialty. Monday morning Gunn set up a meeting for Wild Bill and Ian to brief them on Israeli and Arab cultural differences. Ian and Wild Bill will have to bridge the East-West cultural divide for the trip to succeed. If they don't get useful info, it will set the investigation back a couple of weeks. Hundreds of deaths at today's fatality rate.

Schedule conflicts put the meeting at 5:00 Monday but Gunn needed to fill in the young scientists about cultural issues for their trip. After he put it on their calendars he left each a voicemail. "Please come for a few minutes, at least. Your calendars show that the earliest you are both free is at five. If you are both done early, come over sooner. We'll all get home earlier."

Gunn invited them into his office at 4:53. "I want to alert you to some of the cultural differences that you may encounter and brief you on your cover story and your real work." Gunn looked back and forth at them as they sat down.

"Ian, I know you returned from a colloquium last week. I thought you'd like my briefing on Mideast mores anyway." Gunn looked at Ian for confirmation.

"I'm fine." Ian shook his head. His scowl contradicted his words.

"Are either of your wives going?"

They both said, "No." Each looked at the other. They shook their heads.

"Well, as you can imagine etiquette for women is stricter than for you. Let me tell you all I can think of." Gunn glanced at the notes on his laptop screen.

Ian took out a little notebook and a pen and Wild Bill opened his laptop and thanked Gunn.

"First of all, Israelis are as punctual as your image of German trains. I can't imagine either of you being late intentionally, but don't test their patience. If something delays you, *anything,* be sure to call your contact as soon as possible. Never stand anyone up. Find a way to notify them—borrow a cell phone if you have to. A side effect of their schedule mania is you'll need to plan meetings well in advance." Gunn checked their faces for understanding.

"What's with all this? I thought we were going to an avian flu conference." Wild Bill studied Gunn.

"That's only your cover story."

"Isn't it going to be impossible to schedule meetings way ahead? We can't sit around twiddling our thumbs, can we?" Wild Bill looked puzzled.

"Yeah. It'll be tough. I'll try to set something up for you. At least I can provide some intros. You may also meet someone at the conference that can help. Because of the time difference, my part in the meetings won't be easy. I've barely been able to start on it." Gunn stared into space and put his hand to his chin.

Ian didn't seem attentive. He had an angry frown. Gunn assumed the after-5:00 meeting irritated him and he wanted to get home.

"Thanks," Wild Bill said with a nod. Gunn refocused on him.

"As to dress, you'll probably want to dress up a little more than you are now. At a first meeting with anyone at their CDC, you should probably wear a suit." Both of them wore cotton pants and a sport jacket with no tie. "In fact I suggest you wear a suit to the seminar at the Technion. You'll probably find you're in a minority, but it's a good idea, at least for the first day. Actually, it's the senior people who dress and act formally. The guys your age are more Americanized, more informal."

"How do we both get into one suit?" Wild Bill mumbled and smirked. Gunn laughed. Ian must not have heard.

"Shoot," Ian said. "I hoped not to take one. They're such a pain to pack."

"How can they stand to wear suits in that hot climate?" Wild Bill asked.

"Yeah, they're a hot pain in the butt, but take one anyway for the first day and for first meetings with others. And if you have a private meeting with someone, don't be surprised if they answer their cell phones during it. That's not rude for them." Gunn looked at the ceiling for a moment before continuing. "You better not do it to me here, though. I'll kill you."

"Weird business etiquette, huh Ian?" Wild Bill said.

Ian nodded inattentively.

Gunn wondered if was merely the late hour that was bothering Ian. "The real biggie, though, is that Israelis, like Europeans, have a much smaller personal space than we do. You can expect people at the conference to come right into your face, even hold your arm. It's not rude and it's not confrontational. It's just their use of space—the way they act."

"How close? Like about 18 inches?" Wild Bill held up his hand about a foot-and-a-half from his face and looked at it. He crossed his eyes.

"Yes. 18 inches or less, face to face. And holding onto your arm while they're at it. It is hard to get used to. And, in fact, they will probably think you're distant and aloof. Don't take it personally."

Gunn started out of his chair. He wanted to let Ian get home as fast as possible. All three headed for the elevator. "Oh I know. Just thought of this. Until they invite you to use their first names, use full names. Especially for the fogies like me. Call him *Dr. Moshe Eisenberg*, for example. They will probably tell you to use their first names and dress more casually at the first meeting. Don't presume, though."

"I haven't had time to look up anything yet. What's the spring weather like there? Will it be really hot?" Wild Bill walked with with his open laptop balanced on his arm and took more notes.

"Probably hot an humid. Like summer here, only hotter. And

tempers tend to be hot too. The Israelis are very impatient. You'll rarely see lines. They hate waiting." Gunn pushed the elevator call-button and looked at the ceiling. "There must be more, but I can't think of anything right now."

Ian followed Gunn's hand motion and went into the elevator. "That was quick. Thank you," Wild Bill said. He followed Ian.

The elevator doors closed. Gunn leaned against the wall of the box and felt the Berber carpeting on it. He resented the aroma of smoke—someone must be so addicted he couldn't help smoking in the elevator. Couldn't stand to wait another minute. Wild Bill pushed the button for the parking level. "Y'all're registered for an avian flu conference, but I want you to spend as much time at the Israeli CDC, at their Ministry of Health, as you can," Gunn said. "Try to learn everything about the EBOV outbreak. The flu conference is a cover to avoid irritating your hosts. Moshe will help you and I'll be talking to you be email nearly every day."

"So this is some kind of clandestine operation?" Ian showed interest in the conversation for the first time.

"Cloak. No dagger." Gunn smiled. Good to have Ian back in the discussion.

"How come you're not going?" Wild Bill said.

"Amhach wants a lower-profile presence," Gunn said. "He's worried that if we make it appear that we think the Israelis don't have sufficient technical expertise, they won't talk to us at all. He wants us to learn what's what, but don't do anything they might consider threatening. Especially to their reputation."

"So if we act like tourists, ask to watch, and only very discreetly offer to help however and whenever we can, it should be about right?" Ian looked down and studied the floor. The elevator stopped and the doors opened.

"Yes. Sounds good. Oh. One more thing," Gunn said. "You may want to warn your families that there is an eight-hour time difference so they should only try to call you in the morning Atlanta time. And, if I think of any more sociological issues, I'll email them to you. You've got the highlights, anyway."

"Hemorrhagic fever viruses are your baby," Ian said. "I think you should attend too, or probably instead of one of us."

"I agree, but the specter of an American Ebola epidemic died in 2015. Now politics reigns, not science." Gunn shook his head. "Thanks for your vote of confidence. The bastard in the corner office has his own ideas, or at least he forces someone's ideas on us all." Gunn bit his lip and looked down. I should never have let my disapproval show. He *is* a bastard, but he's our bastard.

Wild Bill grimaced in apparent dismay. "Thanks for the instructions and etiquette lesson, especially since it's way past our normal quitting time."

Ian smiled for only the second time. He seconded the complement and the thank yous then spoke to Wild Bill, "Be sure you drink lots of water and start right away. Those long flights are dehydrating. You need a reservoir."

"Yeah." Gunn agreed.

"What a day." Ian came in early and looked very tired now.

"Ditto." A headache was about all Gunn had to show for the day. "Maybe the ideal is to act like high school kids—curious+ but no threat to anyone."

#

Gunn and Pauline's one story brick house was typical of most of the nicer, older houses in Atlanta or most anywhere in the South. The abundant deciduous trees in their neighborhood reduced air conditioning costs. The Shorehams' trees were oaks, live oaks and two magnificent pecans. The bricks of their house were deep red with touches of white, black and orange that had given it an old-brick look, even when it was new. Like the big trees, it now said *old money.*

Pauline and Gunn sat under the pergola on their patio in back of the house each with a glass of Staglin Family 2007 Cabernet Sauvignon. "You seem to be in a funk over not going to Israel on this Ebola case," Pauline said. "Why don't you call Mele Mele. She always cheers you up."

"Yeah. I can't think of anything better than a talk with her and Jeanne Anne. Except a talk with you. But I'm so mad about that idiot Amhach that I might get carried away and swear. I'm trying to stop and I'm determined never to let either of them hear me swear again." Little girls should not hear their grandfathers swear.

Gunn took a sip of his wine and looked up at the pecan tree that shaded the patio all summer. An epiphyte grew on the stout branches giving the appearance of leaves sprouting all along them. The aroma from a neighbor's magnolia and their own tulips and hibiscus combined with odors of leaf mold and moss to define spring in Atlanta. There was a slight yellowish cast to the entire back yard from the dusting of oak, pecan and other pollen. The air movement from the ceiling fans kept any thirsty mosquitoes at bay. He gave a kick so their swing started its slow rhythm. He put his arm around Pauline and pulled her to him.

She snuggled up to Gunn. "I'm so happy to hear you say that." She stroked his chest, put a finger between the buttons on his shirt, then unbuttoned one button so she could put her hand inside his shirt. "Dinner can wait." She unbuttoned his shirt. They adjourned indoors, but only made it as far as the plush carpet in the family room.

\#

After putting the dinner dishes in the dishwasher, Gunn stretched and kissed Pauline on the cheek. "I feel so much better, I think I'll bake some bread and call Mele Mele. No four-letter words. Promise." Baking helped him solve puzzles of all sorts.

Gunn took out his bread flour, sourdough starter, KitchenAid mixer and dough hook. He put the flour, salt, water and starter in the bowl and started the machine. How the hell can I characterize this damn virus?

As the mixer did its job, he set the bottom oven to bake for one minute and the top one to turn on at 350 in an hour. He put his baking stone in the bottom oven. When the mixer was done, he kneaded the dough for a couple of minutes and put it back in the steel bowl. He dampened a dishtowel, put it over the bowl and placed the latent bread in the bottom oven to rise.

The Israeli Ebola was getting into the news much faster than the West Africa outbreak. Pretty soon CDC will be under pressure to answer inane questions from journalists. What's the newsworthy equivalence? One case in U.S. = 10 in Israel = 1000 in Africa?

While the yeast did its magic he telephoned Hawaii. Mele Mele answered and they talked for a moment about her science fair project, the working model volcano. She groaned and announced she had a sunburn.

"You live in Hawaii. How can you get a sunburn? That's for tourists."

"I don't know. I got it last night and it hurts."

"Last night?"

"Well, it started hurting last night. I was on the beach all afternoon."

"Have your mother put something on it. Some Solarcaine or something like that. And, please, Mele Mele, be more careful. You've got to SPF 30 yourself. Please protect my favorite granddaughter. I've made a promise not to use naughty words. Will you make a promise to yourself to use a sunscreen?"

"Okay, Grandpa. I promise."

"I want you to promise yourself, not only me. It's more important for you to want to protect yourself."

"'Kay, Grandpa."

"May I speak to your mother?"

Mele Mele called Jeanne Anne who tolerated the lecture from her father on the dangers of skin damage and cancer from the sun. "You're still at a vain age when you probably insist on a tan, but Mele Mele isn't that old yet. The sun's effects are cumulative over a lifetime. Protect her now while she doesn't care too much."

"Dad, when were you ordained? Don't be so preachy." She scolded him.

"You're right. I'm sorry. Take care of my girls, please." He looked at the ceiling and shook his head. All he saw was Jeanne Anne rolling her eyes.

After the call Gunn felt tired. He knew his kids would do what they wanted, but they might heed him enough to slow the damage to their skin. Damn, he should have asked questions instead of lecturing. He was too upset.

His mind wandered back to the Ebola outbreak. Could somebody be behind it? The scattering of cases over areas that are hard to travel between seems to indicate deliberate distribution. Obvious speculation. Shit, the conspiracy theorists would have fun with that one. Nothing to help combat the disease or its spread. Gotta stop it. But how?

In their bedroom he thought CNN's news was aimed more at ratings than informing. He barely heard the clip from Abu Bakr Al-Baghdadi proclaiming Ebola the *Fist of Allah*. "He smites our enemies and unbelievers with a plague," an Al-Baghdadi spokesman quoted the *Caliph* as saying.

"What about the case of Ebola in a Palestinian?" a reporter asked the spokesman.

"That man was not a true Sunni." The spokesman and translator closed his eyes as he spoke. No eye-contact with the reporter or camera.

Thus spake the Sunni Caliph. Gunn left the room. Bound to be more nonsense.

Chapter 6 – Day 14, Tuesday

Atlanta

Pauline called Gunn to watch the news. He put down the *Atlanta Journal-Constitution* he'd been reading during breakfast and went into their bedroom with his coffee. Ahh, citrus-vanilla-jasmine. She had already put on Allure, her favorite Chanel perfume.

"Pentagon spokesperson Vera Schmidt has confirmed one case of hemorrhagic fever in Baghdad and refused to deny there may be more. We asked Ms. Schmidt about the relation of this outbreak with others in the region."

A young woman in uniform continued, "We have no information to indicate that the hemorrhagic fever virus cases we have seen in Iraq are linked to the other reported viral outbreaks in the region, and no information they are not."

"What the hell's going on?" Gunn yelled at the television. He almost spilled his coffee.

"The confirmed case is a Sunni woman who has had no contact with any American or Israeli personnel according to the Pentagon spokesperson." Gunn thought about the politics of this outbreak as Ms. Schmidt continued, "In a rare case of support for a Sunni, Iran's leader, Ayatollah Ali Al Khamenei, has attacked the Israelis and blamed them for the Ebola virus. He has issued a fatwa and is demanding a jihad. Al Khamenei has asked his followers to single out Israelis and Americans for assassination.”

“Oh, great,” Gunn said to the television. “Ayatollah Cheerful. A world renowned expert on disease. When in doubt, start another holy war.” We need an interactive television so I could punch that idiot war monger through it. For Gunn, punchable TV was only a step below punchable computers on his *needed inventions list.*

The camera changed to a hospital scene. The caption said the news item footage was an exclusive from an Israeli hospital. As the camera zoomed in on the patient's face, the voice-over read the caption. “The following footage contains graphic scenes that may upset some viewers. Viewer discretion is advised.” Pauline left the room.

At least the network digitally blurred the faces in the TV picture. Viewers couldn’t see anything but the patient’s mouth. He had purple lesions on his left cheek and chin. A gloved hand put a tongue depressor in the patient’s mouth. The open mouth showed blood had oozed out of the tongue and gums. Once the patient aahed, the camera showed a black lesion on the roof of his mouth. This one actually oozing blood. The voice over repeated the message of the caption. “CNN obtained this exclusive footage of a patient in Israel with his permission. Viewers are warned that the scenes are graphic and may upset some individuals.”

The doctor, or at least a male, pulled down the sheets and the patient rolled onto his side. “Is this a sweeps month?” he asked the TV. The doctor untied the patients gown to reveal his back, covered with yellowish pimples and purple blisters, some oozing. There were blood marks on the patient’s gown and some on his sheets, where the blood must have soaked through. The gloved hand pushed lightly on the man's back to roll him further onto his side, revealing more morbidity. As the hand moved to touch one of the bruises, the skin where the thumb had pushed on his back started seeping.

“God. What an awful invasion of privacy. I hope that poor bastard got a bunch of money for showing off his ecchymoses and maculopapular rash. Or, rather I hope his family got it.” Gunn took a sip of coffee. Poor guy is probably dead by now. Can't have lived much after they made that damn video.

Pauline called, “Are they done showing that awful stuff? Is it safe to come back?” She came back into their bedroom. “Oh. That's sickening." She gagged and ran out of the room.

A moment later Gunn called toward the door, "Yeah, it's safe. They're back to talking about blowing each other up in their civil wars. Mangled cars, houses, buildings, civilizations not body parts. No more hemorrhagic fever scenes for a while."

CNN showed an ISIS video of the self-proclaimed Caliph of the Islamic State. "The Ebola Plague is the hand of Allah striking the unbelievers." The subtitle translated the madman's rants.

Gunn turned to Pauline when she returned. "Would it violate the First Amendment to ban sickening and invasive material like that?"

She shrugged. Apparent agreement.

If the Iraqis use the typical Mideastern approach to embarrassing problems he wouldn't be able to trust their epidemiological data. In fact the variety of wars and Al-Baghdadi's pronouncements virtually guarantee the dominance of their and our conspiracy theorists. He wondered if his friends could get past that cultural barrier. Could the Iraqis screw up the samples in a way he wouldn't detect? Will the Iraqis let American or Israeli doctors help treat the woman? Certainly not the Israeli ones.

Gunn had to learn the viral transmission mechanism. The key to understanding the outbreaks was to determine the relationship between the various strains of hemorrhagic fever virus and how the humans had been infected. If this Baghdad strain is the same as the one in Tel Aviv, at least we have a head-start on studying it. If it's another strain, I'll have to decipher this new virus. We should know in a week or two. If it's contagious, then easy and rapid person-to-person infection may occur. Fuck. Too gruesome to contemplate.

Come to think of it, with political hacks running us, can we trust ourselves? If a case of hemorrhagic fever turns up here, what kind of lies will Amhach tell, in the name of spin? Gunn finished his coffee and sat on the bed staring blankly at the television. Would the government quarantine an entire city like they virtually did after the Boston Marathon bombing? "Never open your mind, facts might leak in," he said to the room. "They might encourage you to change your theory to conform to reality." Why can't they wage wars with bumper stickers instead of guns. "My Allah is Higher Than Yours" or "Shi'as don't believe in the True

Allah." That'd be like our bumper sticker battles. "Antagonize a Liberal: Work Hard, Be Happy" versus "Antagonize a Conservative: Think."

Gunn gritted his teeth and looked at Pauline. "Hey. You lawyers like complex hypothetical situations. Right?" Gunn looked at Pauline. He carefully banished the angry tone that pervaded his diatribes at the television.

"Yeah." She looked at him and thought about the unreal examples lawyers study by the dozen. The basic pedagogy for law school is unbelievably weird cases.

"Okay, so here's one for you. We can shoot down an airplane with 500 Americans on board to prevent it from crashing into the White house, right? That's our current protocol isn't it?"

"Yes. I think so." She stared through him and nodded.

"All right. Suppose a major hemorrhagic fever outbreak occurred in Pyongyang and let's say a quarantine has already failed." Gunn watched Pauline's reactions. "Now, if we think the only way we can stop its spread to South Korea is by sterilizing Pyongyang with a firestorm, would we be justified in bombing the city into oblivion?"

"That situation has legal, political, medical *and* ethical aspects." Pauline frowned in thought. "No pat answer will work. Legally, even if a quarantine has already failed, the President probably does *not* have the authority, but I'm sure he could get away with it. If we happened to have a really smart President at the time, he'd certainly try to get the Chinese to do it."

"In the last few decades most of our Presidents have gotten away with war despite no declarations. Is that the sort of precedent you're referring to?"

"Yeah." Pauline looked like she was considering many angles. "Since 9-11 the Secret Service's rules say they can shoot down an airliner full of Americans to save a few others. I guess that probably means we can destroy a foreign city to save our country."

"Okay, that's what I thought. Now you'll see where I'm going. Could we nuke Pyongyang? H-bombs could be rationalized as a cheap way to sterilize the city, right?"

"I don't know. That's much dicier because of treaties that deal specifically with nuclear weapons. Where else are you going with this?"

"After an *Axis of Evil* city, how about the city of a neutral country, then a friendly country, then a city in the U.S. Is there a legal stopping point?" Gunn rubbed his forehead and shook his head.

"A legal one? Probably not." Pauline massaged Gunn's shoulder. "Lots of political and moral ones, though."

"Politically and morally uncrossable lines?"

"Well, any ethical person, even a president, would worry a lot about crossing some lines." Pauline continued her massage. "Different lines for different people and at different times. And a clever negotiator would never admit the position of his or her line."

She paused and stopped rubbing. "And Trump probably isn't smart enough to know if he's being unethical."

"Eisenhower and Johnson used the Army against American citizens, here in the U.S., right? Could the President use weapons against a dying city to contain a disease that threatened a whole state?"

"The National Guard, not the Army." Pauline stared blankly at the TV. "I think he has the legal authority. He'd need lot's more than law on his side, though."

"Yeah, and the Secret Service can shoot down an airplane full of Americans with no authorization, right? Isn't the new protocol to fire on an airliner that might hit the White House? They have to act too fast for the President to assent. So how much more can we Feds do with no prior authorization or accountability?" Shit, am I the nexus of some new nuclear non-proliferation effort? God damn it. We have to find out what it is and how to stop this before some asshole in Washington thinks as evilly as me.

#

When Gunn saw the pictures of Pauline, Jeanne Anne and Mele Mele on his desk at CDC, he felt like he'd been in rush hour traffic for a week. He checked his watch and was actually a minute earlier than usual. Gunn searched his electronic Rolodex for contacts at The Walter Reed Army Medical Center. Linda Steiner's infectious disease specialty looked promising. He called and was pleased to reach her. After re-introductions Gunn asked, "I heard about a hemorrhagic fever virus case in Baghdad. We have a filovirus library and would like to categorize this one. Can we get a sample? Or maybe a slide of some infected tissue?"

"I hoped you'd be able to analyze it," Linda responded in a friendly tone. "Army politics mean it has to be done so that no one here finds out you're working on it, though."

Gunn's spirits rose. This was going to be a great day. If nothing else, the "DNA analysis" should determine any link between the Iraqi and the Israeli cases. Probably it would show there was only one Ebola strain in the region.

He clicked through the menus on his computer while he spoke. With a little luck he might find an unreleased lab report on the Israeli sample's RNA analysis. "Pending." Still, this shouldn't be such a bad day. "We don't have anything on the Israeli virus yet, but we're analyzing it and I expect it'll be done very soon." Gunn clipped his description as he realized he shouldn't reveal that he had tissue samples from Tel Aviv.

"I'm not comfortable FedExing this virus-infected tissue," Linda Steiner said. "I'll send it down by courier even though it may take a day longer. I don't think there's a danger of viral escape, but the Brass will kill me if they think the Press might find out we're not super-careful."

"I appreciate your viral *and* political prudence. I'm glad we have time to work on this while the weasels in the press don't know anything about it." Gunn blew a pffft of exasperation.

"The Press would never forgive us for a release of the virus even if an airline crash allowed it."

"Yeah, can you imagine what it'll be like when they start hounding us."

They lamented working under the scrutiny of the Fourth Estate and the time constraints of politicians and anxious families. Gunn and Linda exchanged email addresses and finished the conversation. Gunn hung up his phone and punched the air. Time to celebrate. He took a Werther's caramel candy from his desk drawer.

Maybe some Iraqi or ISIS jerk lost control of his toy. Nah, probably not. They're so hard up for publicity, they're more likely to claim credit than actually spread the bugs.

As he savored the butterscotch his phone rang. U.S. Representative Cynthia McKinney's assistant identified himself. "Director Amhach's secretary referred us to you. We have two people requesting information and she says you are the best person to help us. The first one is Dr.

George Austin. He's a virologist at a startup Bio Tech company who wants to learn how to do business with the CDC.”

“He should be interesting to talk to. I'll be glad to meet him.” A talk with a young virologist would stimulate his ideas and ego. It's always fun to see what the next generation was being taught. Wonder where he studied?

“Thank you. The second is Robinson Winter, the *Journal-Constitution* columnist. He's working on background about the Ebola outbreaks in the Mideast. They both said they will call you soon.”

At least a talk with a young virologist should be fun. If he tried to delay the inevitable meeting with the reporter, McKinney would probably go back to Amhach to force his cooperation. If he was curt with the reporter, it would probably lead to more time wasting in the future, and under greater pressure. Better to pretend amicability all through the interview with the reporter. Damn. Odd Amhach would send a reporter to me. Hmm. Maybe the interviews are punishment.

He wondered if Amhach knew about the interviews. Wait. Oh, crap. Can it be true? Amhach would never send them to me. He must have bumped it to Josh, who sent them to me. That clown was being coercive saying Amhach referred them. Oh, and Josh would send a reporter to me with no implied assignment to Purgatory.

It was worse than that. Austin, damn. He's that obnoxious guy who accosted me at the BtEA meeting. Yeah, that was George Austin. From a perfect morning to a perfect storm. Shit. Shit. Shit.

While he awaited the dreaded calls, he turned to his computer and found email from Ian Powell.

> Gunn. It'll be a day or two before our bodies are on local time. We're dead after the flight in. We stopped by the Israeli CDC, but couldn't get past security. The place looks like an Army barrack, both the dingy, nondescript building and barricades around it. Boy, Tel Aviv sure is crowded and hot. Even the air-conditioned offices and rooms are hot. Of to the Avian Flu mtgs tomorrow. Hope we stay awake. It's more than an hour drive to get there. More tomorrow. Ian.

Someone should have taught him English and proof reading. Gunn took a sip of his coffee and thought that today he needed a Cabernet, or maybe a Bourbon, instead.

    #

The phone rang. The guard informed him Robinson Winter was on his way up. Gunn braced himself for someone who pulled high strings. Never heard of a visitor running around unescorted. He left to meet the reporter.

After introductions, Robinson asked, "I've been looking at your articles and can't really understand them, but you are *the* expert on Ebola, aren't you?"

"Yes. Hemorrhagic fevers are my specialty. Ebolavirus is probably the best known family of hemorrhagic fevers." This huge man had more initiative than other reporters he'd talked to. This was the first time any reporter bothered to look at what he'd done, let alone admit he couldn't understand it.

"Can you explain to me, in little words that I won't misinterpret, how hemorrhagic fevers are transmitted?" Winter took his small reporter's notebook from his jacket pocket. It was like the shirt-pocket one Gunn always carried. Gunn noticed the nicely tailored jacket Robinson wore. About a quarter inch of shirt cuffs showed. Perfect fit.

Robinson must know reporters have a reputation among their subjects for getting stories wrong. He might still screw it up, like they always do, but at least he seemed to be trying to do better. Robinson asked questions and made more deprecating remarks about his capability and profession. He often repeated Gunn's answers in his own words. He understood Gunn's work about as well as any non-doctor. He asked about specific papers Gunn had written, details of Ebola, Dengue and Hantavirus hemorrhagic fever outbreaks, and about the difference between RNA viruses and prions. They discussed the Falcons, the Braves, and the miserable job the politicians were doing with the "War on ISIS."

As the meeting was drawing to a close, Robinson said, "In my research before I came over I found an old article on Jeanne Anne Shoreham as president of the of National Honor Society at Galloway School. Is she related to you?"

"Yes, she's my daughter. She, her daughter and mother are the lights of my life."

As Robinson prepared to leave Gunn said, "Our talk has been fun, even though I haven't been able to answer some of your questions. After the call from McKinney's office, I expected the worst."

"Yeah, what can I say. My boss gets carried away with her heritage and connections and uses them to impress *us*. Someday she'll learn that she should save her chits to open important doors." The huge man had a gentle way of speaking.

Gunn felt like he'd had a chat with his brother. "Oh, Jeez. Is there any business where you don't have jerk bosses? Does yours have pointy hair or is that only males?"

"Nepotism is alive and well in journalism. It used to be the good-old-white-boys networks. Now the good-old-boys include the DAR as well as the SCV. The names change; the methods don't."

"Yuck. Sounds familiar." Gunn made a face at the thought of the Daughters of the American Revolution and the Sons of Confederate Veterans running journalism. He shook Robinson's hand. At least they are probably better than the KKK, probably a lot more literate, too.

"Maybe I can buy you a beer from time-to-time to see if you've got anything I can use." Robinson's smile was huge. "I might even learn something about your palace." His grand gesture encompassed the large 1600 Clifton Road building. "I'll keep studying. Maybe, eventually, I'll understand what you tell me."

"You've got a deal. And if I have or come across something I think you can use, I'll call you." Gunn looked down at Robinson's card. As Robinson left, Gunn noticed he had a lurking gait. He must want to hide his height. He hunched slightly and took long strides that seemed awkward, especially for a former varsity athlete. Gunn returned to his computer and sent Representative McKinney a thank-you email, "I had an enjoyable and productive meeting with Robinson Winter. He and I plan to meet again from time to time so I can help him with background for future Ebola articles."

\#

Gunn thought about the genetic, polymerase chain reaction, and enzyme-linked immuno-sorbent assay tests that would be needed on the new hemorrhagic fever virus samples. He sent his lab a note, "More HFV samples are on the way for RNA analysis. We will have to do antibody,

PCR and ELISA tests as well. Are the cyclers scheduled completely? How soon will we be able to get this work started?" The PCR analysis is performed on a slide with 96 test reagents, yielding a quick but crude analysis as the slide cycles between room temperature and almost boiling.

With some time of his own, he picked up the top journal from a pile in his desk drawer and opened it to a pink PostIt note and started reading. While reading and without breaking his concentration, he walked down the hall, filled his coffee mug, and returned to his desk.

\#

The next evening Gunn met a young soldier at the entrance to 1600 Clifton Road and picked up the virus samples from the Army's courier. He locked the tissue samples from Linda in a refrigerated safe. When it was 6 PM in Atlanta it would be 3 AM in Tel Aviv. No point in checking for more news from Ian and Wild Bill. Tomorrow should be a good day. Starting off with a discussion of virology should be enjoyable, even with a jerk like Austin. Austin might be able to help with the damn Ebola. Anyway, he needed to ask Austin about his virus work and his company's capabilities. Wonder if Austin knows whom he'll be seeing. Hell, bastard's probably not even aware of how rude he was the BtEA meeting.

\#

Gunn and George Austin had talked for a quarter hour about requests for proposal and research interests. "The RFPs that will interest you and be within your capability are those in the SBIR and related programs." Gunn watched Austin. He eyes were not focused and his body wanted to yawn. "The Defense Department and NIH do many more SBIRs than we."

"Yes. I understand that. You gave me several good ideas in Chapel Hill, but I thought I should tell you about some of our special capabilities. I hoped you might have something that is a perfect fit for us—the sort of thing that hasn't made it to the SBIR stage yet." For a few seconds Austin looked lost in concentration. "For example ProteinGen has extraordinary lab equipment for protecting researchers from pathogens. We can handle anything. If BSL-4 is required, we got it."

"Oh, that's a surprise." Gunn blurted his remark, interrupting Austin. Extraordinary. Just what we've been needing more of. "I didn't know any startups could afford that sort of protection." How cheaply could a bio-safety lab with level-4 worker and environment protection be built.

"We got lucky and bought a lab that was being abandoned by HateSheet when their lab was closed. That's why HateSheet, one of our angel investors, is such a big investor—we paid for it with equity. Hell, we're one of only about a dozen BSL-4 labs in the whole country."

For the rest of the meeting Gunn listened to Dr. George Austin brag about ProteinGen's great equipment and people. Bragging that prompted Gunn to suspect duplicity or exaggeration. Another one of the fact-free Trump supporters, no doubt. And a rechtaberei. But, he did have the sort of equipment Gunn needed to speed his work.

Chapter 7 – 12 September, 2001

CM in Virginia

The Candy Man worried. Could his kid sister, the little girl he'd raised, have been killed? For 15 years he had been father to Françoise. Ever since Mom had to take a job when Dad was killed on a visit to the Holy Land. Dad had been caught in a crossfire in Bethlehem. The Israelis claimed he was just unlucky to be there, but CM was sure it was the Mossad's bullets that had killed Dad.

He had protected and comforted Françoise more like a parent than a big brother. She worked in a law office on the fourteenth floor of the World Trade Center. She should have escaped. Sometimes a person exposed to a virus never gets sick. Sometimes a person in the middle of a disaster walks away unscathed. He had not heard from her and had not been able to reach her. He called home. "Mom, have you heard from Françoise?"

"No, and I've tried her number many times. I also called a few of her friends, all the ones I know." Mom's voice was choked and halting. "No one's seen or heard from her." Mom was an RN/PA at Mountainside Hospital. He took a piece of licorice from his candy dish, the same candy he, Françoise and Mom preferred.

"I think I'll go out and kill me a couple thousand Arabs." CM used a hick Appalachian accent. He pronounced the last word with a very long A sound, "Aaeee rabs."

"We may have lost Françoise, but I don't want to lose you too." Mom cried her plea. "Please don't talk like that. Anger from within kills as surely as bullets from without."

"Yeah, you're right. You know I only talk that way. I wouldn't ever do anything." CM reflected on the way he reacted to perceived wrongs. "Well, I guess I've always have been a little hot headed, haven't I?" At least she doesn't know anything about bashing in the window on Jason's car.

"The desire for revenge will eat you like Staphylococcus aureus," she said.

Staphylococcus aureus, popularly called a flesh eating bacteria, causes necrotizing fascitis. Leave it to Mom to pick a description that only she and I would understand.

"I was so proud of Françoise when she volunteered at the ASPCA shelter." Mom quietly sobbed. "Now I'll never see her again."

"Yeah. She's okay Mom. She loves animals. And she is so smart. Her paralegal job is beyond the dreams of most actresses." CM tried to think of ways to comfort and reassure his mother and himself. "She's so beautiful. Those jobs as a department store model last year opened the doors for the acting she loved."

"Her delicate features were exactly what the stores wanted. I think they're what attracted the producer to hire her." She cried again. It sounded like the doors to a nursery had been opened.

"She'll call soon. She has to. She's probably too busy. I'll bet she helped get her play relocated so they can restart." CM felt his eyes tearing. If Mom doesn't stop the waterworks, I'll be a crybaby in no time. "Did you know that she always asked me about her boyfriends?" CM wanted to turn the conversation to something more positive.

"No. What do you mean?" Mom was quiet now.

"When she was in middle and high school, she'd ask me about guys before her first dates with them. She wanted to be sure we'd approve." What else can I say to buoy Mom's spirits? To take her mind off Françoise?

"Oooh." She ululated. "She's gone."

"Don't talk like that, Mom. Amnesia is not uncommon in cases of severe trauma." CM still held out hope. Only a little. He mostly hoped to help his mother. "Everyone downtown is susceptible right now."

After the phone call, CM recalled when he had kissed a badly cut knee. Françoise had fallen down their front stoop. He held her in his lap and rocked her in their old wooden rocking chair. He vividly smelled Françoise's blood and remembered its roughness on her leg. He combed her beautiful blond hair with his fingers. "You'll be okay. Blood is always scary. Mom will be home soon. She'll take care of you."

When Mom had gotten home from work, she took Françoise to the Emergency Room because the gash was so deep. The doctor had put three stitches in Françoise's knee. She'd hardly cried, either before or at the ER. She may have been delicate, but she wasn't fragile.

He cried quietly. How can I bring back the time when Françoise brought me flowers every day when I had pneumonia. A bunch of dandelions one day and daffodils another. Different flowers picked with love. What a world-class sister. A week in bed and five different bouquets.

A decade and a half of shared experiences. He cried. First time in years he'd been this bad. He'd pummel the Arabs who had hurt Françoise. He'd fly at them with every weapon he could find, like John Wayne in the final scene of "True Grit." He'd have all his *guns* blazing.

And the Jews who killed Dad. How can the Israelis garner so much sympathy when they kill an innocent bystander and claim they had no responsibility. "Just collateral damage." Bullshit.

Revenge only eats at your soul when it's unfulfilled. Revenge taken is sweet.

Chapter 8 – Day 20, Monday

CDC Headquarters, Atlanta

Despite his negative expectations and dislike of Amhach's politics, Gunn always liked the sparsely decorated office. The dark wood paneling and leather upholstered chairs in the CDC Director's Office reminded Gunn of his study at home near Chastain Park. The office smelled of a leather cleaner or polish that Gunn didn't recognize. There were no pictures of family or any personal items visible. Sterility was a virtue at the CDC, one that often extended from lab to office decor, as it had here. But how could Gunn convince the Director of the importance of getting information from the Israeli CDC.

Gunn liked the feel of the leather and the decorative crown nails on the arms of the side chair. He answered the Director's question, "The preliminary tests suggest that the Israeli and Iraqi cases are probably caused by the same virus family. We haven't yet determined the source, or even the species, but we're working on them." Hmm. He had said almost nothing. Probably what Amhach was capable of assimilating.

"And what help has your team gotten from the Israelis?" Amhach did not project the presence in his office that he had in campaign appearances for his presidential mentor. Well, what can you say, the World's full of dorks in high places. If he hadn't spouted that outrageous right-wing claptrap, D.J. Strumpet never would have appointed him.

Amhach's intelligence seemed very artificial, perhaps he was a robot. "Ian and Wild Bill haven't gotten any significant info or assistance from the Israeli Ministry of Health. I recommend we send a more senior person, one that will get more cooperation from the authorities there. Our effort has to be very low profile—it can't be a Ready Team. I don't think young guys will ever get the level of cooperation they need to see the Israeli's work. I think we'll have to see their results to crack this case. If Mid-easterners weren't so status conscious, Ian and Wild Bill would be a great team."

"If only you could be a little more diplomatic, Gunn. You're a loose cannon, if you'll pardon the pun. Even your request is abrasive. 'You didn't say A more senior person might learn more.' You had to say, 'I recommend a more senior person.' Do you realize that you are saying, in effect, 'you made a mistake.' We want team players, ones who support everyone in the Center. Ones who stay on message."

Gunn focused on the clashing twisted mustache and barbiche. They made Hamhock's face look like a question mark. So? Should I say you made a mistake that's likely to cost many lives? Should I tell you what an ass—no don't even think it—what an idiot you are? "Yes, sir. In the case of almost any disease outbreak that might be related to terrorism, we should be involved, and at a very high level. We have a better capability of tracing the origin of an outbreak than any lab in the world." Gunn stared at the Director's chin. He tried to speak directly to the dot at the bottom of the question mark and the clashing paisley tie that made an upside-down exclamation point.

Flatter the airhead. "You've sent a team that is technically far more competent than most and as good as any, but they do not command the same sort of political respect that you or Josh would, especially in the class-conscious Mideast. Ian and Wild Bill are too young to be treated as well as we'd like, Dr. Amhach. It would help our investigation to have a senior representative. Dr. Ikeya or yourself might be too high-profile, but someone like one of us would be a good choice." What a kiss-ass, Gunn thought. If QestionMark Hamhock went, it would even contradict my suggestion of staying below the Israeli political radar.

"Dr. Hickok seems to have come to the same conclusion. He's requested that you be sent to help. I'd like to send you, but I need you to play from the game book the Administration's using." Amhach fidgeted in

his large executive chair and rarely made eye contact with Gunn as he
spoke.

Boy, he had me fooled. This jerk was about as different from his
TV and rally-the-troops personality as a person could get. "What part of
the party line have I contradicted?"

"It's not that you contradicted some policy, it's that you don't
inspire confidence that you will continue to be aware of the ramifications
of your pronouncements." Amhach pounded his index finger on the desk.

Gunn thought about the Greek Statistics Office a few years back,
where there had been talk of charging the technocrat director with treason
because he published the correct data on the state of the country's budget.
His predecessor, and deputy at the time of the incident, demanded that
they vote on data before publication. Vote on computational results? Vote
on facts? He recalled the Statistics Office, then under the predecessor
director, had published a deficit rate of something like 6%, then revised it
to about 12% in the midst of their budgetary crisis. The technocrat found
the true number was something like 15%, which he published. For the
truth, a mathematical truth, he was accused of treason. No wonder no
science or technology came from anywhere near the Mideast in the last
thousand years.

I gather you don't want the truth. "Do you want some fabrication?
What should we do if we find evidence of a terrorist or ISIS backing for
the hemorrhagic fever outbreak?" Gunn's tone was pleasant, contradicting
his words. His Georgia drawl added to the "I want to help" body
language. Be careful. Better not say much to Amhach. He'll think or
recognize I'm calling him a lying asshole. Truth always hurts.

"It's not at all that we don't want the truth." Amhach leaned back in
his chair. "It *is* that there are always many ways to present a set of facts.
When you imply I don't want the truth, that's abrasive. If you were to say,
'I like to put a positive spin on a story,' that would be better. Of course if
we find evidence of a terrorist plot, we need to take action. That doesn't
mean we need to inform the press in such a way that we cause a panic.
This sort of tact is important in international relations, and especially
important when Mideastern countries are involved. You would have
accompanied the original team to help in Israel if I'd been sure you'd be
circumspect and tactful."

"I've been trying to find ways to help our guys from here, but it's nearly impossible. With an eight-hour time difference and only a few personal friends at the Ministry of Health, it isn't feasible to offer much assistance from here. The two-plus hours per day of commuting from Tel Aviv to the Avian Flu meetings in Haifa also cuts into Ian and Wild Bill's time at the MoH. They have not been able to study the hemorrhagic fever research." Gunn looked down and frowned. He tried to think of other ways of tackling the problem. "You know. Sometimes a panic might be useful. Perhaps nothing but a panic would raise the population's awareness and fear of the HFV enough to save them. There are times when we mustn't let them be complacent."

"That attitude is dangerous. I doubt that a panic is ever needed. But if it is, it must come from politicians, not us."

"I'm sure you're right." Gunn thought of climate change scientists, some of whom wanted to start a panic to scare people into protecting the Earth. "Politicians are much more effective at inciting large groups of people to act rationally or irrationally, dispassionately or emotionally. And if the effect is bad, Science won't take such a hit."

Amhach nodded. "I know you want to help. I hope you can keep your mouth shut. I'm sending you over to help Ian and William." Amhach droned on.

Finally. Wonder if this idiot realized a policy reversal would be much more of a negative with his constituency than any specific position? Billy Bob Amhach treated policy like gospel—believe and follow it, even when it is obviously a fairy tale. And now an about-face. He imagined an ad, "New unused brain. Donated by right-wing politician who put principle before thinking. Spouted platitudes. Relentlessly avoided facts and thinking.'

William? Nobody calls Wild Bill that. Amhach has never even bothered to talk to anyone who knows his staff. Hell, what should he expect? Gunn realized Amhach asked a question about the travel authorization. "I'll collect the equipment we'll need right away and get you a TA within 24 hours." Gunn wanted another Ready Team virologist with good teaching skills, but would have to make do with Ian, Wild Bill and himself.

Oh, God. He'd completely forgotten when Ian and Wild Bill went there. The Israelis didn't have a Bio-Safety Level 4 rated lab. The lack of a BSL-4 space meant he should take the same sort of equipment he'd take to a third-world country. We supposedly require a BSL-4 lab for work on dangerous agents like EBOV. I better pack as though it's a trip to the Liberia or Sierra Leone and take pressure suits, for sure. I'll have to ensure that nobody at MoH, not even Moshe, finds out I brought them. I'll hide them until they're politically acceptable or required.

"The worst news, at least from where I sit, is that Robinson Winter will be going to Israel about the same time you do. You have to be especially careful with The Press. With a little luck you will miss him entirely. If he or any other reporter catches you, be sure you only feed them properly filtered data. Or better yet, refer them to me. A casual remark to him might create a situation where I have to take some sort of drastic action."

Does *drastic action* mean firing someone? Shit, what was he supposed to do if a reporter approached him? Mr. Idiotsuit couldn't answer anything, anyway.

#

The next evening Gunn checked his bag and a CDC equipment trunk for the flight to Tel Aviv. As usual Gunn upgraded his seat to business class. "You'd think that TSA would have gotten its act together by now." He muttered to a passenger next to him in line. "They're still wasting all this time with their ineffectual luggage search. I'll bet they've confiscated more tons of nail clippers than they've scared off grams of contraband." The waste was a universal byproduct of security and bureaucracy. More damn federal intrusion of the obnoxious sort he had to deal with on a daily basis. In the waiting area for their flight Gunn saw Robinson and started to walk over. He stopped and sat behind the reporter.

Gunn was absorbed in a Nevada Barr Mystery and missed the call for business class passengers and got in line to board with the hoi polloi. Robinson came over to say hello. They chatted on the jet-way.

A night later, jet-lagged and exhausted, Gunn and Robinson waited to retrieve their baggage. "You ride in first class?" Robinson looked at Gunn. The luggage conveyor had not yet started to move.

"No. Business. I dozed off a little, but I never get much sleep.

Never found a non drug-induced way to sleep on planes, even in a lie-flat seat. I can read and work better in business. If I were as big as you, I think I'd be in front all the time." Gunn straightened to the blare of a horn and watched the carousel start to rotate. "It's one of the luxuries I pay for myself. CDC would never split for it. Waste of taxpayer monies." The dingy cave housing the baggage claim felt gritty and smelled of dirt, mold and unwashed bodies. When his trunk came around he noted the CDC seal had been broken as he started to pick it up.

"Where are you staying?" Robinson stepped in front of Gunn and hefted the CDC equipment footlocker from the conveyor and put it on Gunn's trolley.

"I'll be at the Crowne Plaza on the beach in Tel Aviv." Gunn grabbed his checked bag and put it on the trunk.

"Oh, good. It'll be nice to know one face. I'm staying there too. Want to share a ride?"

"Yeah. The bean counters will appreciate saving a little." What would Amhach say about this? "I think two of us can split a cab for about 25 bucks each."

"Whoever gets through first can get us started." Robinson cleared customs quickly and went ahead to find a cab while Gunn and his trunk were singled out by Israeli customs inspectors for complete baggage search.

Twenty minutes later he opened the trunk for the Israeli customs inspector and saw a TSA announcement that it had been searched. Gunn knew that TSA inspectors regularly lost or stole items from luggage and wanted to check to be sure all the equipment was there. He started to reach for the neatly arrayed equipment in the locker when he was warned, "Al tiga adoni, titracheck. Don't touch. Stand back, sir."

Crap, is that a tear in the hazmat suit. Gunn straightened and put his arms behind his back in a parade rest position. Damn inspectors are endangering us. And for what? By the time Israeli Customs returned the trunk, fatigue had chased the TSA danger from his mind.

When Gunn cleared customs, Robinson came over to him. "I called the hotel and they agreed that a taxi was probably the best choice for two of us."

"Thanks, Robinson. I feel like such a zombie, I probably need your help."

"Let me take your things." Robinson grabbed the trolley with Gunn's luggage and the CDC trunk. They went outside and headed toward the taxi stand.

The generic reception and check-in area at the Crowne Plaza Hotel in Tel Aviv spoke to Gunn. "Welcome to Atlanta, or is it Kansas City or maybe Bombay." Gunn spoke quietly to Robinson. "Boy, the institutional look of this lobby makes it indistinguishable from any other. Even smells generic."

Until the clerk greeted them in Hebrew they couldn't tell they were in Tel Aviv. The clerk said he had only one room ready so Gunn took the early check-in. Robinson went for a sightseeing walk on the Mediterranean beach while Gunn collapsed in his room, envious of the reporter's youth and ability to sleep on the flight, especially in the more crowded tourist section. Or is it steerage?

After a long nap Gunn awoke to the aroma of detergent from the linens. He tried to call Ian Powell and Wild Bill Hiccock at the meeting in Haifa and left a message for Ian on the Crowne Plaza's voicemail. "Ian, we, meaning all of us, need to get together. Let's plan on dinner here. I'll see if Moshe can join us. I'm about to call him and I'll try to talk him into coming or at least stopping by." He left contact specs and requested that Ian confirm acceptance. He repeated the message on Wild Bill's Crowne Plaza voicemail.

With the meeting set up to the extent he could, Gunn felt better and relaxed. By mid afternoon, when Atlanta was awakening, Gunn started to get a second wind. Actually his body was awakening about an hour earlier than his Atlanta get-up time. Now he wished he'd toughed out the jet lag. Sleeping all day would slow synchronization of his biological clocks to the local diurnal cycle. He reached Moshe on his second call and talked him into a drink with them after dinner.

The concierge gave Gunn directions so he was able to connected to the Internet. He checked his email and monitored the CDC news line. So, by now everyone knows about the hemorrhagic fever virus in Iraq. Gunn would tell Moshe the Americans had nothing to do with Ebola outbreak. God help me if Moshe doesn't believe that. Actually, could the CIA be behind it? He was sure CDC had not spread Ebola, but he couldn't be sure about other parts of his own government.

He wondered if other mid-easterners would believe the claim? Gunn scanned the news and realized that the Israelis would be accused of spreading the Ebola. Maybe the accusations had already begun. These would come from many quarters not only from Khamenei and Al-Baghdadi. The Israelis had plenty of enemies, plenty of hemorrhagic fever victims, and one of the most effective espionage and sabotage teams in the world. In fact, they could have created the HFV virus and the outbreak here might be a symptom of insufficient biological protection. Could it even be a diversion? Could they be that devious?

#

Gunn, Ian and Wild Bill walked toward the hotel's restaurant. Robinson came up. "Mind if I join you?"

Gunn was perplexed. Should he follow Amhach's warning and arouse Robinson's curiosity? Before any approach occurred to him Wild Bill and Ian both told him they'd be glad for his company.

"I brought pressure suits, but I've remembered something," Gunn spoke to Wild Bill and Ian as the three waited with Robinson Winter for dinner. "I think I saw a tear in one of them when customs inspected the trunk. I'd completely forgotten about the rip until now so I didn't recheck. It was probably damaged by those incompetent obstructionists at TSA when they rifled our equipment. What a creep Bush was. Campaigned for smaller government then adds TSA making him the greatest peace-time government enlarger in decades. Lying bastard. Typical pol."

"Hey," Wild Bill said. "At least the current President can't lie. Not enough brains to have volition."

"The leader of the fact-free faction." Gunn shook his head.

"May I ask a question?" Robinson turned toward Gunn but did not give him time to answer. "How serious a problem is the tear in one suit?"

Gunn looked at Robinson. "Hmm." He was about to elaborate.

"The suits are important." Ian gestured in a sort of grabbing motion showing a feeling of protection. "But even one with a big tear provides virtually complete protection. Duct tape will keep most viruses out. The nosocomial Ebola infections, I mean viruses acquired in hospitals, are from incorrect procedure, not defective equipment."

"Oh. So your 'pressure suits' are like the hazmat suits I see on TV, right? *It's* the suit you depend on to protect you from the Ebola, isn't it?"

"Bingo," Ian said. "You got it. But most of what you see is the disposable outer suit, not the pressurized underwear that our Level 1 Suits have."

"Because they're pressurized a modest-sized hole in most parts of the suit shouldn't endanger us." Wild Bill seemed to want to convince himself more than anyone else. "I think Ian's right, Robinson. We'll reseal the tear, if there is one, and the pressurized air is drawn from outside our work area and filtered before it's pumped into the suit. So it'll blow any virus out any remaining holes. Most leaks in the suit oughtn't to expose us to any danger."

Gunn contemplated. "It is a gruesome virus, but it can't leap tall buildings in a single bound. At least we don't think it can. And we'll use the torn suit last."

Ian nodded agreement. His gesticulating hands showed the strains of his personal life—he had almost no finger nails and raw spots from chewing his nails.

"By the way, Robinson, the CDC is not officially here." Gunn frowned and studied the reporter. "We don't want anyone in Israel to feel we don't trust them. Please don't report anything about the suits until the Israelis accept our help."

The discussion veered to the hassles of flying since 9/11 before they returned to the reason for their junket. "I think we'll get more from our hosts if I hover instead of trying to help," Ian said. "What do you think, Gunn?"

Gunn nodded. "Helicopters are us."

"And I want to check everything I can," Ian said. "So far we've done nothing useful but attend the Avian Flu Conference. That idiot politician Amhach should have sent you to begin with." Ian made a screwing gesture with his index finger toward his temple as he spoke.

"Thank you for the vote of confidence." Gunn savored a bite of lamb and nodded in thought. "We'll find out soon if it's justified. I talked to my friend at the Ministry of Health. He should stop by for a drink this evening."

"Doesn't it take a lot of fancy lab equipment to get anything done that they can't do already?" Robinson ate his salad deliberately and studied the scientists' faces.

"Well, I hope we can help more than simply watching over the MoH tech's shoulders." Ian squinted in thought and ate the last of the bread the waiter had put on the table for everyone.

Robinson frowned a little as he ate. "You don't need any special chemicals or machines? They'll have everything you need?"

"Gee. I hope so," Ian said. "Never occurred to me they might not have what we have in Atlanta."

"They'll have everything we want, Robinson," Gunn said. "The only thing they lack is a lab with the same BSL-4 level of protection against accidental viral release. Their equipment may be a bit older and that means it's a little slower, requires a little more time for calibration, or needs a slightly larger sample for its analysis. On the other hand, some of their gear may even be newer and faster than ours. That big Ebola outbreak in '15 was 2500 miles and probably 2500 techno-years from here."

"You like to talk about all this gory stuff?" Wild Bill looked at Robinson. "Has your job so inured you against these evils that you enjoy blood and guts?"

"Enjoy it? No." Robinson had a contemplative half-frown. "I tolerate it as a part of my job. I know I need details to tell a compelling story. There's another factor too. Maybe you haven't noticed, but people's tolerance for sordid details is much greater in print than in visual media. It's easier to read or write about a gruesome event than watch it or be in it."

Ian smirked and nodded. "Let me ask you something, Robinson. How'd a vegetarian get to be so big?" Robinson was a couple of inches taller than the six-footer Ian and was built like wrestler. "Didn't you play football?"

"You're the doctor, Ian. You tell me. I figure it's 90% genes, 9% nutrition and 1% meals."

"Your basic point is probably right." Ian scratched his lip. "I'd guess its more like 70%, 25%, 5%, but your idea is right on."

"And doesn't good nutrition mean vitamins, minerals and proteins, not meat?" Robinson said.

"Yes." Ian nodded vigorously.

"And, yes, to answer your final question, I was a tight end at Ole Miss. I'll never be able to play the invisible reporter. *And here,* I'm even more conspicuous than in Georgia."

"I hadn't made the connection until a minute ago." Ian looked at Robinson. "Weren't you also a basketball starter?"

"Yeah. Not much good on offense. I was the defensive wide-body to block, or at least fill up, the whole lane."

"Hey, just the guy I wanted to meet." Wild Bill smirked. "Can you explain three football terms?"

"I hope so, what are they?" Robinson squinted at Wild Bill.

"What's the difference between a *tight end,* a *split end*, and a *loose end*?"

Before Robinson said anything Gunn, who faced the restaurant's entrance, spoke. "Hey guys," he said in a low voice. "Moshe is coming over. He's the only local who's allowed to know why we're really here. Keep voices down so no adjoining tables can hear us. We have to be sure our presence doesn't upset anyone."

Chapter 9 – Day 22, Wednesday Evening

Tel Aviv

The four Americans sat in the bar at the Tel Aviv Crowne Plaza. From the tall bar-chairs and small tables no one could really distinguish this bar from any American hotel bar. The biggest differences from saloons in American businessmen's hotels were the more intense tobacco aroma, brighter lighting, and the more polyglot background chatter. The wine list was more international. Gunn and Robinson's bodies said, "morning" and they were ready to go for many hours when Moshe arrived at their table.

Moshe was dressed in green jeans, a bolo tie with silver and turquoise clasp, and cowboy boots that made him look almost 6 feet tall. "I decided I should dress American to meet you. And, anyway, I never get to wear these clothes." Quite a contrast to Robinson and Gunn's jackets and ties. Ian and Wild Bill were in slacks and polo shirts. Moshe took a chair from an empty table and joined the group.

"Moshe, I'd like you to meet Dr. Ian Powell. He's been with us for about six years. I'm sure you heard about our E. coli outbreak a few years back—here's the guy who broke that mystery. He demonstrated his extraordinary gift for very fast lab work when he coaxed the genetic secrets from the bananas." Ian's work had allowed the CDC to implicate wild hogs in the contamination. He proved the outbreak came from an organic farm that leased the plantation the season before. He found the link before anyone else.

Moshe and Ian exchanged greetings. Moshe made eye contact and shook his hand. "Doctor Ian Powell. Glad to meet you." He added the title and repeated the full name for Wild Bill. He sustained eye contact and shook hands. When Gunn introduced Robinson Winter from the *Atlanta Journal-Constitution,* he said, "I'm glad to have the Press here, Mr. Robinson Winter."

Was that a touch of the typical Israeli formality? More likely a tic to help him remember the names. He couldn't recall any such stilted introductions from previous trips to Israel.

After introductions Moshe turned to Ian. "Well, we'd sure like to know where the virus came from, but even more important is to find the transmission mechanism. If we can identify the source it ought to help us, but it's not what we really need." He turned his head to look at Gunn.

"We hope you have a lot more data here," Gunn said. "We haven't gotten anything since before I left. I came to improve the data transmission."

"And most of our disease transmission is from an unknown source or sources. And, I think only 2 or 3 cases were caught from sick people." Moshe looked apprehensive. "We're up to something like 80 cases now and we've had 18 deaths so far."

Robinson looked shocked at the tally. He took out his notebook and wrote for several seconds.

"This has turned into an epdemic fast." Gunn realized he shouldn't have used that term. It was like noticing Trump had lost the vote, even though he'd won the election. Some phrases were verboten. Or at least Amhach-verboten, like *loser Trump* and probably *Mideast epidemic.*

Gunn turned to the reporter. "Robinson, please don't use the term *epidemic,* at least don't associate it with any of us. Dr. Amhach might have a cow. Please let someone else use that word first."

"No problem. I'll avoid the term until others have used it." He made more notes in his shirt-pocket notebook.

"Good work, Gunn. You've done it now." Wild Bill had a smirk. "Now he'll call our outbreak an *pandemic* and we'll get in even more trouble with Amhach. Be careful what you wish for, you might get it."

"I'll be circumspect about using either term." Robinson continued writing. "I could call it a plague, if you prefer."

Gunn rolled his eyes. The doctors discussed the novel ways that this hemorrhagic fever might propagate and possible ways to break the hypothetical cycles. Most RNA viruses can't be transmitted by food because they break down in the stomach—too acidic. Most hemorrhagic fever viruses were carried on microscopic water or blood droplets from coughs or sneezes, but that aerosol mechanism seemed unlikely here because of the geographic spread of the cases. Several of these viruses, including those of the Ebola genus, were transmitted in body fluids. Sometimes using ticks or mosquitoes as vectors. Sometimes in blood from coughing or sneezing. Sometimes via dirty medical supplies like needles, dressings or hazmat suits. Robinson listened and took notes. Eventually Moshe excused himself and they agreed to meet mid morning at the Israeli disease control office in the Ministry of Health.

"Thank y'all for letting me listen to your discussion," Robinson said. "I'm going to try to talk to some of the patients and their families tomorrow, so I won't join y'all for breakfast."

"Be circumspect about specifics, Robinson. Please don't tie us to the speculation." Gunn pounded his forehead with the heal of his hand. "We're clueless at the moment and non-scientists rarely understand all the blind alleys we explore before solving a riddle."

#

At noon the Americans were still working in a dingy MoH lab that smelled of tobacco and sweat. Moshe had talked three of his co-workers into translating for the Americans and all six of them were ready for their lunch break. They had spent the morning trying to put themselves to sleep by combing the medical records of all the hemorrhagic fever cases and awaken themselves with a discussion of the effects of alcohol on concentration.

"I didn't see any patterns but I did notice one thing, at least in the reports I read." Wild Bill looked in his notebook as they prepared to leave the lab. "There wasn't anyone from the poorest ranks of society. Could this HFV be a rich man's disease?"

"Ooh. Hey. That's right," Gunn said. "I can't remember any poor patients in my pile, either." Gunn scrunched his face to one side and rubbed his chin and mouth. "Wish I'd explicitly looked at socioeconomic status."

I didn't see any indication of poor patients, either." Ezer had been translating for Gunn.

"I had one janitor who moonlighted as a guard." Ian's scowl disappeared. He leaned back on his stool and looked at the ceiling. "He can't be more than one rung up the economic ladder. But if we have 79 out of 80 who are middle class or higher, we may have a start. Maybe we need to look for factors we can eliminate in 95% of the cases instead of trying to look for a link. I can't think of any other commonality in my 23 reports." Mor, Ian's translator, nodded in agreement.

"Oh, God. I was beginning to think we'd have to start with eliminating non-common factors too." Gunn shook his head as he spoke.

Wild Bill put his files in a neat stack on the lab table. The files now included summaries and translations of some sections into English. He put his laptop on top of the stack with an expectant sigh. Gunn had stacked his work a few seconds earlier. Ian's stack looked a little messier because some files were turned cross-ways to the main pile and he had nothing for a paperweight on top.

The Israelis agreed to check with the American team after lunch. Most of the reports had been checked and key portions translated. The Israelis would top to see if more language help was needed.

"It's got to be ten times as hard to find a common omission as a common thread. There has to be a tie." Gunn looked down at the piles of reports. "It's going to be a bastard to find it. To make matters worse, I'll bet we can't even talk to most of the HFV patients because they don't speak English."

"What languages spake the deceased?" Wild Bill talked to himself more than to the others.

"We'll need a lot of help from Ezer, Mor and Charles to be able to do anything there."

"Yeah." Ian stood up straight, stretched his spine. "Half are dead and we can only expect a few of the others to speak English."

"Is that right?" Wild Bill frowned. "If the victims are upper class, most of them will speak English, won't they? I don't want to unnecessarily endanger anyone. We need to at least try talking to people before asking for help, don't you think?"

"Hebrew is written backwards." Ian addressed Wild Bill in a too serious voice. "Does that mean they speak backwards too?"

Wild Bill guffawed and nodded agreement.

"I noticed the types of data on the charts varied quite a bit." Gunn's voice tone was serious. "I'd bet they don't even have a standardized questionnaire for patient interviews. "

Ian took out a notebook and pen for the first time today. "That means we need to make our own list of questions. If I write them from the bottom up, is that close enough to backwards?"

"Okay." Gunn's voice showed anguish. "From what I've seen I can't believe all the interviewers have asked all the patients the same questions. By now we've already lost all possibility of getting answers from about a quarter of them. We definitely need more commonality."

Ian took notes as Gunn and Wild Bill brainstormed their questionnaire. They wanted to know everyplace the patient had been, what animals they had contacted or been near, especially exotics. The patients' complete sex and travel histories. "And we should ensure our info covers a full month preceding their first symptoms."

Ian looked up from his notes, "Do we really have to go back that far? Isn't the longest incubation period of any HFV well under three weeks?"

"I think we better do a full month," Gunn replied. "There are cases of HFVs with incubation periods of weeks. If we don't go back at least a month or so, we might miss the one data point we need. It'll be nice if our fever's incubation period is only a few days. The most recent parts of patient histories will be most accurate. In fact, if this damn virus has a month's incubation, we may miss it because of lost memories."

"Come to think of it, think how much easier it'll be to find commonality if everyone uses a standard form. We'd know right where to look and which parts need to be translated for us." Wild Bill made a exaggerated eye roll and stared at the piles of reports.

They finished lunch. "Keep working on the list of questions, make them as specific as you can." Gunn rubbed his forehead. "I'll swing by the American Embassy to see if there's any news we've missed. They may have something that isn't in the papers or some communication from Amhach. His ego's so big he probably thinks he has to use diplomatic security. I'll be back sometime late in the afternoon. Let's plan on giving the list to Moshe today. We'll have to have it ready by five o'clock. But then we'll have complete and standardized interview forms from now on."

Gunn returned after 4:00.

Wild Bill presented him with a complete set of questions. "Ian's gone to the lab. He wanted to check out all the samples he can," Wild Bill said. "He hopes to do some of that immuno-PCR he likes and who-knows-what-else. It's a good thing he's here."

"Yep. Even if all he does is watch over their work, it'll be easier to trust the results." Gunn stared into space and nodded as he pondered. "Filoviruses are so poorly understood. I hope that suit protects Ian and that the vaccine is as effective as we've been promised."

"Oh my God. You don't really think he could be at risk, do you?" Wild Bill looked as alarmed as if he'd been told his brother had Ebolavirus.

"Let's pray not." Who knows about this beast?
#
Three days of conferences, lab work, reviews of Israeli work, results, and interviews. Finally the American doctors thought they'd made real progress in understanding this virus. The virus killed 2 people yesterday, probably as many today and tomorrow. And those numbers will double every week or so. If that weekly doubling really happened, that would be the whole world population in less than a year. Much less than a year.

They still had no clue of its cause or how to stop it, but they'd been told the results from the PCR analysis in Atlanta were due, which should tell something of the similarities of the viral outbreak here and the one in Baghdad and a new one in southern Iraq.

Moshe spoke quietly to Gunn as the group left the Ministry of Health lab. "I see what you mean about Ian. He not only works faster than anyone else, he's much faster. He seems to jump from one insight to the next."

"Sounds like what we've seen in Atlanta. Let's hope he nails this so we can seal the virus's coffin."

Moshe nodded. "One important factor. One question."

"Yeah?" Gunn glanced at Moshe as they reached the end of the dingy Ministry of Health hallway.

"Does he always keep everything in his head? So far, he hasn't documented anything. One of my techs asked him about it and he said, *I'll do all the paperwork at the end, while you're stamping out the virus.* Is that what Ian always does?"

"Yep. Just like every other time."

"Crap, Gunn. We have to protect him. Anything happens to him and we loose weeks."

Gunn looked at Moshe. "Got any budget for body guards?"

"I wish. I only wish." Moshe shook his head.

An hour later the three Americans sat around a table in their hotel's restaurant. They waited to order dinner. "Look at these pictures." Ian took out some gas chromatographs and put them on the table. "This virus is amazing, like nothing I've ever heard of. These things have some iron and tungsten." He pointed to some of the line groupings he'd labeled *Fe* and *W*. "Can you believe it? I never heard of a virus with that much metal. Have you come across any hemorrhagic fever with heavy metals like this, Gunn?"

Gunn shook his head. "Guess heavy-metal's not just for listening anymore. Never saw one dance around like this bastard."

"Wow. Extremophiles." Wild Bill mumbled. "Like the Yellowstone bacteria. Man, those W-lines are strong. I have never seen so much tungsten."

"If that's right, this may be a defense mechanism," Gunn said. "It could make the virus as tough as a prion." Prions are a sort of super germ that usually survive normal sterilization temperatures. Prions cause brain-wasting disorders like Creutzfeldt-Jakob disease, commonly thought of as the human version of mad cow disease.

"Funny you should mention prions." Ian placed a electron micrograph on the table that showed a pile of spaghetti. "Perhaps it's an aberration or perhaps this virus is developing some of the folding characteristics of those buggers. Lots of work to do on its structure."

"How will all that metal affect our vaccine's efficacy?" Wild Bill asked.

"Not sure. Might render it useless." Gunn turned the chromatograph, as though one orientation made it clearer than another, and studied it and the micrograph. "And if it picks up some of the prions' bad habits, we're in serious shit. We need to notify the doctors and nurses how dangerous it looks. Can I have some of these pics, Ian?"

"Sure. There's nothing secret about them."

"Maybe there should be." Wild Bill studied Ian and Gunn.

"I *am* sure the isolation facilities here are excellent and the medical approach is adequately cautious." Gunn studied the charts. "But in Baghdad, who knows. And we need to be sure morticians and hospice workers as well as medical people and patient families are warned. If this keeps spreading, what about Cairo or Damascus?"

"Has a scary ring," Wild Bill said. "And if ISIS or Al-Qa'ida or Assad get their hands on it, we can be sure they'll spread it faster."

"Wonder if it is from ISIS." Gunn shook his head. "Al-Baghdadi's rants seem to imply their participation or at least their wish for involvement." Wonder if we should tell the CIA, so their assassins would even work harder going after ISIS operatives.

"And further." Ian rubbed his forehead. "We ought to get histories from the families of the sickest and the deadest." Ian tapped his fingers on the table. "In fact we should get histories from the families of all potential victims. From everyone who's sick with MEFV-like symptoms. We've got to get the information before death." Ian huffed. He used Gunn's new term for the Middle East *Filoviridae* Virus. They all pronounced it mef vee.

So far the disease in Iraq followed an outbreak pattern eerily similar to Israel's, with more rapid spreading than last year's African epidemic. "At least our questionnaire will be available everywhere," Gunn said. "Hope we can convince everyone to use it. Especially the anti-American countries."

"And anti-American non-countries." Ian bit his lip.

"You know," Wild Bill said, "Robinson is a great guy and he really is working hard at understanding our geek-speak and accurately turning it into English. I think we should get this to him first. It would be nice to give him a scoop. He can spread the word better than us, anyway."

"Yeah, I like him." Gunn nodded and ground his teeth. Would Amhach fire him? No easy solutions. Protecting people was more important that protecting his career. Definitely.

"Why don't we call him with the story tonight," Wild Bill said. "Time is of the essence. What do you think?"

"He's much more thorough and careful than I expected." Gunn nodded. "Never trusted a reporter before. I hope we can help him. But even for Robinson, I want to have a written press release. The press'll get it wrong no matter what, but a written statement'll help."

"How can they get it wrong if you give them a written version?" Ian asked.

"I don't know, but they always do. Their wordsmithing inevitably changes the meaning someplace." *Amhach is so sensitive, perhaps I can hold off a day or two.*

Throughout dinner at Tel Aviv's tony but modern Carmella Bistro, the three discussed how to word the press release. It had to alert the medical community but not cause a panic; scientifically accurate but in plain English. And the big requirement, to make the wording so clear and well written that reporters and especially translators would not mangle it. That requirement would fall primarily on Gunn. He knew, and the others reminded him unnecessarily, not to use CDC bureaucratese or scientific jargon. At least no tipplers were close to them in the partly empty restaurant with many hanging plants and restored tile-work.

Gunn recalled a recent talk about communication at a Unitarian Church. The speaker had noted that a few words are used in opposite ways by scientists and the rest of the world. A *theory* is practically certain to scientists, much more solidly established than a hypothesis, but most people viewed theories as what engineers call *wild-ass guesses*. A *coincidence* to a scientist is the basis for major investigation and may lead to a *theory*, but to anyone else it is a chance occurrence that should be of little scientific interest. When scientists *believe* something, it means that nearly all scientists agree. Scientists' belief has nothing to do with religious or non-religious faith. Scientific *models* are targets of checking and verification. They are unlike the rest of the world's models, which are concrete objects. He would avoid all those terms too, hoping the Hebrew and Arabic versions would be as accurate as his. Hell, he hoped the editor-massaged English version was as accurate as his.

Chapter 10 – 17 July, 2008

Candy Man in Herndon, Virginia

CM's office was spartan—no pictures of family and no mementos of school or work. Neat and clean. The beginning of the "Great Recession" was on the news every day, even though the term had not yet been coined. At ten o'clock CM walked around the company's offices to say hello to everyone. "Everything going okay?" The replies were nearly all affirmative. One negative answer was on a personal issue—Henry's girlfriend had dumped him. He reminded everyone, "Don't forget our staff meeting at 11:30 in the break room." He made another stroll again at eleven and again mentioned the staff meeting. CM spoke privately to one researcher and one technician-secretary, "Be sure to see me right after the all-hands meeting."

CM's employees knew his tan slacks, a blue blazer and geeky tie meant meetings with people outside the company, bankers, venture capitalists, or customers. In other words, meetings that paid their salaries. Most of their customers, like their lawyers, did not expect him to dress up to talk to them, but CM thought he made a better impression in a suit. His fashion education came from his technical college peers. He thought a blazer and tie was the same as a suit.

Luck is as important a factor in company success as it is in determining who contracts diseases. CM believed in the truth of the saw, "You don't get to choose your diseases." Or your investors.

CM tasted metal. A sign of fear—nothing metallic in the environment here. He leaned back against the counter with a Coke dispenser, a microwave, and a Bunn coffee machine. The counter's Formica corner dug into the palms of his hands giving him something to concentrate on. Anything to stop thinking about the odious task at hand.

"Let me start with a personal story." CM looked at his employees. All were there. "Many years ago my father was visiting the Holy Land and was killed by Mossad agents. That had nothing to do with Virein, but they may be trying to silence us now."

"Virein could have survived this economic collapse. We could have survived the loss of the contracts from the Government. But we couldn't survive all that with the Israeli-controlled banks cutting off all our credit. We are broke though we have enough money so everyone will be paid through the end of next week. Today I sent the State notification that we have laid off virtually the entire staff."

He explained what little he knew about collecting unemployment and advised everyone to apply for it. "There's a one week delay before any benefits are paid, so file right away. Some normally reputable companies say people are fired, not laid off, to reduce their unemployment insurance premiums. We would never do that. I've done everything I can think of to make sure your transition from Virein is as smooth as possible." He looked each of his employees in the eye as he apologized for letting them go. "You shouldn't have any trouble getting unemployment relief. It isn't a lot but it will help to pay your bills until you find a new job. I hope you are each able to get replacement jobs quickly. I will write recommendations for any who wish them. I hope everyone of you stops by to see me. Maybe I can help you find a new position."

CM felt the welts on his palms for the first time since he leaned on the counter edge. He answered questions, praised everyone for their help and wished everyone good luck. The meeting ended when a local caterer brought in a three-foot sub and salad. Drinks were from the machines on the counter. He invited everyone to share lunch. He returned to his office, closed the door and pounded his fist on his desk. "Fucking Jewish bankers. They're the ones that really killed us. If those bastards had extended our credit line for one more month, we'd have made it."

The knock on his door sounded timid, like his most underpaid employee. He invited Darrel Li in and told him his job was secure. The company had enough cash to continue his paycheck for several months. "I've reduced my salary to the same as yours," CM said. He hoped to inspire continued hard work and cut off any requests for a higher salary. He looked around his office, trying to evaluate it as others would. The office was spartan with few decorations, but much larger than he needed. He took a breath, but noticed no odors. "We'll have to move to more economical space at the end of the month. No money wasted on rent."

CM did not know what to do. He decided on openness. "One other thing I'll do is give you some pay in stock. That way you'll be much better off when we get back to profitability." He wouldn't waste money on lawyers to make sure the stock distribution was entirely legal. He'd just copy what the lawyers had done in the past and hope. Anyway, the lawyers were Jews so they wouldn't get anything more out of Virein.

After talking to his favorite and cheapest scientist, he made a similar offer to Lab Tech Ingrid, the only other employee invited to stay.

Chapter 11 – Day 24, Friday

After dinner Gunn retired to his hotel room with its obligatory yuck painting over the bed. This one was orangish with an ornate fake-gold frame and a pastoral scene of what Gunn thought were ibexes in the Alps. The closet inside the door had non-stealable plastic hangers. Everything was clean to the point of sterility. The room even smelled of bleach and the industrial cleaners used in hotels.

As though in apology for the institutional decor, the corridors were filled with the familiar odors of hot and humid areas. The moldy Mediterranean aroma in his hotel reminded him of Georgia when he was a kid. By the time he returned from Harvard the whole state was air conditioned. Cooling, done primarily to lower the humidity rather than the temperature, kept the indoor South below 70 degrees all summer. Mold would not grow in the new dry South. The molds that had defined the aroma of the South were gone from indoors.

He pounded the wall with his fist. If only he could return to those simpler days when diseases themselves were the threat. Before serious bio-terror weapons. How could he tell if this was even a weapon. Times like this the constitution got in the way. The bastard who unleashed this, if it was done by a person, deserved cruel and unusual punishment. Heh, heh. And I'm as good a shot as William Tell. I'd shoot his cojones off. Gutless terrorist bastard. The death penalty is too good for these ISIS slimes. We ought to put them in jail with some big guys to rape them every day. Much better. Like the joke. Give them 70 Virginians, not virgins.

He had to get off the revenge kick and back to work. He needed to learn more details of the reported *Ebola* cases in Baghdad. Now the press has me doing it, talking about the hemorrhagic fever viruses as *Ebola.* The CDC news line had no info he hadn't read. He sent an email to son-in-law John Dalton in Baghdad.

Gunn imagined target practice on the balls of ISIS fighters. He thought a high-powered laser would be nice to use on them—permanently damage their eyes. Or maybe burn their nuts until they beg to be shot. He had to stop thinking that way.

Gunn prepared to sign off and looked at his inbox where he discovered a return email from John. "Damn. Now's the one time I wish I had one of those chat programs on my system. I should have listened to Wild Bill when he recommended that IM thing." Gunn spoke to his computer as he opened the message.

Haven't heard much about the Ebola. Lotsa rumors. G2 is the sick person is a wife of some politician. Army may know more. Want me to poke around? Give a big hug and kiss to Grammy for me. Sure will be glad to get home. I miss Jeanne Anne and Mele Mele more than ever. Love John.

Gunn smiled. He realized he sometimes called Pauline "Grammy" when he talked to Mele Mele, but somehow it seemed more incongruous for this big, tough Marine to use his daughter's diminutive for his mother-in-law.

G2, that meant sergeants, right? The military's most reliable source of information. If they said it's some pol's wife, must be. John could poke around, but he's more engineerical than medical. I wonder if he could help one of us get into see the doctors there.

John,

Thanks for the quick reply. We're not even sure of all the questions we need to ask. But you could help a lot if you could get one of us into the right places to talk to the doctors and health system bureaucrats.

Would such a visit be safe (in terms of military *and* personal safety)? Could one of us talk to people there who know about the "Ebola Outbreak?" Whom do we need to contact for permission to go to Baghdad? Any ideas?

Will relay your hug to Pauline in a moment and give it to her in person as soon as I'm home.

Gunn

Gunn reread his message and hit send, hoping John would still be on-line. He sent messages to Pauline and Jeanne Anne then checked his inbox again. Luck. John had replied.

Gunn. Just talked to COL Passpartoo who said he can get you in here and into the hospital where the Ebola case is. He's scared of Ebola because it's in the Green Zone. Free day after tomorrow. Can you make it by then? Have a Navy plane in Cyprus coming back through Istanbul. Departs IST 2030 tomorrow. Have reserved 1 seat. John

P.S., If your Israeli visas are in your passports, you'll have to come on one of our planes. The Iraqi's will not let anyone with an Israeli visa in their passport into the country. Our planes bypass their passport control.

This seemed as good as chat could be. There was so much to do in Israel. Would Wild Bill or Ian would be interested in going?

John,

Please hold that seat for us. One of us will be on the flight. How soon do you need the name? Is clearance important?

They finished with the arrangements. Gunn sent an email to Mele Mele while he awaited John's reply one time and checked El Al's schedule to Cyprus and Istanbul another. He sent John thanks for suggesting flying from Istanbul because the connections to all the airports on Cyprus looked so bad.

#

The next morning, the CDC threesome were at the breakfast table in the relatively empty Crowne Plaza. "Bad news for the people here. I did not work on the Press release. I'm trying to determine if I have to get Amhach's permission. I don't know how long I can put it off, but I decided to wait till the end of the weekend for both Amhach and Moshe."

Wild Bill shook his head. "We don't dare put it off very long. It'll only make the matter worse."

"Yeah. And now we have another issue. We need someone to go to Baghdad to collect any samples they'll let us have and learn how much of what we've heard is true. If the disease develops there as it has here, we can expect a bunch of EBOV cases soon." He leaned over the table and spoke in a low, keep-the-message-at-the-table voice. The others leaned forward to hear. "I can't directly ask anyone to go because of the danger of visiting so close to a war zone, but if anyone will volunteer, it would help. You should leave this afternoon."

"I'll go." Ian looked eager. "I've always wanted to see the Tigris-Euphrates Valley. I probably won't get to do much sight-seeing, but I'll see more than by driving up and down the coast to Haifa."

"Are you sure? I don't want you to feel pressured to travel to an area where terrorists and those murderous anti-Islamic, Islamic State thugs are so active just to pick up some tissue, blood samples, and possibly-interesting information." Gunn stared at Ian's eyes searching for any hint of dissembling. "Also, I hate to ask you to travel on a Sunday."

"Yes, I'm sure. Colleen and I discussed the dangers of this assignment before I left and she knows I'm really anxious to get to see the Fertile Crescent." The conversation was exclusively between Ian and Gunn.

Gunn worried about the risks of a trip to Baghdad, so close to ISIS held territory. "Okay. One thing that should make the trip a little safer and more productive is that you'll have a marine escort and guard while you're there. My son-in-law is on TDY at the Embassy in Baghdad. He's one of the military who are *no longer there* since the redeployment in 2011. Maybe he's ordered to wear moccasins, you know, to keep his boots off the ground. He's set up a meeting with a colonel who's afraid of the virus. He's also made a reservation on a Navy flight from Istanbul into Baghdad tonight. Both he and this Colonel Passpartoo have agreed to give you directions anywhere and I have the impression they'll escort you wherever you need to go. I think John's glad for the excuse to break the monotony of his job. I don't know anything about the colonel." Gunn sat up straighter and made loose fists in a problem-solving sign.

"Oh. That should make it a piece of cake. I figured I'd be entirely on my own. I was more worried about Army bureaucracy than Sunni or ISIS slime-balls." Ian still leaned forward in his seat and talked in a low voice as he ate another slice of toast.

"Turns out the Navy flight may be extremely important," Gunn said. "Do you have an Israeli visa *in* your passport?

"Yeah. I had to have the visa to come."

"Well, the Iraqis would never let you in the country. The Navy flight bypasses them at Baghdad Airport. Given your Israeli visa, it's the only way we have to get you there."

Gunn looked around the room to be sure nobody seemed to be listening to them. No one sat at any of the tables near theirs. He took a deep breath. "My son-in-law, Major John Dalton, plans to meet the plane at the airport and escort you into the Green Zone. I'll email John that you're on your way so he knows who to look for. Come to think of it, I have some pictures of him on my laptop. I'll show you them when we get to work this morning so you'll know who to look for. Perhaps you have a selfie of some sort you can send John?"

Ian nodded. "Copy me on one of those emails to John and I'll send him my pic."

Gunn returned to his room to retrieve his laptop and stopped to check his email before he left the hotel for the Ministry of Health. As he worked back from the top of the list he came to one from Ikeya, sent Friday.

Gunn, Amhach very upset. He says he specifically warned you not to talk to Robinson Winter and you violated that order. I don't know how long I can keep you out of trouble. This is dicey. ...

How did Amhach know I had talked to Robinson? How was he supposed to do his job if he couldn't fly on the only plane the Government rules allow him to fly on?

He then found a message from Amhach:

> I gave you a direct order not to talk to any reporters and specifically to avoid Robinson Winter and I have learned that you've been talking to him. This sort of insubordination will not be tolerated. ...

Gunn thought about the information paths that allowed Amhach to know what had happened. He composed a reply.

> Dr. Amhach,
>
> I saw Robinson Winter in the boarding area for our flight and specifically avoided him because of your order. Even if there had been no charge, I could not change to another flight because we are only allowed to fly U.S. flag carriers.
>
> By coincidence Robinson Winter's saw me and **he** came to talk to me while we were boarding. Again in Israeli customs, I could not avoid him because we were trapped in the small area between our gate and customs waiting for our luggage. In fact, it was a help to me to have a strong athlete hoist the equipment trunk from the baggage conveyor to my luggage trolley.
>
> Also, he is staying at our hotel and frequently asks to join us for meals. What am I supposed to do, tell him **his** government won't talk to him? (Can you think of anything more inflammatory to do to a reporter?)
>
> The only conceivable thing I could do to lessen contact is pass your order on to all three of us. I thought that inadvisable because Robinson Winter would learn about it (he is a reporter, in other words a professional snoop, after all) and antagonizing the press seemed much worse than talking noncommittally to the Fourth Estate.

Gunn wondered if Amhach was literate enough to know the term. Tough. He realized the others awaited him so he bcc-ed the message to Ikeya with no review and hurried out.

Chapter 12 – Day 27, Monday, Afternoon

Tel Aviv

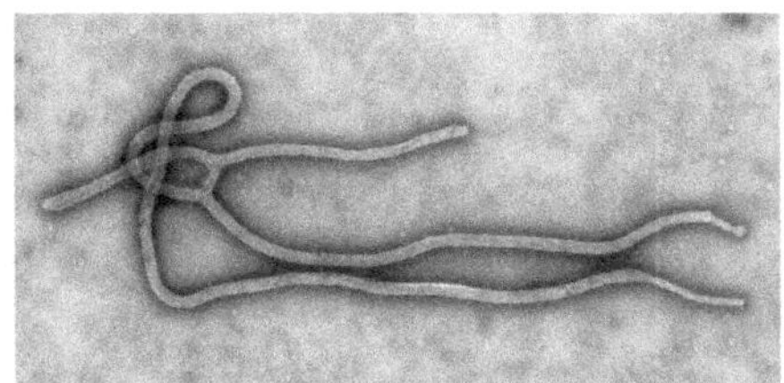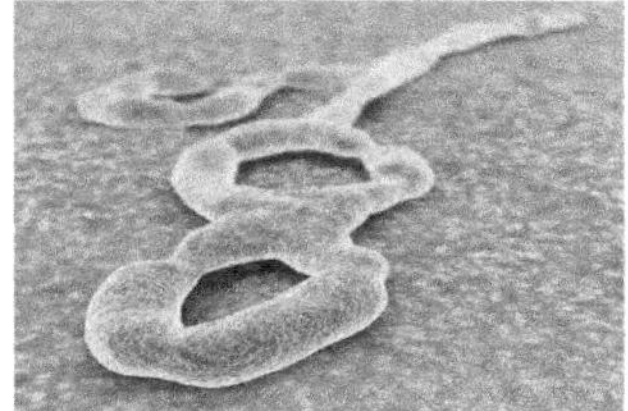

Ebola Electronmicrographs

When he was alone Gunn opened his laptop, touched the power button and waited for it to come out of hibernation. His ThinkPad, like his Crowne Plaza Hotel room, was deluxe. Deluxe, dated and generic. Both relied on South Asian manufacturing, the computer for its parts, the Crowne Plaza for its fittings and furniture. He pulled up a press release template, which the CDC's IT department in Atlanta insisted they use, and worked on an article.

When he ran out of words, he went to Moshe's office. "We have to do something quickly and publicly to alert people in other countries to the danger of this virus. Hemorrhagic fever is bad enough to begin with, but this one seems to have some sort of thermophilic protection in its RNA."

"Protection? What sort of *protection*?"

"We've found lots of iron and tungsten in its structure. We think the metals will make it more resistant to autoclaving than most viruses."

"That's new, right?" Moshe said.

"Yeah. And we're concerned alcohols won't kill it."

"What about medicines?" Moshe raised his eyebrows, wrinkling his forehead. "Our patients are mostly recovering."

"Most? I thought we were seeing something like 75% mortality." Gunn rubbed his chin.

"Well, I was discounting the early cases, before we properly diagnosed anyone. Those poor souls who were treated for flu and things like that. The ones whose Ebola treatment was delayed by misdiagnosis."

"Oh, yeah. Good point. And I was taking into account the fact that many of the current patients will die soon, even though they are still alive now." Gunn looked down and shook his head. God awful disease.

"Anyway, we brought a little of our experimental vaccine and a little Zmapp and other drugs. You must be about out of everything. Problem is, we're worried nothing'll offer much protection against this beast." His hand moved to cover his face. He rubbed the bridge of his nose.

"Crap. Bet you're right. And I think we're out of Zmapp already" Finally signs of concern in Moshe's voice.

"Oh. Damn. Damn. Damn. Maybe even worse." Gunn pounded his forehead with his fist. "Just occurred to me. If this was designed by some maniac, he may have engineered some Zmapp and other med resistance into it, too." Gunn rubbed his temples. "The way this is popping up, I knew the Zmapp had to be about gone. Hope none of us ever need it. God. There are so many cases we want all the defenses we can muster for everyone here." Gunn looked out at a regatta. A fleet of spinnakers gently pulling their boats toward the marina.

"Wait a minute. You also said *other* countries. What other countries? " Moshe sounded more concerned. Did he now realize they really were up against a widespread superbug.

Gunn thought of himself pulling Moshe along. Moshe turned into a boat, Gunn the sail and sitting in the back, slowing the boat by dangling his hand in the sea, Amhach. Their boat sailed toward a school of sharks, only these sharks looked like long pieces of rope with messy knots for heads. "We need to be sure the warning news is delivered to all medical personnel, both here and in Baghdad."

"I don't know," Moshe said. "I worry about any public pronouncement that doesn't go through normal channels. Why can't you send your message directly to other outbreak sites and let them worry about it?"

The sharks parted for the boat and went off toward the beach. They looked for other victims. The out-of-body Gunn tried to yell to swimmers but no sound came from his mouth. Even with Gunn at the helm, the badly loaded boat wouldn't stay on course. He blankly stared at the regatta. "Several reasons." He spoke slowly as he answered Moshe's question. "We don't have any good method for direct communication and our own messages will only go to hospitals we know about."

"I don't like it." The Moshe-boat morphed into a Moshe caricature which shook its head in distress. This dark-haired obese Harpo Marx pulled a lit blowtorch from his pocket and sterilized everything in sight. "Why not use diplomatic channels. Put the onus on the politicians."

Gunn turned back to face his friend. "Hadn't thought of diplomatic channels. Guess that should work." Gunn's drawl gave him time to consider this distribution technique. "And the diplomatic channel should be fast. I assume we can ask the diplomats to alert everyone. To immediately forward it to all medical and mortuary personnel. Good idea Moshe. I like it. Amhach's continuous harping on political repercussions should have made me think of the diplomats. Or maybe his one-track mind, fact-free approach to management drove the political solution from me."

"Yes, that's it. With the diplomatic connection no heads will roll. It should even get to people faster."

"Yeah. Sounds good. Very good. Maybe not perfect, but this'll keep Billy Bob Amhach happier, for sure." Gunn briefly thought about the political fallout, an item he normally forgot. "Damn pols will never accept blame, but this approach will protect us. Thank you, Moshe, it'll help us all." Gunn contemplated the communication. Damn I hope they're careful in Iraq.

Gunn studied his friend. "Can you come over this evening? Maybe after dinner? By then we'll have our draft press-release done. You can review and critique our plan and med-alert and help us figure how to actually get it into distribution." Gunn wondered about the dark forces so common in the Mideast. Would they mock the CDC and ridicule suggestions of great care? Hell, it happened in West Africa, where we're less despised. Would the jerks here say it is all a CIA plot to slow urgent care? CDC's humorous, though actual, 2011 use of a Zombie Apocalypse in its example of how to do warning for a possible plague or epidemic may have changed the notification landscape. It was a humorous and eminently readable way to demonstrate catastrophe planning, but it was a gift to the fact-free faction, the conspiracy theorists, who want to claim the CDC is behind the MEFV epidemic. No time to worry about that. Maybe the zombies hadn't made it this far east.

"I won't be able to come over this evening. My in-laws are coming for dinner." A few second's silence and a sigh. "I'll find some way to get away. You'll have to help me make peace with Ester's uncle."

#

After dinner Moshe arrived at Gunn's room dressed in a navy blue Izod polo shirt, khaki slacks, and a yarmulke, conveniently hiding the balding spot on his head. Gunn paced while Moshe reviewed the written plan and draft medical alert and suggested a few minor changes.

"Okay. New topic." Gunn rubbed his forehead. "Have you seen Ian's chromatographs?"

"Yeah. You showed them to me last week. Remember?"

"Oh, crap, that's right. This shit's getting to me. I don't even know what *I'm* doing." Gunn repeatedly slapped his forehead with the heel of hand.

"Okay." Moshe spoke slowly and made a beckoning motion toward Gunn. "Tell me what's new and special about the chromatographs. What important new stuff do you see in them now?" Moshe sounded tired, not angry. Virologists often think of the bars on a chromatograph as a picture of a sample the way a criminologist thinks of a fingerprint as a picture of a perp.

"The chromatographs are in that envelope." Gunn pointed at the large envelope again and shuddered a little.

Moshe shook his head and closed his eyes. He sat, pulled out the charts, and studied them for a few seconds. "All right. What's so special about this virus? All I see is another random bar code. I'll bet you peeled this off a bottle of bourbon." He had a slight twinkle in his voice. Moshe was returning to the old friend Gunn had known for years.

"No, actually it's from Mogen David." Gunn used the patronizing tone that men often adopt with each other. He verified his old friend saw the sarcasm and was not offended at his suggestion of using a Kosher wine bar code.

Moshe smirked.

"Sorry. Guess you're not so used to chromatographs." Gunn reached over and pointed to the iron and tungsten lines in the graphs. "You saw these? We've never seen such prominent lines for refractory metals in a virus. We've compared them to other viruses. " Gunn pulled his laptop over and clicked away for a few seconds then turned it to Moshe and showed him a pair of chromatographs. "This is what the Ebolas we've seen in the past look like."

"They do look somewhat similar. Is that EBOV?" Moshe pointed at the chart on the top of Gunn's screen.

"ZEBOV, at the top and Marburg on the bottom." Gunn described the original Zaire Ebolavirus and the Marburgvirus, the one that had been considered an Ebolavirus for a couple of decades, but was now classified as a separate genus, but the same stringy virus family, *Filoviridae*. He turned his laptop back toward himself and moved the pointer and tapped on the mouse button a few times. Gunn turned the laptop so Moshe could see the screen. He now had pictures of Zaire, Marburg and Tel Aviv hemorrhagic fever viruses on the screen.

Moshe studied the laptop images. "Oy veh. If you throw out the metal lines, our baby looks sort of like a cross between the other two. Is that what you see?"

"Only the RNA will answer for sure, but yeah, that's what we think. That's our starting point. Our current hypothesis. We ought to get at least some word within a week or so on the analysis. I've never seen anything like this." Gunn shook his head and rubbed his temples. He looked past the drapes through the glass doors to his tiny patio with its view of the Mediterranean.

Gunn shuddered. "And, it only gets worse. Now a third item. We must have two outbreaks in the Mideast. I mean two outbreaks outside Israel. Got an email from Atlanta. Says there are rumors of a case in Southeast Iraq. That makes four cities, two countries, and probably over a hundred people infected already. No fast diagnosis. No cure. Few preventative measures."

"You're a lot more scared than this morning, aren't you?" Moshe looked up and raised an eyebrow, in his trademark gesture.

"Yes. This looks grim." Gunn bent over, still rubbing his forehead. Your doctors are pretty safe. In Iraq, who knows? Nosocomial transmission infected those two nurses in Texas in '14 and has been especially common in countries with poor hospital protocols. Hell, it's the norm without great care. I doubt the Iraqis are as careful as you, especially now that our military is officially out of there."

> \#

Moshe blessed Gunn's circumspect med-alert and cover letter requesting rapid dissemination to all hospitals, medical personnel and mortuaries throughout the region. The press release emphasized that West African Ebola outbreaks mostly occurred before medical personnel realized what they were dealing with. Most people got the lethal disease from other people because of inadequate or unsanitary medical or mortuary practices.

It also stressed that this Mideast Ebolavirus survived normal sterilization procedures. All material from infected patients, including needles, must be burned or flame sterilized. They sent it to the public relations officers for the Ministers of Communications, Defense, Foreign Affairs, and several lower level functionaries.

For days the epidemiologists poured over records and family and patient interviews. They monitored the new cases, which were now occurring at a rate of dozens each week, and brainstormed. They had days of collecting samples from sick people, their families and their environments.

> \#

Ian returned from Baghdad with slides from thirteen victims. "They haven't really admitted any cases. The ones we'd heard about are all in American and British hospitals. I found many more likely EBOV cases hidden in Iraqi hospitals. It's exactly as you feared, Gunn. Their Government won't admit the disease exists. If our embassy staff weren't so huge, we'd never have learned about most of these. I had tons of help getting into hospitals, both from John and from other embassy people with acquaintances on various hospital staffs."

"Oh, crap." Gunn shook his head and bit a thumbnail. "That means we have two full-fledged outbreaks. It isn't only another couple of cases over there. Damn, damn damn. This rules out most non-intentional sources. I guess it's possible that birds or bats might spread it in isolated pockets like this."

"Yeah," Ian said. "Looks really bad. I tried to convince the medical personnel of the importance for really serious sterilization and data collection, but their secrecy and denial mean the message only went to a few safe friends. It will only move to other hospitals by word-of-mouth."

"Damn. How many unreported or unrecognized cases do you think there are in Iraq?" Gunn cradled his head in his hand.

"Oh my God." Wild Bill spoke before Ian replied. He looked like he'd had an epiphany. "In Iraq we have to assume there are all sorts of cases in areas that Ian couldn't or didn't get to, don't we? We better assume it is rampant in ISIS-controlled areas."

"Yeah. And maybe in other countries. We'd probably never hear anything about the virus in Syria." Gunn looked as pale as the others.

"Syria is not very open. Half-assed Assad is about as closed and isolated as they come." Wild Bill shook his head.

"Maybe we should hope our pet is an ISIS development," Gunn said. "If they are responsible, we can hope it didn't get loose in their areas."

"Does that make sense?" Ian asked. "They couldn't develop this, could they? Some Russian, Chinese, or even Israeli, would seem more likely to me. They have the scientific and espionage chops. ISIS doesn't, do they?"

The Americans entered all their info into a database. They twisted and turned the data to new orientations looking for common threads. They made graphs, charts and maps and looked for patterns. Though exhausting, this analysis of the thousands of samples they had now amassed from many people and many places was easy and safe because it kept the team members away from the virus. And away from treating dozens of sick and dying people, who presented real dangers and big risks.

Thursday evening Gunn called Moshe, "This is frustrating. We need more analysis and more techs to localize the virus. Can you come over to the hotel so we can discuss it without continuous interruption?"

"Without interruption?" Moshe said. Gunn imagined his eye roll and his mouth in a half sneer as he shook his head. "Every time I've met you in the evening you waste all my time. You're only interested in a drinking buddy. I'm glad to go out for a drink occasionally, but not every night like you bachelors." The argument went back and forth for a full minute.

Moshe, like American bureaucrats, left work and expected not to return until the next morning. They argued until Gunn said, "We've come 5,000 miles to try to help with this epidemic and we've been working on it 80 hours a week. Hard work. Don't you think you can give us one evening away from your family? It's only the second this week."

"Yeah, sure," Moshe said. "Twenty hours hard work and sixty hours hard drinking."

"You bastard. Thirty or better on hard work, I'm sure." Gunn felt like pounding the telephone. His image of Moshe had become a great curly haired boulder—completely immovable.

"Okay, I'll come to meet, but in your room. I want this done quickly without distractions or alcohol on your side."

"Deal." Gunn immediately put his bottle of wine inside the armoire and closed the door. He brushed his teeth. Yuck, what an awful taste right after wine. He gargled with Act to drive off the yuck. When he heard the knock on his door he popped a Certs in his mouth.

They had been working less than fifteen minutes when the phone rang. Moshe picked it up and handed the phone to Gunn, who stood to answer the call. "Gunn Shoreham." Silence. "Oh no. What else can go wrong? I'll be right over." Click. He collapsed back into his chair.

"What happened?"

"That was Wild Bill." Gunn buried his face in his hand and trembled. He held his breath in an attempt to dissipate the nausea, to force the elephants out of his stomach. After many seconds he let out a gasp as his body complained about the lack of oxygen. He started breathing again. "Wild Bill took Ian to Sourasky Medical Center. He had flu symptoms."

"Eyze chara baleben," Moshe swore in Hebrew. It was an epithet Gunn had heard him use when they were at Harvard but had little idea of the specific meaning. He used it rather than the more common Anglo-Saxon terms often heard in Israel. It was less offensive to Americans. The emotional meaning was clear—something along the lines of *What the fuck will happen next.* "What the? Why didn't he call before they left?"

"Wild Bill said he tried to call. He must have called while I was on the phone to you."

"Crap. Damn awful timing." Moshe hung his head and shook it.

"Yeah. And Ian's sure he has hemorrhagic fever, not something as benign as the flu." Gunn rubbed his glabella.

"Oy veh. Much worse than that, from our standpoint anyway. He was close to finishing his analysis. Nobody works as fast as he does. This is bound to slow the MEFV fight." Moshe rubbed his chin. "And his documentation is so sparse... Lots of his work will have to be repeated."

"Damn. You're right. Ian takes pretty shitty notes. I think he hates writing. I've noticed his English is poor—lots of misspelled words or typos and such."

"I won't have much to go on, will I?" Moshe gently punched his temples with his fists. "I won't be able to repeat only the last two steps to catch up with him."

Gunn shook his head but said nothing.

Moshe looked toward the door. "Lousy timing, Ian."

Chapter 13 – Day 3, Friday

Darrel Li in Herndon, Virginia

Darrel Li had assumed his wildly non-Chinese given name when he first came to America for graduate school. He picked it for weirdness. An unusual first name was important when you have the most common family name in the world. He didn't hear the oddity of his combined first and last names.

He received his doctorate, with specialization in gene splicing, from the University of Virginia in Charlottesville. He never noticed the inconsistency between getting his degree from the school Thomas Jefferson founded and his hypothetical espionage work as a one-person sleeper cell for Ministry of State Security, the Chinese version of the combined FBI, CIA and NSA. He was the vanguard of new experiment by the MSS in Beijing created for technology espionage. Darrel never saw himself as a spy. He knew he had been forced into MSS service as a condition of going to America for graduate work. He began working at a biotech start-up in June, 2004.

The MSS wanted to infiltrate high tech start-ups with their own young scientists, a move well beyond their traditional work to extract information from the American government labs. The Ministry of State Security hypothesized they'd glean new technology from these small companies in areas where the American Government did no work itself, areas like information-tech and bio-tech. And they hoped one of these young PhDs would create another Alibaba.com. Darrel knew his job was exactly what MSS desired.

Like many gifted scientists, probably most of them, he was blessed with autism spectrum disorder, which manifested itself in poor sense of humor but an extraordinary ability to concentrate on a single problem for long periods of time. That first symptom showed when he gave papers on his graduate work and at Virein during his job application process: he had read the entire paper to his audience, the start-up's scientists.

With coaching during his first few years on his job at Virein, he learned to be much more personable to audiences. He continued to withdraw into his own world when he talked, but his improved speaking skill meant his audience rarely noticed. His boss, CM, always accompanied Darrel at presentations and intercepted questions, greatly increasing Darrel's comfort.

By Thanksgiving 2008, he was one of only three people at the company to have anything to be thankful about. All employees except their tech, Ingrid, and him, had been let go—laid off because the company's cash reserves were so badly depleted. CM let Ingrid go 18 months later. He had given Darrel only one raise in six years.

Darrel and CM took Ingrid to lunch on her last day on the job in the spring of '10. CM had selected a Chinese restaurant for the going away party for the secretary/receptionist/lab tech. She had a glass of white box wine. Darrel and CM had tea.

"Darrel, something I've wondered for years." Ingrid studied the scientist. "Do you have more than one suit?"

"Yes." Darrel always kept technical competence as his highest priority. True, he wore one style of charcoal gray suit, even under his lab coat, but his microbiology skills were the best. He even wore one of his gray suits when he accompanied CM to give a technology presentation to venture capitalists or other potential investors. "I have four of these suits."

From 14 employees in '06 to three in '08 to two in '10, Virein needed a financial breakthrough. CM always seemed to be looking for money: venture, contract or angel. This time in Research Triangle. Last month it had been overseas.

The company had nearly developed a technique for splicing genes into vegetable DNA. Darrel had made presentations where he showed the splicing would allow companies to tailor resistance to specific diseases for almost any crop. The venture capitalists didn't buy it. The government didn't buy it.

With the company close to gone, CM redirected their efforts to yeasts and fungi. CM put only one demand on Darrel's work, that he always think about productizing his ideas. He told Darrel he hoped to get money from the beer, wine, or mushroom industries. "We'll have no competition," he told Darrel and investors. He managed to keep enough money for the two scientists. Darrel often talked to CM, both for brainstorming and for the dish of licorice always on his desk. The candy dish remained full, even through all the cutbacks.

Darrel decided to try his own hand at raising money for Virein. Two days after the first signs of the Ebola outbreak in Israel, Darrel Li took his boss to Dulles Airport. After driving the Candy Man to Dulles Airport, Darrel called the Chinese embassy from a pay phone by the taxi stand. "This is Darrel Li. Is Chen Kwok Pun available, please?" He looked at his watch.

Forty-three seconds later a man picked up his call. "Hello, Dr. Li? Mr. Chen is not available right now. Can you give me a number and I'll have him call you back?"

Darrel had assumed the name was fictitious, a key to tell the receptionist to treat his call specially. "No. I have no number. This is pay phone at airport. When can I reach him?"

"Hmm." The man paused. "Go to the Dragon Café on Arlington Boulevard in Falls Church. Mr. Chen will meet you there." He switched to the Mandarin dialect of Chinese.

Darrel's abs cramped as he recalled the day of his pre-employment interview. He felt as nauseous as he had then. He had a rented a Toyota Corolla. After the day of interviews, Ingrid walked to the door with him. "How do I go to get back to Dulles Airport?" he asked.

"Nothing to it. Go out to Centreville Road." Ingrid pointed to their left, west. "Turn right on Centreville and go about 100 yards then turn left onto the Tollway. Its well marked, All you have to do is turn left right after you go under the Access Road."

"Sounds easy enough."

"The only thing to worry about is the four-lane change across traffic. You'll have to cut across the toll road to make the left exit into Dulles."

Darrel thanked her. He repeated the directions to himself and started driving back to the airport, slowly and cautiously. He saw the sign to the Dulles Airport access road, as Ingrid had told him. His directions said to turn left, but he couldn't. Too much traffic. He turned right at the next chance and went down Woodgate Drive, unsure of what to do. After a ten minute stop in the Woodgate Centre's parking lot to recover his composure, he turned around and retraced his route back to the company. On the second try as soon as he saw the sign to Dulles Airport he pulled across the traffic. Three lanes to cross. It nearly killed him changing lanes under the overpasses.

He shuddered at all the errors and the recollection of that drive. He could not drive where he was not familiar with roads. Was he going to be sick here? He looked down and put his hand to his mouth and tried to concentrate on the image of a field of flowers. He had needed three and a half hours for the 10-minute drive to Dulles. He rarely ventured as far as Falls Church.

"I cannot find that place." He also changed from his Pidgin English to Mandarin. "It is unacceptable to me. Is there another meeting place you can suggest that is closer to Reston-Herndon?"

Again more than ten seconds of silence greeted his question. "Can you find the Golden Panda on Lee Highway in Chantilly?" Darrel thought he could hear sounds of paper shuffling.

Darrel had seen the Golden Panda but had never been in it. Thank goodness. I can find it again. "I will go there and wait."

"Sit in the very back booth. It will take Mr. Chen more than an hour to get there."

"How will I recognize Mr. Chen?" Darrel said.

"You don't have to worry about recognizing him. He will recognize you."

Darrel felt more sure than ever that Chen Kwok Pun was a code name, not for a person but for a service or office. They were probably scrambling to find someone to meet him. "That's not sufficient. I will not talk to anyone if I do not know who he is and that he can be trusted."

Another ten second delay that felt like ten minutes to Darrel who now felt accustomed to the American pace of conversation.

"He will wear a Mao pin on his shirt pocket. You will only be able to see the pin after he sits down, unbuttons and opens his suit jacket. He will also know your father's birth village.

"Okay. I will be there." Darrel returned to his car and slowly started the drive back to Herndon. He looked at the gold building standing on its corner, the one that looked like someone dropped it there by mistake. No Feng Shui.

Chapter 14 – Day 30, Thursday

Tel Aviv

Gunn and Moshe caught a cab to Ichilov Hospital in the Sourasky Medical Center, a mile due east of the hotel. Gunn felt at home with the institutional decor, gurney-width doors, and rubbing alcohol aroma. The machine-gun armed guards were unfamiliar and unsettling in a hospital.

At Ian's room they were stopped by an armed guard. The guard spoke and Moshe translated, "Nobody's allowed to go in there. He's been told only the people on the hospital's list are allowed in."

"Tell him who we are. We should be on the list." Gunn's voice was conversational. Perhaps it was his Georgia drawl, perhaps his southern manners, but people thought he sounded pleased with nearly every situation.

Moshe spoke to the guard. Gunn could only understand their names. The guard called on his radio and waited. Gunn visualized a bored clerk clicking away on a computer, trying to find the list of allowed visitors. Then his image changed to a bored clerk looking through stacks of paper files in manila file folders piled in her in-basket, trying to find a folder with a list of names. Eventually the guard's radio retorted, "Dr. Shoreham yecholim lehicanes. Dr. Moshe Eisenberg lo al hareshima."

When the radio finished its pronouncement, before the guard could say anything, Moshe turned to Gunn and explained. "You're on the list. I'm not. Go on in and I'll go find the Security Office and try to straighten this out. You'll have to show the guard some ID to get in. I hope you brought your passports or something."

Gunn looked at Moshe and shrugged. "All I have with me is my driver's license." He took his license from his wallet and turned and handed it to the guard. Gunn kept searching in his wallet. Moshe watched the proceedings in seeming amusement. After another 15 seconds Gunn found his government ID card, which he also handed to the guard. Moshe turned toward the elevator but returned when the guard spoke again.

The guard spoke sternly to Gunn. Moshe translated, "Be careful. Put on a mask, gown and booties to protect yourselves and everyone else. Don't go close to the patient and don't touch him. Make sure your skin is all completely covered. Don't stay in more than 30 minutes. When you come out keep your gloves on until you have put all the other stuff, including the goggles, in the red can in the anteroom. Be sure everything is completely in the can. Don't open the outer door until everyone's done changing and the burn can is tightly closed."

Moshe spoke to the guard, who pointed to the door from the hallway into Ian's room as he spoke. The anteroom's large window would allow the guard to verify that all Ian's visitors properly followed all the procedures. "He also says to make sure the inner door stays closed while you change. Never more than one door open at a time and obey any orders the nurse gives you." Moshe pointed to the two doors. "Sorry, I know you know all this, I translated what he said."

He entered Ian's anteroom. A pile of surgical wear filled a shelf inside the door. It looked like the Israeli's had been scared into believing in nosocomial transmission. From this angle the bio-hazard symbol on the red steel garbage can was prominent. "Thank God they're taking this seriously," he spoke to the empty room. "They must be burning everything that's been exposed to Ian or any of the other victims. Good precaution."

In Ian's room a nurse sat in the corner, clad head-to-toe in a green hazmat suit. He or she looked up to see the new comers, then turned to watch the blood pressure and oxygen monitors connected to Ian. Ian's IV drip said it was operating properly.

"I feel like I have the flu," Ian said to Gunn.

"That's what he told me as we came down here." Wild Bill spoke through his mask. Like Gunn, his ears were protected by the green hood and his face was covered by a surgical mask and a plastic face shield. No skin showed on Gunn or Wild Bill.

"Yeah, but I don't think I've been exposed to the flu," Ian said. "I can't recall seeing anyone with it. Hemorrhagic fever is too dangerous to take a chance. I had to get down here. So far no one will say I have only the flu. Be very cautious. I thought I was, but I'm worried. I'm awfully tired."

Gunn noticed some blotchiness on Ian's hands and face. "Have they started you on Zmapp?"

Ian shook his head. "I think all the usual Ebola antivirals are used up. Think all they have is regular ones."

"We have a little. I'll make sure you get it starting in the morning." Gunn studied his colleague. "That's about all we can do to help. Do you want us to have the CDC fly Colleen over?"

"She's in the midst of two years of oral chemo for the APL she had. I worry that she isn't very strong yet. Please don't call her till we're sure of the diagnosis. I don't want her to be concerned unnecessarily."

As they talked, Moshe came in. "Hey, Ian."

Ian didn't seem to notice the greeting. "Anyway, I don't think she's allowed to travel. She's supposed to avoid crowds because the chemo drugs destroy her immune system. And even if she did go on the plane, it would be too dangerous for her to come see me."

Gunn shook his head. Crap. Why did this happen to him. "If you have Ebola, I'll kill you, Ian. I've never lost a team member to the target infection. You break my record and you're dead meat."

"And if you think you're getting any of my blood, you've got another thing coming." Wild Bill put his hand to his chin in a contemplative gesture that distorted his mask to an even more cartoonish shape. "You may be A positive like me, but I like my blood where it is." Wild Bill and Gunn continued their feeble attempts at humor while Moshe mostly listened.

#

On the elevator down from Ian's floor, Gunn said, "Did you notice Ian's skin? Petechial rash, I think. If I'm right, we should have an easy diagnosis by tomorrow morning." The rash was like a severe case of acne about to erupt. With Ebola, it would look like hundreds of pimples within a day or so, each pimple would be twice as big as any acne pimple.

"Yeah. And he shows all the other early symptoms, too. Even if it isn't Ebola, it sure looks like some HFV." Wild Bill grimaced as the whole group acted like they were standing around Ian's grave watching the sod being dumped onto his coffin, not going down in an elevator in one of the World's best hospitals. "At least no western hospital has lost any early-stage Ebola patients."

"Not yet, anyway," Gunn said. "Remember those pics Ian had. This bastard is harder to cure and harder to sterilize against. And, so far most of the patients have had Zmapp or something like it."

"Do you think Ian's procedures were at fault?" Moshe asked the morose group. The big man abruptly dominated the elevator. The Americans looked at him.

Except for his frown Wild Bill looked quite collegiate in jeans and a light green tee shirt sporting a Dilbert cartoon. Silence. Ian needed help and hope.

"I doubt it," Gunn said finally, as the three exited the elevator on the ground floor. "If I were to pick one issue like that right now, it would be Ian's onychophagia."

"That's right," Wild Bill said to himself. "He didn't have any nails, did he?"

"No. And his fingers had numerous open wounds. He's provided more openings for the virus to get into his body than most people. A slight porosity in some gloves or mishandling of them, and the virus could get through onto his hands and into his blood before he has a chance to scrub."

"Damn. Even regular Ebolaviruses are tough. Really hard to stop." Moshe shook his head and looked at the floor. "Hemorrhagic virus. Any blood transferal and the virus goes with it. And this tough bugger is more likely to survive on a hard surface for some time. Oy vey."

"Even careful sterilization might be useless," Wild Bill said to Gunn. "If your guess that the virus has some sort of thermophilic adaptation, he may have picked up the virus in an area he thought safe and clean." Two heads nodded in agreement. "Damn it. Why does this happen to him? He's so careful. What are his chances now? Ten percent?

Fifty percent?"

"It's nowhere near that bad, thank god." Gunn looked down. "No implication of belief in a supernatural force implied by that," he mumbled to himself. "Those are the numbers for third-world hospitals in sub-Saharan Africa."

During the silent return to the hotel, Gunn worried about others getting the disease. There were continuous reports of shortages of anything medical in Iraq. He wondered if the Iraqi conditions could be much better than those in Sierra Leone or Liberia. "We've got to be sure we've notified all the medical personnel in Iraq."

"So that's what's bugging you," Wild Bill said. "I could see something on your face but hadn't deciphered your frown. What exactly are you suggesting? What additional notifications should we send?"

"Sorry, that was rather out of the blue, wasn't it. The primary vector for the spread of hemorrhagic fever viruses has been insufficiently super sanitary medical, hospice and mortuary practices. It occurs to me that the reported conditions in Iraq are almost as poor as those in Nigeria. We need to find a way to notify all the orderlies, nurses, doctors morticians and what-have-you in Iraq."

"And family members," Moshe interrupted Gunn.

"Yeah." Gunn nodded. "Damn. I have to warn John, too."

"Who's John," Moshe asked.

"Oh. My son-in-law. He escorted Ian around Baghdad. Ian shouldn't have been contagious until long after he got back here, but whatever got him may have gotten John too." Gunn rubbed his forehead. How could this be happening to him? He decided to send John a warning as soon as he was back to his computer.

"Oh God, yes." Gunn continued messaging his temples. "We have to hit all the family members in Baghdad and wherever else this may pop up. Oh crap. We've got to scare the bejeesus out of damn near everybody. And everywhere. As it pops up in more countries we'll need to make sure everyone understands that the bodies of victims should be cremated."

"Uh Oh." Moshe almost sounded like he was crying. "Cremation will be another toughie. Neither Muslims or Jews are allowed to cremate their deceased. It's considered mutilation of the body."

"Yuck, will anything less kill our MEFV." Wild Bill shook his head.

"Wonder how long this damnable virus takes to die underground?"

They discussed various ways to disseminate the news. The Americans thought the press was the key. They seemed ready to go for splashy news reporting to be sure everyone was informed.

"Wait a minute," Moshe said. "This might start a panic."

"You mean like the ones in New Jersey and Maine?" Gunn smiled and shook his head. "The asshole politicians in those states panicked when Ebola showed up in 2014 but the only people they bothered were the nurses, the exact people who needed support. Did you hear what Ian found in Baghdad?" Gunn looked at Moshe, his face begging for an answer. "A dozen cases there."

"I thought there were two *possible* cases. He found a dozen? But your embassy only reported one or two?" Moshe paled. Gunn had never seen him look so northern European.

"The Embassy had heard about two. The others were in hospitals Americans don't use. He found a dozen patients, in smaller Iraqi hospitals. He found more flu, but the dozen were cases he was pretty sure were EBOV. For all we know there are dozens in Iraq. In fact, it's hard to believe there are less than dozens there." Gunn tried to sound sympathetic. He didn't want to come across as abrasive.

Wild Bill was ashen. "We've got to tell them all, don't we? And fast."

"Diplomatic channels should be as fast as the news." Moshe shook his head. He didn't seem to be paying attention to anyone.

"Ian said the only cautions adopted by hospitals were from word-of-mouth." Wild Bill bit a fingernail. "The diplomats must have been too worried about embarrassing their governments to disseminate our med-alert."

"And even if it finally gets through, we can be sure the message we give them won't be accurately transmitted, perhaps not even to the right people. This is really scary." Wild Bill was still ashen. "And what about other countries. Neither Syria or ISIS will admit any cases. Or the other rebels, either."

Gunn nodded and looked at Moshe. "And if we bypass your bureaucracy somehow, it'll still go through several others. The way this erupted here, we should be worrying about a hemorrhagic fever pandemic." This outbreak could really get that bad. "MEFV could be much worse than the bubonic plague in the Middle Ages. Even with the best treatments currently known, this filovirus would probably have a fatality rate worse than the medieval plagues. Death count in the billions for a pandemic."

The first plague, the one in the middle Sixth Century called the Justinian Plague, was probably a significant contributor to the great recession now called *The Dark Ages* because it killed such a large fraction of the population of Europe. At its current growth rate, this MEFV could infect everyone in the world in about six months. It had to be stopped.

"Hell. Damn. You know you're on your own on this." Moshe's anxiety sounded similar to the time he'd been arrested in a sweep of a party at Harvard and couldn't prove he was 21—not frightened, but apprehensive. The three scientists entered their hotel and headed for the elevator.

"I think we've got to use the news media." Gunn thought about Israeli TV. Damn reporters. Damn journalists. Israeli TV will want an interview and they're bound to get something wrong. "The only way we can quickly reach everyone is to use CNN and Al Jazeera. They're bound to make lot's of mistakes, but the dissemination will be faster with them. Y' know, Robinson's the first reporter I've met who even cared enough to try to get everything right. So maybe it will be more accurate than usual." Israelis listen to Al Jazeera all the time even if some members of the American and Israeli governments consider the Qatari news channel to be Al-Qa'ida News Inc.

"Now wait a minute, Gunn. You're going way to far. You tell Al Jazeera and heads will roll even if everything else is kosher. My bosses will kill me. Their bosses will sack them. The Prime Minister will go after all of us. You can't do it." Moshe stood between Gunn and the door to his Crowne Plaza room. Very confrontational. His poor attempt at belligerence actually showed how conflicted he was.

Gunn edged around Moshe and slouched into a chair. He looked at the ibexes over his bed. "What do you mean *can't do it*? How else can you reach the doctors in half a dozen cities that we know of plus who knows how many dozen more. Cities all across the Mideast? All those we didn't reach on our last attempt? What about orderlies, morticians and families in Baghdad or Cairo or Damascus?" His slow drawl pleaded for an answer. He looked into his lap. "I'm desperate. You're aware of repercussions here and I suspect Amhach will use it as an excuse to fire me." Yeah. Just what I need. Another career-threatening report.

"And this is one that needs to be picked up by Al Jazeera," Wild Bill said. "If they don't broadcast it, we'll miss contacting many of the people who need to protect themselves. Hell, we'll miss most of them."

Gunn turned reflective. "Try to imagine the possibilities and consequences. If we tell no one, Israel and the U.S. are blamed for the pandemic and annihilated. If we use diplomatic channel, the pandemic is blamed on Israel, and it's annihilated. If we use the press, the pandemic is averted and only we, ourselves, are annihilated."

"Talk about a horny dilemma." Moshe sagged.

"Hmm, Amhach's been gunning for anyone who doesn't toe the line." Gunn felt pale. "Actually the Trump line. Might as well give him the ammo he needs to get me.

"And if the outbreak extends to Iran or Syria, those governments will never even admit they have the virus." Wild Bill looked at Moshe. "Other cases will appear. But we'll only know when the sickness reaches the bloodiest, terminal stage when it is unmistakably a hemorrhagic fever."

"You're right. They need to know." Moshe appeared resigned and scared. "Crap. Everyone has to know."

"Yeah. Everyone." Gunn pursed his lips as he nodded. "At least anyone who might be related to any possible victim."

"So you agree, Moshe?" Wild Bill said. "No more euphemisms and circumspection. Plain language: assume people with flu symptoms have the Ebolavirus Plague."

"*Plague*, that's a good word for hoi polloi," Gunn said. "It'll cause extra action, probably panic."

"And we have to be sure all needles used for people with flu symptoms or Ebola, are destroyed in fire." Wild Bill nodded. "We have to be sure hospital administrators know that no water-based sterilization suffices. One hundred degrees is probably only half the temperature needed to kill these bugs."

"The anti-western sentiment we arouse with our panic will be nothing compared to what would follow the millions of EBOV cases if we don't do a broad notification." Gunn studied Moshe to be sure he agreed, or at least understood.

Chapter 15 – Day 7, Tuesday

Darrel Li in Herndon, Virginia

Darrel went into the Golden Panda, past the Buddha on a chair holding a sign "Please Seat Yourself." Opposite Buddha, on the wall next to the cash register a handwritten sign, "No Tipping," in Chinese logograms only. He walked to the back of the long narrow restaurant and found an isolated booth, but six people were sitting in it. He sat at a table where he could watch the door and the booth, the one for the meeting with the hypothetical Mr. Chen.

The odors of soy sauce, burnt sesame and peanut oils, and black tea permeated the dimly lit dining room. Some North China music covered the sounds from the front of the restaurant, but not those from the corner booth. Those people spoke too loudly, anyway, and probably wanted even less lighting, like most American restaurants. Plexiglas covered the Ming Dynasty pattern table cloths. A broken corner adorned the clear plastic cover on Darrel's table.

The waiter came to his table. "Can I get you something to drink?"

"Tea, please." Darrel checked the entrance and the corner table. "How long will table be occupied?" He pointed to *his* corner table. "I'll need more space when my friends join me."

"I think it will be quite some time." The waiter looked. The six Caucasian business people were chatting and drinking tea. "They haven't been there very long. They are regular customers and always eat a long and expensive lunch."

Darrel scowled and wondered what to do. He studied the table. *Expensive* Hmm. The waiter won't move them.

"We have another large table. Our other corner booth in front." The waiter pointed past the kitchen which occupied the center of the restaurant. The cook sat by the stove in his glassed-in kitchen, waiting with the materials for the lunches he would soon wok.

"I'm expected here. I better stay at this table. It'll probably be hour before anyone else gets here, anyway." Darrel returned to the Chinese paper he'd brought in from his car.

News about Daw Aung San Suu Kyi greeting crowds in Yangoon in one news item and the glee aroused among separatists on Taiwan from Trump's tweets in anoother. Darrel read the articles. He slowly realized he did not want to be seen with that paper, not by MSS. He folded it and put it back in his pocket. He doodled on the napkin, working to better understand his latest work on inserting new genes into yeasts using viral modifiers.

After 68 minutes, a man walked up to his table. Darrel was so deep in planning his next days' work he jumped at the sound of the voice in front of him. He looked up blankly, still lost in thought. "Hello, Dr. Li, my name is Chen, may I join you?"

He recalled why he sat in the Golden Panda. He looked at the corner booth. Still occupied. He checked the newcomer. Chen's dark gray suit looked baggy and ill fitting. I guess Beijing wants our agents to be obvious. "Yes. Please sit down." He pointed to the chair across the table.

So this is Mr. Chen. No, that's probably an alias. He is some staff member of our embassy, here to find out if they should spend any time talking to me. Actually, he is probably with the Ministry of Security Services and attached to the embassy. Lots of American embassy personnel are CIA. Lots of our *diplomats* are MSS, too, I'm sure.

Mr. Chen sat in the chair and faced Darrel. He looked around toward the entrance then turned to Darrel. "May I change places with you or sit there?" He spoke in Mandarin and pointed to the chair next to Darrel, one with its back toward the corner that would give him an inconspicuous view of the restaurant's entrance.

"Yes. Go ahead. Sit there." Darrel pointed at the empty chair and also switched to Mandarin. He continued to watch his visitor. Definitely MSS.

Mr. Chen moved to his new chair next to Darrel. He could now watch the door and the sidewalk near the Golden Panda's entrance. "I gather you're from northwest of Beijing?"

"Yes." Darrel recalled that the contact would know his father's village. He continued to study the visitor.

"Oh, good. I should be less formal." Mr. Chen unbuttoned his suit jacket revealing a red Mao pin stuck on his shirt pocket. "I never met your father, but I gather he was from Xinxing Fucun. Is that where you were born?"

"Yes. I grew up there." The ersatz Mr. Chen had satisfactorily identified himself. Whoever he is, Darrel should be safe talking to him.

"How far is Xinxing Fucun from Beijing? I've never been there."

"It's about 100 km away. An easy train ride." Darrel remembered that he should try to stay in the conversation. Ask questions as well as answer them. More small talk followed. "Say, I have a problem I hope you can help." His voice was very low, as it had been for the entire conversation.

"Go ahead." Mr. Chen nodded.

That's an unusually American gesture of understanding. "We, meaning my company, have made significant strides and are on the cusp of being able to insert new genes into fungi. This has tremendous commercial importance because it should allow us to design mushrooms that have high protein. That would make them even better for meat replacements than the Portabella burgers you can get in American stores now."

"That's very interesting," Mr. Chen said without seeming at all interested.

Darrel frowned and tried to think of all the things he was supposed to do. "In addition to providing a better diet in China, it will provide a tremendous export product and allow millions of farmers to increase their exports."

Mr. Chen brightened. "Oh. Now I see how it's interesting and important."

Darrel quieted and looked up at the waiter when he approached their table to see if they were going to wait for other arrivals or if they wanted to order. He took their lunch orders. Darrel ordered stir-fry pork and mushroom. Mr. Chen ordered cashew chicken. The waiter left.

He's interested. Time to spring the trap. "Our problem is that we need a little more money to finish the project and perfect our techniques. The Great Recession has taken away nearly all of our money. Can our government help my bio-tech start-up finish the project? Do we want to be a leader in the next generation of bio-technology?"

"I don't know, but I'll relay your question back to Beijing." He seemed to lose all interest in the conversation.

Mr. Chen must have expected some great piece of espionage. Darrel had disappointed him, but something might still come from the request.

Darrel held a Chinese black mushroom in his chop sticks. "Suppose this had as much protein as pork." Darrel pointed the mushroom at a piece of pork in his bowl. "It would revolutionize the Chinese diet. And give us a whole new menu of exportable foods."

"Yes, I suppose it would." Mr. Chen sounded skeptical.

"But that is the technology we have. It's nearly marketable. We are at the point where we need some very small additional support to finish. If the Government supports the final stage of our work, then it will own the technology for making high-protein mushrooms." Wonder how good Mr. Chen's English is. "It will own the *MeatRooms*," he said in English. "We could be creating them within a few months. In Beijing." Mr. Chen doesn't believe me.

Chapter 16 – Day 31, Late Friday

Tel Aviv

When Gunn and Moshe returned to Gunn's room in the Crowne Plaza, he checked the press release and inserted one more comma. He added copies of two posters he found on the Internet. One graphically warned, "You mustn't touch a sick or dead person or monkey." The other showed that effective sterilization of needles required fire. Water could not get hot enough to kill MEFV. It also warned of the danger of even a single touch to a wound. "These posters don't relate directly to our press release, but they'll emphasize our point. What do you think?"

"Looks good. Guess we better get going." Moshe's voice indicated resignation and forced acceptance.

"But look, Moshe. There's no point in destroying both of us. I'll get this out to everyone. There will be an English speaker somewhere near the phone for Al Jazeera. Go on home and make sure you have a good alibi."

"I hate throwing you to the lions. Are you sure you'll be okay?" Moshe looked skeptical.

"Hell, the worst that can happen is that I'll have to join Doctors Without Borders. Get out of here, but let me know if there's anything else I can do to hide you."

He frowned and shook his bowed head. "Probably jail us for copyright infringement with those posters."

"We'll probably be lucky to be jailed for the posters. Hell, copyright infringement jail might keep us treason jail for the MEFV announcement. Probably me out of Guantánamo and you out of Ayalon or Shata."

"Well, I'll need some help making peace with Ester's uncle, the rabbi. He'll be really upset at me because I drove on the Sabbath."

"I'll do what I can. Blame that on me, too." Gunn made a shooing motion to Moshe. "Tell him it's not yet sundown in Atlanta. We still have plenty of time to pretend to drive legally. Get going."

Moshe thanked him and left. Gunn looked at his watch and the clock radio. Too late to get the announcement to any of the ones who need it tonight, but 5:15 PM in Atlanta is good for tomorrow's papers. He emailed the press release to Robinson at the *Atlanta Journal-Constitution* and called him. No answer on Robinson's phone. His call was routed to voicemail on the first ring. He described their plan and finished his recorded message for Robinson by reading a few parts of the press release. "When you get this message, please call me back with some local media contacts, if you have any. I also have something more for you but I don't want to delay sending this news to go to CNN and Al Jazeera right away. Call soon, please. We have to warn all the medical and mortuary personnel around here. By tomorrow morning, our time, you should have the story out. I hope the scoop is as big a deal for you as it is for reporters in old movies." He collapsed into his bed.

    #

Gunn jumped awake when the phone rang a few inches from his head. He fumbled for the phone, dropped it, then answered. Robinson Winter identified himself and said, "I emailed some contact info for CNN. I don't know anyone with Al Jazeera, so your contacts there will be as good or better than anything I can provide."

Gunn mumbled. Even to himself, he was unintelligible.

Robinson continued, "Oh. Sorry to wake you up. You called only a couple of minutes ago. I thought you'd still be up. Go back to sleep and thanks for the scoop. It *is* a big deal for me."

Gunn looked at the clock radio and was surprised to see 2:25. He shook his head to clear it and awaken himself. "No. That's okay, Robinson. We want to help you. Thanks for letting me know you got my call. You saw the note to make sure you skip the radio and TV. If you put it in your paper tomorrow, it'll buy me a couple of hours." Before

Amhach would know about and the crap would hit the fan.

"Yeah. I got that. I won't tell anyone but the *Journal-Constitution* press people."

"Now, are you in a private location? Can I give you some off-the-record info." Gunn thought about Ian. "Don't let anyone know where you learned it. Okay?"

"Guaranteed source anonymity. Confidentialities are us. Shoot."

"Ian has what we think is the hemorrhagic fever. We're almost certain he's come down with MEFV but we won't have a histological proof for a few days. The symptoms look grim. If you report this, do not identify Ian. Nothing worse for his wife than to hear about this from your paper or the TV."

"Wow. Did the torn suit allow him to get Ebola?"

"Nah. Almost impossible." Gunn explained their Ebola transmission theory. "That part's all in our press release. No mention of Ian. Right?"

"Yes, sir. No problem. No mention."

"TSA is so incompetent. Blame them if you want." Gunn groaned. "Actually, it would be better not to mention the torn suit. Ian's wife might connect Ian to the Ebola case if she read that tidbit."

"You suggest I beat up TSA for tearing your suit even though you think that has nothing to do with Ian's Ebola?" Robinson had good diction that went with his good dress and no noticeable African-American accent.

"They deserve it. Culpable if not guilty. You want a story about how inept they are? I found a Spiderman toy in my suitcase after a flight. Some poor kid lost his treasure. Apparently the TSA baboons put it in my bag, probably when they rifled his stuff and mine at the same time."

"Are you serious?"

"Yes, sir. It happened to me. If you lose a toy or tool, you assume you forgot to pack it or lost it. But there's no way to add anything to a bag except for some inept inspector to stick it there. More inconsiderate than sloppy."

"I begin to see why you're down on TSA."

"Wait, you haven't even heard the really bad one. Pauline found some thong panties in her suitcase once. Can you imagine what your wife would say if she found girlie underwear in your suitcase after a business trip. At least that time, the panties were in her bag not mine, so she knew it was TSA's incompetence, not my philandering. That incident really scares me because it means that TSA has probably destroyed some marriages with similar clumsiness. They should privatize that whole mess. They have no right to be federal employees. Bastards give us all a bad name." Gunn heard from a female coworker, Komiko Yomato, who was surely groped by a TSA agent. Dr. Yomato was so cautions and supportive of TSA's basic effort that she'd never complain to anyone. She even demurred when Gunn urged her to write letters, at least to her congresswoman or a senator.

"I'll see what I can write," Robinson said.

"Yeah. And remember, you only have to talk to feds once a month. Your occasional interviews with us can't be too awful. Think how exhausting it is for people who have to deal with bureaucrats every day. The biggest drawback of being a fed is I have to deal with them daily." Gunn chuckled. Robinson seemed to pick up on the satire. They hung up. Gunn picked up his crossword puzzle magazine to bore himself back to sleep.

In the morning, after only four hours sleep, Gunn contacted the two international news networks to deliver his press release around noon— very early morning in Atlanta. He emailed Pauline to let her know that he'd probably ended his career at CDC. He also asked her to monitor the news and let him know when the warning appeared on the news.

Gunn retrieved his passport from his locked laptop bag and left to join his colleagues for breakfast. After a hasty meal, they walked to Ian's hospital. This time the guard spoke to them in English as soon as they walked up. "I know you'll be careful about the virus. Make sure anything that might be contaminated goes in the red burn can, Doctors." He held the door open as Gunn and Wild Bill entered the anteroom.

"Thank you for speaking English. I know it's rude of me not to know more Hebrew, but this trip came up too fast for me to have a chance to brush up on it. Do you have a card? I'd like to relay my appreciation to your supervisor." Gunn stood with his heel holding the door. He held out his hand.

"Thank you, sir," the guard replied. "I appreciate your complement, but I don't have any. Only detectives get cards. Please do let the door close right away, though."

Gunn stepped back into the hallway so the outer door could close and noted the supervisor's name and email address on the back of one of his own cards. He put it in his shirt pocket and returned to the anteroom. The door latched behind him. "The guard must have been given our pictures or something, Now that I have my passport, he opens the door without asking for ID. These guys are pretty damn competent *and* considerate."

As soon as Gunn saw Ian, he shook head in dismay. Ian spoke first. "It's pretty clear now, isn't it. As soon as it's 8:00 in Atlanta, I'll call Colleen and tell her my diagnosis."

"This has to be the World's best Ebola hospital," Wild Bill said. "These guys have so much experience not even Emory could touch it by now. Got to be the best."

Wild Bill tapped Gunn on the shoulder. "Why don't we send him home?" He spoke quietly. "CDC could afford an air ambulance."

Gunn turned toward Wild Bill and whispered. "I doubt that Colleen would be allowed near him. Her chemo makes her so vulnerable to infection, it may be better for him to stay here."

Ian did not look at all happy at the prospect of days, even in the World's best Ebola hospital. "And though the vaccine didn't prevent infection, it may have conferred some protection. I'm optimistic. They got me on Zmapp last night."

"Oh, it finally came in." Gunn felt a little relief.

"Yep. Ups my chances a bunch."

The group's distress still showed. Wild Bill discussed options and commiserated with Ian.

Gunn grimaced and listened to the conversation. He did not hear it. Finally he broke his silence. "Ian, I hope my questions don't upset you, but I have to ask. Do you have any more ideas how you contracted the virus? Any safety hints you can pass on to us?" Gunn took a deep breath, frowned and coughed. When he reflexively put his cubital fossa to his mouth, his double covered arm hit his mask. He frowned.

"You know I'm very careful in the lab and I can't figure it out. Only thing I've come up with is that somehow some of the virus particles were carried out of a lab or hospital room, probably on some equipment. My hands have been so dry and chapped, especially since I visited Baghdad. They have open cracks all the time." Ian held out his right hand. In addition to the cracks in the cuticles from nail-biting that Gunn had seen, there were dry-skin cracks in the fingertips.

"I'd noticed your dry hands but hadn't thought about how dry Baghdad is compared to Atlanta." Gunn shook his head and looked down. Why'd he send him to Baghdad?

"It felt like desert. Somehow, something I picked up must have been ebolized." Ian's laugh quickly turned into a cough. "I'm sure the infection occurred when I wasn't even in a patient room. Some surface must have had the virus on it."

"Maybe even your gear. Did you use your gloves to undress yourself and only touch the insides of your gloves?" Wild Bill asked.

"I can't remember for sure. I always do. I think I did, but how can I be certain?" Ian coughed, more violently and for much longer this time. His eyes sagged. "Whatever happened there, whatever I did, I am certain I was much more cautious than anyone else in Iraq. Years of training and practice that no one else could have." He shook his head slowly and gently.

"You need to get more rest, Gunn." Wild Bill tapped Gunn on the shoulder. "Your stress and fatigue increase the likelihood you'll come down with something." He pulled Gunn back from Ian's bedside.

"Do you have Skype at home?" Wild Bill spoke to Ian. "Because travel is problematic for both you and Colleen, we should fix you up with a video link."

"No," Ian said. "Our computer's too old."

"Well then, we'll make sure Colleen gets set up with a new system so you can at least skype each other." Gunn stepped back from Ian's bedside, but still studied him. "Amhach should be able to make that happen pretty quickly." *At least that bastard better make it happen fast.*

"Think the MEFV can be caught over the Internet?" Gunn watched Ian.

"Maybe we can put a surgical glove over the computer." Wild Bill pulled gently on the tips of his gloves.

As his friends tried to cheer him, Gunn wondered if it was his imagination or was Ian worsening by the minute. That Zmapp worked pretty well last year. Damn. It better work for Ian. Was this EBOV variant engineered to tolerate it? The rash seemed more distinct and Ian's catarrhal lips had a distinct blackish cast. "We should give Ian a chance to rest. We can return a little after four, after he's had a chance to call Colleen. Got to be some way to get someone at CDC to quickly set her up with a Skype system."

"Can he make an international call from here?" Wild Bill asked.

"Oh, yeah. I have no idea," Gunn said. "No wait, he won't need it with Skype. He needs WiFi, right? He'll only need to make international calls until we get Skype working."

"Oh, right." Wild Bill's voice was soft and his eyes teary.

"I'll see if Moshe can call you and patch you through to Colleen somehow so you don't have to fight with Sourasky's switchboard..."

"Thank you," Ian said barely audibly. He pressed the top of his sheet to his mouth and coughed again. As he relaxed, they could see a splatter of blood on the sheet. The door between Ian's room and the ante-room closed. The two left, doffed their hospital gear and put everything in the burn can. Gunn watched as Wild Bill removed his gloves last. They were both careful to only touch the insides of the gloves. It's amazing how watching near-death increases self-preservation care.

#

The Americans met Moshe at the Israeli Ministry of Health, which was empty for the Sabbath. He led them to his virus lab, which smelled like their lab. A little smaller and quite a bit more crowded than theirs in Atlanta because there were more and larger machines, some quite old. They brainstormed on transmission mechanisms and the implications of Ian's hypothesis on transmission. At 3:15, Moshe looked at his pager and left the lab. He returned in two minutes and motioned to Gunn who followed him through the unlit labyrinthine halls the short distance back to his office. On Sunday afternoon 1600 Clifton Road probably looked as deserted.

No uncovered horizontal surface in Moshe's office. The H Law: Nature abhors horizontal surfaces (and conspires to cover them with junk). Moshe picked the handset from atop a pile of papers, handed it to Gunn, and left.

"Gunn, what is the meaning of this story on Fox Morning News?

And in the *Journal-Constitution* too, I see. This is your way of being a team player? Get yourself back here right away and keep your mouth shut."

"Yes, sir. I planned to call and leave a message by 8:00. I'll get my return ticket right away."

"Good," Amhach was a gruff as an exasperated drill sergeant. "And don't talk to anyone until you get here. Come straight to my office."

"Yes, sir. There is another matter that demands your immediate attention."

"What do you mean, *demands my attention*. How dare you demand my attention." Gunn visualized Amhach as a falcon, a scowling Atlanta Football Falcon from their logo.

"I didn't demand anything, sir. The situation did. Ian Powell has hemorrhagic fever and he may have only a few days to live. CDC owes him his wife's presence, even though she can't travel to be here. The situation is that CDC needs to help her get set up with a Skype system as fast as possible. CDC may need to lend her a computer, perhaps all she needs is the camera. That way they can at least see each other and talk."

"Why didn't you tell me that immediately?" The falcon developed bulging eyes and prominent varicose veins. Its eyes popped out of their orbits and dangled by the optic nerves.

"I did. I don't have your home phone so I planned to leave a message on your office line. It's only 7:15 there now, right? Leaving a message is the best I can do, right?"

"Yeah." The deformed falcon became a mutilated mockingbird.

"And how early do you check for messages on a Saturday morning?" Gunn asked.

"Humph." A sheepdog lying in an heap in front of a cage of screaming hyenas. Obedience to idiocy. How did this guy ever get a medical degree?

"And in case you didn't know, Ian's wife has acute promyelocytic leukemia. She's in long-term chemo now. We need to do whatever we can for the Powells. They're both so nice. It's like Job—they do the right thing and the worst is handed to them." Gunn's normal benevolent voice and Georgia drawl contradicted any abrasiveness of his words. His tone of voice said, "We need to help them a lot, don't you agree?"

"Yeah." Probably mumbled to avoid admitting egocentrism.

"I used a press release to reach the Egyptian and Iraqi medical personnel so fewer of them will suffer Ian's fate. Ian found that the med-alert had reached only one of the hospitals he visited." A dozen hospitals with probable Ebola that had never been warned. No way all these bureaucracies would let any official word through in a few days. Too many ass-holes like the CDC boss to bottle up communication. "Probably take weeks for any official message to reach the doctors and nurses, and that assumes it is given to the hospitals at all. I hope that between CNN and Al Jazeera that everyone gets the word."

"You told the terrorists at Al Jazeera?" A hyena braying from beside a dying animal.

"It's the only way to reach all the Arab world fast. You are aware that there are outbreaks in at least six cities in three countries. It's now confirmed in Egypt and Iraq. We have only our hope that the outbreak is confined to these three countries. Ian found a dozen probable cases and we have to assume there are many more. The situation looks the same as here." Gunn spoke in his usual drawl, though he wanted to shout at Amhach and shake his lapels. He explained that everyone needed warning because so many people come close to bodies. "If we don't slow the spread, everyone in the Middle East will be infected in a few months."

More unintelligible mumbling from Atlanta.

"This may be the pandemic we've been fearing. Because it's a HFV, it's much more lethal than anything in centuries." Gunn no longer cared if Billy Bob Amhach knew what *huff-vee* meant.

To get through a thick skull, messages had to be repeated. "And, because cremation is against both Judaism and Islam, we have to be sure the warning is simply and clearly worded and sent to hospice workers, morticians and families." Gunn paused to let the severity of the predicament sink in. "And furthermore, think of the much greater repercussions against us if there are a million fatalities because people aren't warned." Because ass holes in America stymied their own *free press* from spreading the word.

Chapter 17 – Day 7, Tuesday

Darrel Li in Herndon, Virginia

Nearly a week had passed since the first reports of the Ebolavirus outbreak in Israel and it would be several days before the first case would be admitted elsewhere, but Darrel had not yet heard about it.

He was aware of his gene-manipulation work and helping his company stay afloat. He had missed one paycheck because the company needed equipment more than he needed pay. He decided MSS was only be in the business of stealing technology, not supporting it. Any interest in supporting Virein should have been obvious within a few days—MSS would have asked for some info about the work or details of how much support the company needed. It was time to seek financing elsewhere. CM might still get something, but the financial situation was grim so Darrel had to help.

Four days after meeting with the hypothetical Mr. Chen, Darrel went early to lunch at the Tianjin House, a small Northern-Chinese restaurant. This restaurant felt cleaner and smelled fresher than the Golden Panda. The glass table covers did not feel at all oily, like the plastic ones at the MSS restaurant. The Tianjin House also seemed busier, but that may have been because of the time of day or day of the week.

He sat in the back of the long narrow dining room and watched other diners and the road for more than 6 minutes. He could see no sign of anyone paying any attention to him or watching the restaurant. He went to the pay phone in the corner and dialed a memorized number.

His call was answered in English and another language he did not understand. "Hello, this is Dr. Darrel Li. I am virologist. I have information that may interest you and have request for you. I want meeting." He talked slowly and distinctly and watched everyone in the restaurant.

"Please hold on a moment, Dr. Li." The phone answer-er put him on hold. Woman, probably middle-aged. Maybe American, maybe not. Should he have told her he was Jewish? Probably not yet.

Darrel faced out of the old English phone booth, an odd decoration for the Golden Panda. Looking through the red-mullioned windows he could see all traffic through the restaurant door or anyone close to him. The 96 windows of the booth allowed him to watch everything nearby but no one could hear anything he said. The booth could be bugged or the phone tapped, but any such intrusion would not be directed at him.

After 27 seconds, a male voice spoke. "May I help you?" No identification.

He repeated the message he'd given the Israeli Embassy receptionist. "I have nearly-developed technology that can increase productivity of overworked farmland and put worked-out land into production again. I would like to meet someone to discuss it."

"Where are you located? Where do you wish to meet?" The voice was pure business. "When do you want to meet?"

"I am in Herndon. I want to meet near here as soon as you are able. I cannot travel far." Darrel thought about the intergovernmental relationship between the United States and Israel. "This is not project for America. We are private company, not U.S. Government agency." He thought about *Herndon* and decided it was such a well known suburb everyone would know about it.

"Can you suggest a place that is good for you the day after tomorrow?"

"Let's meet at Tianjin House in Reston at 11:30. They should not be too busy early on a Thursday. I will try to sit in back of restaurant."

The agent agreed, noted the address, and got the phone number of the pay phone, which Darrel warned him might not work for incoming calls.

"I will wear a blue blazer and tan slacks," the agent said.

"Thank you. I will wear dark gray suit. I need to know your name." Darrel took a pen from his pocket and prepared to write on his hand.

"I am Herb Rosenthal," the man on the phone said.

"Thank you. I also need distinctive garment or trait so I can be sure I know you. When you see me in restaurant, greet me in traditional way with the Hebrew word for peace, okay?"

"Okay. I'll do that." Mr. Rosenthal paused for a moment. "To make it easier for you I am five foot nine, weigh 175, and look Jewish."

"Thanks. That'll help" Darrel nodded into the phone.

"Thank you Dr. Li. There's one more thing that may help. I have discolored hair due to chemo-therapy. I can assure you it's all me and no wig, but it looks like the worst hairpiece ever made. It's not something you'll see on anyone else. I do look forward to seeing you Thursday."

Darrel thanked him and hung up. He returned to his table where his lunch had arrived. The chop sticks felt rubbery. He decided not to try to pick up the pineapple from his plate, at least not for a few minutes. He looked at a table opposite his booth and wondered if he should sit there on Thursday. A table is harder to bug than a booth, but easier to overhear. He would think about that.

Chapter 18 – Day 32, Saturday

Ministry of Health Offices, Tell Aviv

Gunn moved a few papers aside and returned Moshe's phone to its cradle. What the hell was he supposed to do? Go home? Stay? He didn't even know what Amhach wanted and he still didn't know how to reach him. Gunn sat in Moshe's chair and surveyed the books around the office. What the devil was he supposed to do? Moshe's phone rang.

"Dr. Eisenberg's Office," he said.

"Medaber Chaim Lackel mihadshot arutz ehad, efshar ledaber yim doctor Eisenberg?" came from the phone.

"I'm sorry," Gunn said. "I don't speak Hebrew. I'm an American. I'm using Dr. Eisenberg's phone. Can you repeat your request in English." Gunn carefully enunciated his staccato message.

"I beg your pardon. This is Chaim Lackel of Channel Two News." The accent sounded Israeli. "I wanted an interview about the hemorrhagic fever virus press release that went out to CNN this morning. Are you one of the Americans involved with treating the Israeli Ebola patients?"

"Uh, yeah. No, *no*. I am only observing." Gunn paused while he pondered how to handle the call. "Dr. Eisenberg is in charge here. It is inaccurate to say we're involved. We Americans are not treating anyone." Gunn spoke in his usual slow drawl with extra pauses for thinking. He was about to continue with a description of the need for disseminating the warning on the danger and indestructibility of the virus when Chaim spoke. It did not offend Gunn because colleagues often interrupted him during conversations at the CDC in Atlanta.

"Well, what I really meant, did you have anything to do with the press release? Can we talk to you about it?" Chaim's English accent was tinged with Boston. Gunn wondered if Chaim Lackel studied at one of the Boston schools.

"Yes. We can talk to you. It is important to emphasize that we do not know what virus we are dealing with. It's also important that we warn health care, hospice and mortuary workers about the danger of this new strain of hemorrhagic fever."

"Is Dr. Eisenberg in?"

"Yes." Gunn answered slowly. He wondered if Moshe would be upset when he learned Gunn admitted his presence.

"We're under deadline pressure. We'd like to come over there to talk to him."

"Hmm. I don't know if he's available. I'll try to get a message to him that you want an interview."

"Thank you. Please ask him to call right away."

"I know Dr. Eisenberg has a meeting at 4, so I don't think he can call before 5."

"We have to be on the air by 6:00. Please do whatever you can, as fast as you can."

Gunn collected contact information from the reporter and left to find Moshe and the others. Gunn wound his way back through the empty, unlit halls of the Ministry of Health to the lab where the team worked. Everyone stopped and looked at him for news as he arrived. "Amhach called. He wants me to come back, I think. At first he said, *return right away*, but then he seemed to say, *okay stay and do what you can there*."

"Yeah, sure, no problem," Wild Bill said.

"When I hung up, your phone rang again right away, Moshe," Gunn said. "A reporter, named Chaim Lackel called. He wanted an interview about the hemorrhagic fever press release for the evening news. What do you know about him? I told him I'd try to get a message to you."

"He's a pretty good guy, I think," Moshe said. "He's young and aggressive, so we'll have to be prepared for antagonistic questions. On the other hand, he seems to have more believability and more viewership than most anchors. If we work as a team and try to cover the nasty questions, we should be in good shape to talk to him." The four spent several minutes discussing ambush interviews. Moshe's pager gave the slight buzz of a device on "vibrate only." He twisted it on his belt, looked at it and left the room.

Their discussion often came back to Ian. They worried about the mechanics of making international calls from Moshe's phone. A few minutes later Moshe returned.

"Moshe, can you work with Wild Bill? We have to be sure he can fend off Channel Two," Gunn said. "I need to go use your phone for one more call to Amhach to see if he wants me to return right away or not. Can I call him back from here?" Gunn studied the table as his voice turned into a quiet growl. "That idiot contradicted himself so many times. I've got to find out what the bastard wants."

"Good idea." Moshe gave Gunn directions for calling the U.S. and the access codes he'd need to make an international call from MoH. "Go use my phone. You'll have plenty of privacy there."

"Thanks." Gunn collected a few papers.

"We should do some play-acting for the interviews to practice for ambush questions," Moshe said as Gunn went to make his call.

Gunn left a message for Amhach. "I apologize for the misunderstanding. I need to know if you want me to abandon Ian and return right away. Because it is difficult to reach me by phone I will check email especially frequently for the next several hours and days."

#

The three virologists went over the press release as they returned to their hotel. Gunn was so distressed at his teammate's condition, he changed a few parts, hoping to garner more sympathy for Ian. Gunn and Wild Bill listened to Moshe rehearse. Before he'd finished the second dry run, Chaim and his crew arrived at the Crowne Plaza. Moshe met the news crew in the lobby. The TV crew suggested everyone go to the rear of the hotel because of the good lighting.

"The beach sure makes a beautiful backdrop," Wild Bill said. With the camera rolling, Moshe read the press release. In the middle he read, "Among our patients with the hemorrhagic fever virus, we have one American. His wife is recovering from leukemia and is still too weak to travel. We are fixing a Skype connection so the two can easily visit. When the American became sick he was helping us determine the source and transmission mechanism for this pernicious disease."

Gunn kept a close watch on the news crew as Moshe read the press release in Hebrew. There were enough proper nouns and scientific terms that he knew what Moshe said most of the time. The part about Ian's wife lit Chaim's team up. Gunn doubted they heard the rest. They had their sound bite for the evening news. The rest of the news conference was questions and answers, in Hebrew to Moshe and English to the Americans.

All the early questions related to the identity of the American and his wife. Gunn gave the answer they had agreed on. "For his personal privacy and to protect his wife from being hounded by reporters, we will not discuss or describe either of them in any way."

There were no ambush questions. The reporters had what they wanted before the Q&A started. They repeated questions about the American's "Ebola." The doctors corrected the term several times describing the disease as a hemorrhagic fever and denied they knew it was in the Ebolavirus genus. They pointed out that no definitive diagnosis had been made, but that he, like many Israelis, Iraqis and Egyptians, was *very* sick.

When the news team left, the trio spent an hour in the Club Room where the news ran all the time. The reporting and interview on Channel Two, what he could understand of it, pleasantly surprised Gunn. After the news, Moshe headed home and the Americans sat down to eat and watch the dying day's light turn the waves into bands of pink foam.

Before he turned in, Gunn checked his email and the CDC newsfeed. Oh God. Three more cases in Baghdad including, an American assigned to the embassy. Again, it looked like a disease that would only infect people who are solidly in the middle class. He sent an email to Linda Steiner at Reed. "Are they vaccinating anyone with the experimental Ebola vaccine? How are the supplies of Zmapp? (BTW, it doesn't appear to work as well on Mideast Filovirus as on the African Ebola strains). We had run out of Zmapp here so Ian Powell hadn't gotten any until yesterday when a new supply arrived."

He thought about the time. It was mid lunch hour Saturday in

Washington. He didn't feel up to waiting for an email that might not come for a couple of hours. He googled "baghdad Ebola," "baghdad filovirus," and a few other variants but didn't find any new information. Then he saw a new email. Gunn marveled that a civil servant worked, especially on a weekend.

Gunn,

Nobody in Army vaccinated against Ebola.

Don't know more than you. USAMRIID not involved yet.

Good luck :)

Linda

Damn. Probably no Marine had been vaccinated either. God I hope John is safe.

Chapter 19 – Day 32, Saturday, Evening

Tel Aviv

In the bar of the Crowne Plaza, the two epidemiologists met. As usual Wild Bill ordered juice while Gunn requested a bottle of the Château Fayau Bordeaux.

"Our real job is to figure out how Ian got the virus." Gunn realized he was frowning but couldn't stop. "No sure way to go about this. Just have to cover all bases. I'll ask John if he can provide a complete list of Ian's movements."

"John?" Wild Bill bit his lip and knit his eyebrows.

"Yeah, John Dalton, my son-in-law, who guided Ian in Baghdad. I want you to talk to Ian separately. There is some chance he might say something to you he wouldn't admit to me." Gunn gestured toward Wild Bill. He again rested his forehead on his fingertips. Their drinks came. Most guys are more likely to admit inappropriate behavior to another guy their own age, aren't they? "Your discussion with Ian shouldn't feel as much like an interrogation as mine. I think it's more likely to yield useful data."

Wild Bill wore an Hawaiian print shirt, the type that had helped give him his sobriquet. He looked at the bottle of French wine and asked, "Are you really going to drink that whole thing? A whole liter of wine?" He watched as the waiter finished serving and walked away.

"Not now, I won't," Gunn said. "If you don't help me, I'll smuggle the bottle back to my room. It's not as bad as you think, Wild Bill. The bottle only hold three fourths of a liter."

"But so many people are addicted," Wild Bill said. "It's too dangerous. I won't touch it." He closed his eyes and moved his hands like he was pushing away a tray of drinks.

"Could be a good choice." Gunn nodded vigorously. "A major contributor to alcohol addiction is genetic. If you don't touch it, you'll never need to worry."

"Anyway, no damn drunkenness here," Gunn said. "I only drink enough to be optimal for my heart and arteries." He still felt gruff and sure it was more obvious in his voice than he wanted. He thought for a substantial fraction of a minute.

"We have to figure out what's going on here." Gunn nodded in thought. "We need to know everything Ian touched within a hundred meters of the hospitals, MoH and here. If someone sneezed in the same room he was in, we've got to check them. If Ian was screwing somebody in Tel Aviv or Baghdad, we need to know it."

"Wait a minute," Wild Bill said. "How can we even know if the virus is present on something? Don't we need to start by trying to find a fast detector?"

"Right. I assumed a simple blood test would work. We need a quick and dirty test so we better start by verifying that our HFV will cause cell rupture on a slide and see how much virus we need. Can you do that?"

"I'll verify the test," Wild Bill volunteered. "I should be able to determine both its sensitivity and the speed. Damn, I hope the test is fast."

"Yeah. Ugh. If the test takes very long, the process of determining the virus's presence will exhaust us." Gunn decided that he would interview Ian, then Wild Bill would give it a go. On the way to the interviews with Ian, each would collect surface samples from any likely places, including in his room.

"It may kill us and we may hate the sight of each other," Gunn said, "but we must discuss our progress and speculations several times a day."

"At least we had some time for sight-seeing before this hit. I hate to waste a trip only on work." Wild Bill did not look at all discouraged, maybe even energized. "What do you think I should do for permission? Work through Moshe? Sourasky?"

"Moshe is probably our most powerful weapon to get into places, so we should use him last. Let's start by swabbing what we can at the hospital. First, let's try to collect what we need. If that fails, i.e., if someone stops us, we can ask . With any luck, whoever stopped us will recognize we're helping them and they'll decide to help us."

Wild Bill seemed to feel he had to fill Gunn's pause. "So, we'll sample surfaces all around Ian's room and any other areas where he may have touched things. We keep sampling until we're told to stop?"

"Yeah, and if we're told to stop, we argue. Not too vigorously, of course, but if they tell us to stop, they may not have authority to do it. A *little* arguing may get past any one person. We want to try to get everything we need by ourselves. If someone tries to stop us and we tell them we're fighting the Ebola plague, that ought to scare them off."

"I love it," Wild Bill said. His eyes were ablaze. "If they stop me checking around the Sourasky tomorrow, I argue. If that still doesn't get us our samples, then you try later." Wild Bill looked into the distance and tapped a finger on the table.

"Good approach, Gunn." Wild Bill gave a thumbs up gesture with his right fist. "We hope that if someone stops us it's on his own initiative, nothing official. If he doesn't back down, he may not be there to stop us later in the day or the next day."

"And for God's sake, be careful. We should try to do our work without gloves except in the hospital because it'll attract too much attention." Gunn looked back at Wild Bill. He held his pen by the end and inserted it into the hole his loose fist made. "Hold the swabs far from the cotton and stick them in a vial right away."

Wild Bill nodded. "I'll take every precaution I can. It'll be easy to swab most things without touching anything but the clean end of the q-tip. Should be easy to collect our samples with no gloves needed or involved."

"Great," Gunn said. "Careful and safe." He nodded in thought. "And innocuous."

Chapter 20 – Day 33, Sunday

Tel Aviv

Gunn arose early in the morning and checked his email. A message from Ikeya. He never expected his boss to work weekends. Amhach must have ragged on him.

Gunn,

It looks like everything is about to hit the fan here. Unless you think Ian needs your help, please return as soon as possible. I may need your support.

If you can come, please do, but have Wild Bill stay there with Ian at least for a little while. Repeating, if you think there is any help you can provide, stay and assist. My guess is that Wild Bill can do as much as any of us for Ian and that more people will not improve Ian's prognosis.

Tomas in IT loaned Colleen a new laptop and got her Skype up and running. Hope she and Ian are now able to talk and see each other.

Josh

The message left Atlanta about 6:00 last night. Bizarre it took so long to get here. Electrons must travel slowly underwater.

Gunn pondered the Ikeya problem and what was happening in Atlanta. He thought he had established adequate rapport with a variety of people at the Israeli MoH. He had little reason to stay longer. Ian has the best possible care and ought to be glad to have Gunn in Atlanta where he could help Colleen understand the whole mess.

He started his search for a reservation on the evening's flights. If he'd known yesterday, it would have been easier to find space because of reduced Jewish travel on Saturday. Well, maybe the Christians are less likely to travel on Sunday. He found a seat, but only in Economy.

He arrived for breakfast at the Crowne Plaza's café before Wild Bill and sat down in a corner booth. The Mediterranean aroma reminded him of Atlanta. Not at all the same, but incredibly evocative of the moldy aromas of his childhood. Wild Bill came into the café and joined Gunn.

"Well, it looks like I'll be going back tonight," Gunn said. "At least I think I've done nearly everything I can to help here." He glanced at the masts in the marina and opened his mouth to continue.

"Those slimy politicians," Wild Bill's snarl was punctuated by a frown. He brought his hand down on the table so hard that Gunn's cup jumped in its saucer. "Why can't they keep their hands off our work. Is it okay to write a memo saying Ian and I think you should stay?"

"No, no. I didn't say it right. I am going back because Ikeya wants me. This has nothing to do with Amhach this time." Gunn nodded and sipped his coffee. "There is some internal matter. The message says he wants you to stay to help Ian, comfort him and assist here anyway you can. I'll return tonight. My reading between the lines is that this has to do with Iraq and comforting Colleen, not Amhach."

"Okay. That sounds reasonable, even good. I still wish we didn't have to deal with Dr. Amhach ..." Wild Bill shook his head.

"Yeah," Gunn responded. "I agree. Two things puzzle me. How scientists can be unthinking fundamentalists like Slimehach and how, if they get into positions of power, they think their religious beliefs are better than everyone else's." Gunn studied the nearly flat Mediterranean.

"I think we all agree about Amhach," Wild Bill said. "I've often wondered if he thinks people like Gandhi, Mother Teresa and Siddhartha

Buddha are damned because they don't believe in *his* God. I'm a Baptist too, but not like him, thank God."

"How does a Luddite airhead get the President to name him head of the CDC?" Gunn talked softly, almost to himself. "By being nominated by one," Gunn answered his own question. "Maybe the next change in Washington will change the presidential cronyism and senatorial toadyism."

"Let's hope." Wild Bill sipped his coffee.

"You'll be on your own for all the Ebola testing we planned. I'll make sure you have my son-in-law's email. I don't think he's the right person to go around Baghdad collecting samples, but he'll probably know whom to ask. And he should know everywhere Ian went."

"Anyone can go around swabbing. Moshe may even find someone to help me."

Gunn studied his coffee. "I'm ready to go home. I really want to get back to Pauline. Thirty-five years of marriage and I still get homesick for her. Been pining for her since I left."

"I think all of us, and especially Ian, are a little homesick by now," Wild Bill said.

"But, damn it, I hate to leave Ian. I can't even do anything to help him, but somehow it seems I should stay and try to help." Gunn rubbed his forehead and temples. He shook his head. "I feel like everything I do now is a mistake."

"I'll stay to provide any care we can think of. It may be a bad choice, but you really should go back to Atlanta."

Gunn considered the help Moshe and the Ministry of Health could provide. "I don't think we can get any help from MoH today, but we need to figure out whether there's any important additional samples or even information that Moshe can't FedEx. Maybe I can even be of more use to Ian in Atlanta. I may be able to scrounge up some meds that have run out here."

"Good point. I may be able to brings something, but that won't be quick." Wild Bill made a carrying gesture.

"My own guess is that you've established the personal contacts and relationships you need. We may need to return in a month or two, but I think we're okay for now."

Wild Bill nodded in agreement. "Yeah. Ian needs someone, but the investigation doesn't. If I had to leave today, I'll bet Moshe would get a nurse to collect all the surface swabs we need."

They reviewed their skimpy knowledge of the virus and adjourned to Gunn's room. Soon they departed to see Ian. As they walked to the hospital, Gunn said, "We can't tell if we're in a rut. Let's comfort Ian then go sightseeing. We'll be more apt to think of the missing pieces by walking around the Reuven Rubin Museum than by brainstorming in a hotel room." They agreed to sight-see the galleries and boutiques on Bialik Street until dark with a couple of visits to Ian to cheer him up and break up their day.

#

Gunn arrived at his desk in Atlanta before 7:30, Tuesday, taking advantage of the faster pre-rush hour commute. Until his body clock slowed down to Eastern Daylight Time he'd enjoy the early morning drive. He put himself on Ikeya's calendar for 1:00, the first available time. Email from Wild Bill, encrypted and addressed only to Gunn said,

Ian is barely making it. Pronounced gangrenous appearance. I'll be back to the hospital this evening, if he's still with us.

Oh, dear God. Don't take Ian. He hasn't done anything to deserve this. He and Colleen don't need to be tested. How can anyone believe in a God that does this to good people like Ian and Colleen?

In his trip report Gunn emphasized the need to do everything they could for Ian and that it might already be too late. When he arrived in Ikeya's office at 1:00, he was told to close the door. "Gunn, let me read you something. Please tell me the tone it conveys. 'Dr. Ian Powell may well die within the next 48 hours. No airline will fly him home because of the HFV and his wife can't go visit because of her leukemia. The CDC has an obligation to do what it can for him including sending a plane to bring him home as soon as that's safe for him and Colleen.' Would you say that is deferential or friendly?"

"No, sir. It's factual."

"Gunn, 'Factual' is not descriptive of tone. You know how sensitive Amhach is to things sounding supportive. When he sees this, he'll again see what he can do to get you. You must try to be less abrasive." The meeting continued, going downhill from there. Ikeya tried to convince Gunn only to send memos up the line one step at a time. "Let me buffer them for you. It might mean your career."

Gunn shook his head. "What's left of it."

Chapter 21 – Day 35, Tuesday

Atlanta

Gunn studied the newly arrived reports from the genetic analysts. The data on the virus were bizarre. Now it was pretty clear that this virus had been created in a lab. Somehow its designer had mixed Reston ebolavirus, which had never bothered people, and Zaire ebolavirus, one of the most deadly of the hemorrhagic fevers. He'd also thrown in some iron and tungsten, which allowed it to survive normal sterilization temperatures.

The genetic analysis showed the virus contained some *ladder rung* sequences that matched Ebola isolated from monkeys in Reston, Virginia, that were absent in the original Philippine source virus. Gunn studied the report. Oh my God. That meant this virus wasn't a bio-terror weapon from one of the usual suspects, it was from the United States. From our Reston Primate Lab. Well, at least, the developer had some Reston Ebolavirus from the U.S. to work with.

Dr. Amhach (Eyes Only). I have information that I think you'll want to know immediately. I need to present this information directly to you. If you would call me, I'll come at any time of your convenience.

Well that ought to be diplomatic enough for him. Gunn looked at the email. He looked down and rubbed his temples and read it again. He moved it to his drafts folder. The email was too dangerous. He needed to learn more about the virus's source before he discussed his results with anyone, especially Dr. Asshack. Nobody CDC could find the source of these virus parts this as fast as Gunn.

Damn, maybe it would be better to hire a hit on the virus's creator or shoot the bastard myself. But, first, I have to find the creator and distributor. And it may be some organization, maybe not a just one person.

Maybe brainstorm about it with a completely trusted colleague. Wait. I'm likely to be condemned for the delay notifying Amhach. Damned if I send it and damned the other way.

Gunn opened a new email from Wild Bill.

Gunn. Good News, but don't broadcast it yet. Ian and I have told Colleen. He is beginning to look a little better. I think he may beat the monster. Bill.

Damn, finally some good news. Gunn pounded the air and his desk. #

That evening Gunn and Pauline walked to the nearest Dairy Queen for dessert, a mile hand-in-hand through Chastain Park behind their house. They often selected DQ for its low fat desserts and exercise getting there. The magnolia-scented walk was a joy every spring. Though a few pounds more than he wished, no one would consider Gunn flabby but only a few called him slim. He ordered a dish of non-fat soft-serve and a Peanut Buster Parfait for his slim wife. They sat at an outdoor table to eat. "This hemorrhagic fever virus is awful. It seems as lethal as Ebola. The electron microscope images show its shape is typical of filoviruses like Ebola. But MEFV seems to be transmitted more easily. It's scary. Ian thinks he picked it up enough from some supposedly sterile surface." Gunn mumbled on about his fears of a Mideast *Filoviridae* pandemic. "When we left the number of cases was doubling every five days. That means one case for every person in the Middle East in four and a half months and the World's population in less than six."

"Didn't you say that all these viruses were only transmitted by close contact? Like exchanging bodily fluids? Do I remember right? Are you now saying this is deadly like AIDS used to be, but fast acting like rabies? And it's transmitted as easily as flu?" Pauline sounded like he told her to believe something she knew was either a lie or the end of the world. Gunn remembered hearing that tone when he first tried to talk her into bed decades ago.

"You've got it, babe." Gunn squeezed and caressed her hand. "I couldn't have said it any better. I'm not sure of the last part, but it does seem to spread much more easily than other hemorrhagic fever viruses, at least its growth rate is doubling the number cases every five days instead of every seven or more, like the West Africa Ebola in '14. And that's in addition to its superpowers—surviving normal sterilization and our current Ebola drugs."

"MEFV, UFV, we all fever for MEFV." Pauline shook her head.

"It's sickening, that's for sure." Gunn squeezed Pauline's hand again and pulled her close. "It's so much more robust than most viruses. Some of it survives contact with dry surfaces and it survives many normal sterilization procedures like autoclaving. One hundred degrees doesn't kill it. I mean 212 degrees doesn't kill it." Gunn babbled about the dangers and the work to understand and contain the disease. Pauline's questions had opened the stadium doors and the crowd of ideas came pouring out. Some disappeared into the ether like fans sprinting to their cars, others lingered like tail-gaters, bouncing back and forth, interacting like fans of opposing teams. But this RNA virus was no game.

Gunn yakked on, trying to talk his way out of the guilt he felt. Why had he sent Ian to Baghdad? We could have gotten slides and tissue samples without anyone going to a war zone where Ebola should be much more dangerous. There was no getting around it, he had probably sentenced Ian to an awfully miserable year and possibly exposed John Dalton to this virus. Recovery and rehabilitation often took a whole year after EBOV. Yuck. Hope MEFV is no worse. And even that assumed Ian made it through the next few days.

He poked at his chocolate-vanilla swirl and ate a little. "If this outbreak in Baghdad threatened the entire country or region, do you think the Army would consider using an A-bomb on Baghdad? You know, like we were discussing the other night."

"Let's not even think about that one." She looked shaken at the thought.

They finished most of their desserts and started home. "Oh, wait a sec. I want to check something." Gunn walked across the lot to the pay phone near the Dairy Queen and typed its number into his cell phone. He saved the number as he walked back to Pauline. "Just wanted the number of a more secure phone in case I need one."

"Were you paying attention to see if anyone watched you?" Pauline took his arm.

"Ugh. No. I'm not very good at this spook stuff, am I?"

"I don't think anyone could follow us through the park without being seen. I watched and if you're being followed, the tail is a real pro. Well. Either that or we're so gullible that we wouldn't see him no matter what."

"So comforting. They probably use hedfly-sized drones to spy on us now. Or maybe several people and drones trading off tailing us." Gunn looked around, as though a G-man would wear a shirt with "FBI" emblazoned on it. He blathered on about the virus and political tensions at Clifton Road.

"Why do you need a secure phone?" She hung on his arm. 'Who are you afraid of?"

"Well, Amhach wants to get me, so he might do something. If our government is the source of the virus, they're bound to try to stop anyone prying into the viral source. If this is some renegade CIA operation, sort of half in and half out of U.S. control, then who knows what they might do to protect their identity."

They followed a routine they had repeated several times a week for years, they walked with fingers entwined or arms around one and other. Pauline squeezed Gunn's hand and rubbed her arm against his. When Gunn finally ran down, she said, "You realize this is the first time you've brought your work home?"

"Hadn't realized it. I've never been so scared before."

"You've used a bunch of weird words talking about it. You called it 'not so comical,' 'thermostatic' and some other crazy stuff. What's all that in English?"

"I like 'not so comical.' Never thought of that. I *wish* Ebola were more comical. The word is 'nosocomial.' Means the disease is spread in hospitals. You know, like MRSA and other staph infections you hear so much about."

"How do hospitals spread the virus?"

"We think it's spread the same way as staph infections, by sloppy cleaning and careless or not really hot disinfecting. Many Third World hospitals are so poor they don't use disposable syringes. If they're in a hurry, they may not even sterilize them."

"So it is like that bug your father got at the University of Mississippi Medical Center in Jackson after his operation?" They were alone in the park. Pauline rubbed her breasts against his arm. He savored the gesture. So casual that even in a crowd no one but Gunn would notice.

"Same sort of careless, dirty procedures do it, yes." Gunn looked and felt dejected. "The Israeli hospitals won't be careless and spread it, but I have no confidence in the safety of other medical workers or morticians, especially in other countries. And even if all of them use proper precautions, what about their general populations? The people who'll see sick spouses or children first."

"Oh dear. I never thought about home treatment problems."

"Lot's of home treatment and home body-interment preparation means lots of opportunities for transmission."

"I'm glad you're here." Pauline dropped Gunn's hand and put her arm around his waist. "You're home with me now."

"Let's see Ebola is also zoonotic. That's a good word. It means Ebola comes from animals. Was that one of your words? No one is sure which animals harbor the virus and live with it, but the most likely culprits are bats. It is so lethal in humans and apes that we know they can't be carriers. There must be some animals somewhere that have the disease but live happily with it and rarely pass it on. Just like all the other hemorrhagic fever viruses."

"Like the black death was carried by rats and fleas?"

"Yeah, and we're not sure of the carrier animal." Gunn mumbled again and talked mostly to himself. "Fruit bats are our best suspect."

"Oooh, nasty." Pauline rubbed against his arm.

"Mm. Let's see, this nasty virus seems to be thermophilic. Etymologically that must mean it likes heat, but it really means that it can tolerate heat. It's as though the virus took up with some bacteria from a hot spring. The bacterium taught the virus how to pick up heavy or refractory metals like iron and tungsten. The metals help it tolerate normal sterilization and cooking temperatures."

"It's pretty awful stuff. Is it really deadly? Is Ian in serious danger?"

"It's about as deadly as diseases get. Anywhere from half to 90% of the people who get the old Marburg ebolavirus died from it. With this variant, it looks like it's going to be closer to the 50% mark but that still makes it much more lethal than a cottonmouth or rattlesnake bite even though it's not as bad as rabies, say. Anyway, I'm sure it's accurate to describe it as *deadly.*"

Gunn stopped abruptly. "Oh, I forgot to tell you. Wild Bill says Ian seems a little better. He's not only praying for Ian, he says he expects Ian to make it."

"I thought you needed some good news. Sounds like you finally got it."

Gunn nodded and gave Pauline a hug as they walked up their drive, under the live oak trees, to their brick house. "One really bizarre feature of the epidemic so far—it seems to only affect people in the upper classes, the ones most likely to use professional help, especially in hospitals." Inside their house he confessed to being stumped about the virus and how Ian could have contracted it. "This whole case has so many weird and contradictory facts. I think I'll bake some cinnamon rolls, it'll relax me and maybe I'll get some ideas."

"Which kind are you going to make?" Pauline looked at Gunn and stroked his arm with her fingernail.

"I like that old Kansas recipe because it's quick and easy. Mainly I want to relax and clear my mind."

"You know the way to a girl's heart," Pauline said.

He gave her a peck on that kissable crook of her neck and turned toward the kitchen. He took one step then returned to give Pauline a big hug and a real kiss.

"Well, you do still remember how," she said.

Eighty-five minutes later Gunn found Pauline in their study, looking at a legal brief. "Buns are in the oven and I still don't have any good ideas. You often think of unusual things that don't occur to me. Got time to talk?" He walked over behind her, rubbed her shoulders and kissed her ear. "Maybe some brainstorming will help."

Gunn described Ian's thesis on how he caught the virus and reminded her how the only common thread they found among the early victims was that none were destitute and only one was even borderline poor. "Even before the virus cropped up in Baghdad, the Israelis had seen both Arabs and Jews with it."

"Well if there's no commonality of venue for your MEFV, maybe there's a commonality of victuals. The foods that the middle and upper classes eat are different from those of the poor. We eat more fresh food, things that are not sterilized by canning."

"Oh, I like that idea. *Organic foods kill thousands*. That would put a crimp in organics. I wonder if organic and kosher have any relation." Gunn felt the excitement of a new discovery, like the time he determined that Zaire ebolavirus and Sudan ebolavirus were distinct species. "Muslim food rules are rather like kosher, I think. They both avoid pork, at least." Gunn wrapped an arm around Pauline and gave her a Dagwood kiss.

"Umm. I better come up with lots of ideas like that," Pauline said as she licked her lips in an erotic way. Gunn felt hotter.

"The metallic atoms we've seen in MEFV make it look new to our immune systems and it seems to make it much tougher so it probably survives some treatments that would kill other viruses." He gave her another peck on the cheek. "The protection is enough so MEFV would survive most cooking."

"You always talk as though it evolved this capability. What's the likelihood it could have been designed to have it?"

"I think you're right. I've come to the conclusion it must have been done by someone with access to two strains of Ebolavirus. One, the Reston EBOV, is distinctive to a lab in Virginia. That's in the neighborhood of our government and the people in it. I know there has been talk about weaponizing Ebolavirus and Trump is so anti-Semitic.... The Twit-in-Chief's mad tweets may have pushed someone in a weaponizing project over the edge."

\#

As Gunn dressed for work Wednesday morning, Pauline called to him. "Gunn, there's an Ebola outbreak in Hawaii. Are our kids in any danger?" Pauline and Gunn used whatever excuse they could to visit

John, Jeanne Anne and Mele Mele.

Did she think we should go protect the kids from this amorphous threat? Nah. She's only looking for an excuse go for a visit. "Should be no danger to anyone outside the hospital. I guess it was inevitable. Did some soldier come down with it?" He returned to the master bedroom went over to the clock radio and increased the volume a tad. "God. What if John's the victim? Or if he was somehow exposed when he helped Ian?" Christ. Why had he ever let John help in Baghdad? Ian alone, or better some local doc, could have done everything Ian did. Maybe not Ian by himself, but any Iraqi nurse.

Renée Montagne reported, "... The Navy Hospital spokesperson announced that the patient has symptoms similar to those in the Mideast." A female started speaking. "We are treating the patient for hemorrhagic fever. He is in isolation ...."

"I'm pretty sure the only danger is to people physically close to the patient," Gunn said to Pauline. "We haven't figured out how it's transmitted. We're protecting against the traditional HFV transmission mechanisms, and that should be okay in a hospital. We don't need to worry about Mele Mele." He realized he'd used his CDC jargon for a hemorrhagic fever virus.

Pauline studied her husband for a moment. "You don't really believe that do you?"

"Mele Mele's probably in more danger from my swearing. I think it's true. No. I'm damn sure it's true. No. I don't know. The sailor with the disease must have picked it up in the Mideast. We still don't know the transmission mechanism. I've got to stop swearing." Gunn shook his head and moped.

"It's two more months to Mele Mele's birthday. Is it safe to wait until then?" Pauline asked.

"I'll call Jeanne Anne and John. I've got to warn John." Gunn shook his head. "When we go out there, I don't want to bother Jeanne Anne. You three ladies are too important to me." He closed his eyes and mumbled at the floor. "I have to speak as though Mele Mele is listening to me all the time." And he had to make sure they were all safe. What the hell could he do? This was so scary. God, take me, not Mele Mele. Save us all from it. Damn, and I can't call until this afternoon.

Gunn called Linda Steiner at Walter Reed. Before the phone rang he hung up. The Hawaiian case was in a Navy Hospital. Back to the Rolodex. Gunn had stopped using a real Rolodex decades ago, but thought of his computer address book as one. Dr. Saul Abraham popped up. Gunn couldn't remember anything about the guy, but he had been stationed in Hawaii at one time. He should at least know the correct contact person or organization.

He reached Dr. Abraham's voice mail. After identifying himself in a friendly way, he said, "I have been working on deciphering the history of the hemorrhagic fever viruses from the Mideast. I would like to get a tissue sample from the person in Hawaii who is suspected of having the virus. If you could please call me..." Gunn thought about the message and decided it didn't need any more information. His contact info described where he was and should be adequate. He pressed 1 to save the message and hung up.

At least Mele Mele and Jeanne Anne lived across Honolulu from Pearl Harbor and the Medical Clinic there. He needed to know the transmission mechanism of this damn virus. How else could they be sure they would stop its spread?

\#

Gunn answered his phone on the first ring. "Gunn Shoreham," he said mechanically as he picked up of the phone. He exchanged greetings with Dr. George Austin, the ProteinGen president.

"Dr. Shoreham, I am following up on the conversations we had in Chapel Hill and at your office a few weeks ago. You pointed out the importance of tailoring our pitches to the specific needs of a person or agency." Austin's voice showed no sign of the anger and whining that bugged Gunn in their earlier encounters. Even his lisp wasn't annoying when the message was positive.

"Any SBIR is a crap-shoot. Anything you can do to show you're trying to help solve the requestor's problems will help you." Gunn tried to sound circumspect.

"Yes. Thank you. I learned you were in the Mideast and suspect you were concerned about the EBOV breaking out there." Sounded like Austin had a genuine interest.

"For confidentiality reasons, I can't comment on your suspicions."

Gunn tried to be sure his voice indicated eagerness to continue. He did not want to cut off the conversation, but he distrusted the phone's confidentiality—especially from Amhach.

"Well, I wanted to be sure you know we would be very interested in any work we can do to help with your EBOV investigation. We do have a BSL-4 lab here, so we're fully qualified to do any procedures, isolation, characterization, what-have-you on your samples."

Gunn learned more details of ProteinGen's capabilities, thanked Austin and told him he'd keep Austin informed of anything he could. "Helping startups is one of my duties and pleasures, George." They talked for about 10 minutes.

If ProteinGen has a BSL-4 rated lab, that means they have one of the key pieces of equipment for MEFV development. Not the most important, but the most expensive and and hardest to duplicate. Could they have developed MEFV for themselves or some Federal Agency?

Chapter 22 – Day 8, Wednesday

Darrel Li in Herndon, Virginia

Darrel worked at his desk in the corner of the lab at Virein. In his normal work mode he was so intense that he could miss ringing phones and conversations of people standing at his desk. This morning, he had not yet started, but still jumped when his phone rang. He answered in English with only his name, as he'd heard others do.

"Hello, Dr. Li. This is Herb Rosenthal again. An important meeting has come up tomorrow. Can we meet today? Same time and place?"

Darrel collected his thoughts and tried to re-orient his thinking to the context of the meeting. "Yes." He paused for seconds. "That would be good." He looked at the calendar on his desk where his meeting was described in his own Chinese shorthand, something only he could possibly read. He drew a circle around the info and arrow to today.

"Thank you. Same time, same place, but today. See you in about an hour and a half?"

They agreed. Darrel set the timer on his desk for one hour. He had to be sure to hear it.

\#

He arrived and sat in the back corner of the Tianjin House at 11:17:34 and ordered tea. He waited for the hypothesized agent from the Israeli Embassy to arrive and reveled in the aromas. The evidence of woked pork, chicken, soy sauce, and burnt cooking oil filled the room. All were cooked into the restaurant's woodwork. It was a pleasant combination, like his college dorm. It reminded him of Beijing University. A part of China he hadn't seen since he graduated. Not like home, too oniony.

He liked Tianjin House because it was cleaner than the Golden Panda and the food tasted more like home. Most other restaurant's food was not at all like his mother's. The lighting was a little brighter, but more important, it was less noisy so work and conversation were easier here.

Darrel wondered if Herb Rosenthal was a Mossad agent. At 11:28:37 a Caucasian who could pass for Italian, Arab or Israeli entered. He wore the required blue blazer and tan slacks and a blue and tan striped tie, the type Darrel called a regimental tie. About as inconspicuous clothing as a man could wear in Washington, D.C. He appeared to have black hair, but white sideburns or white tops to his sideburns. He took off his dark glasses and walked to the back of the restaurant and to Darrel's booth. "Dr. Li?"

Darrel nodded and watched. He could now see that the man's hair was black on top with a white fringe and lighter black hair on the sides, as though he had a black toupée that was faded around the edges and a poor match for his fringe of real hair. It did look like the world's worst wig.

"Shalom, Dr. Li. I'm Herb Rosenthal."

Darrel stood. "Thank you for coming, Mr. Rosenthal." Darrel tried to recall all the warnings he'd been given about dealings with Americans or others. "Please call me Darrel."

"Okay, Darrel." He held out his hand. "My name is Herb; that's a lot easier than Rosenthal."

Darrel shook Herb's hand. Darrel was not sure what it was about the man, but he felt relaxed, more so than with Mr. Chen, more like the compatibility he felt with his boss, CM, Charles the Candy Man. He was determined to be guarded. He knew people evaluation was not one of his strengths. Nor was small talk. Or other casual, interpersonal courtesies. Damn autistic leaning.

"Will you tell me about yourself?" Herb looked around. "I did some research and found a Dr. Darrel Li with a PhD in virology from UVA in Charlottesville. He works at a startup somewhere around here. That is you I found, isn't it?"

"Yes. I don't think there is another Darrel Li around. I am one you found." Darrel tried to look up and make eye contact with the man. That was hard. Herb wore his hair very short. Must be military or Mossad.

"Thank you. You gave me some of that background on the phone, but I misspelled your company's name until I found it on-line."

"Spelling is always hard for me," Darrel said.

"Me too. My first language is Hebrew, not English."

Darrel remembered to nod. He'd been told nodding in a conversation showed understanding, not agreement.

"Can you tell me what sort of work you're doing?"

"We were working on inserting genes into plant DNA, but funding for that is gone. Now we apply techniques to inserting genes and modifying genes in funguses."

"I wouldn't have thought there would be money for that." Herb shrugged and looked around again. The waiter looked at their table so Herb held up his tea cup and wiggled it.

"You are right. But we have no competition and think we can modify mushrooms to provide a good source of protein. We hope button mushroom burger or even huagu burger will be as good a protein source as hamburger." Darrel went on to explain more of what they were doing, how it should be salable, and how they needed money to finish.

"I am Jewish." Darrel leaned close to Herb and spoke in a very low voice. "My mother was a Jew. I would like to do something for Israel, if I can. Maybe we could even take all our technology to Israel so we can grow *hamburger trees* on worn-out land. Not literal hamburger trees of course, but mushrooms with comparable nutrition."

Herb sat back in his chair. Did that mean he was bored? Darrel wondered if he'd ruined his chances with the Israelis. What should he have done?

"Wow," Herb said. "That sounds huge to me." Herb's gaze became distant and he rubbed his chin.

Darrel realized he's completely misinterpreted Herb's body language. Not unusual. Maybe this meeting would lead somewhere after all.

"I'm sure you realize I'm in no position to evaluate your offer. I can't judge the science or the finances, but if you can give me some technical details, I can and will make sure the right people see them."

"Thank you. I know that's all I can expect." Darrel gave Herb some papers and received a business card with his contact information. "I'll send you more complete technical information and a business plan for our venture within 36 hours. Is this address the best one to use?" Darrel pointed to generic gmail address on Herb's card.

"Yes. That will be perfect."

"I'll send the information as encrypted files with the password *Shalom*, with only the S capitalized."

Herb took another business card from his wallet and retrieved the one still in front of Darrel. He wrote on both and handed one back to Darrel face down so the "PW Shalom" scrawl showed. When their meals arrived, Darrel described how Virein had developed techniques for making very robust protein enhancers. "They will be well suited to the very high temperature of the Mideastern deserts."

Darrel thought he'd managed to make contact where Charles had failed. This would help everybody, but most especially Virein. He thanked Herb.

Chapter 23 – Day 36, Wednesday

Atlanta

Gunn preferred to think an Israeli or Arab obtained some Reston ebolavirus, Zaire ebolavirus and a thermophilic bacterium and derived this MEFV supervirus from it. The virus might have come from the U.S., but that didn't mean it was created or distributed by an American. Maybe some damned hyphenated American. Some madman.

There must be a gazillion thermophilic bacteria in the Dead Sea and probably as many viruses. RNA viruses are notorious for rapid evolution. If you could work with a metal-loaded bacterium, the virus might co-opt some iron and tungsten from it. Many thermophilic bacteria fit the bill. And extremophiles like them are hardly studied.

Gunn made a list of the steps that a scientist might use to develop such a bug. If Pauline's food transmission idea was right, the metal, or something, had to:

- Protect it from moderate heat
- Protect it from stomach acid
- Be insertable into some food where it would replicate

Wait a minute. Gunn looked at the last item. Yeast. It would be difficult but he thought it was possible to insert a virus into yeast where it could multiply and spread. If the yeast used by boutique bakeries was infected, it would fit all the epidemiological data, wouldn't it? The idea became a mindworm. Gunn could think of no other possibilities.

Gunn composed an email to Moshe. "Please send me a big collection of up-market yeast-leavened products, and put a bio-hazard label on it. I have thought of a possible H5E1 vector—yeast." Gunn went on to briefly outline his reasoning and asked if there were many bakery workers on the infected-persons list. "We'll do DNA analysis. You may want to start checking more samples for HFV to broaden our testing." He added his regards to Moshe's family and clicked on send.

Gunn sent messages to his daughter and to his son-in-law warning them to avoid baked goods. He realized he had no idea of the temperatures reached in a loaf of baking bread. He had baked thousands of loaves of bread recreationally, but paid little attention to the chemistry and physics of baking. For Gunn, baking was an escape from science, not an application. Because of its size, bread ought to be about the lowest temperature yeast-based product so it is the one most likely to contain viable virus after baking. And this virus is so virulent that killing 99% of it would leave a lethal dose.

Gunn felt a warm glow. He had a plausible explanation for the major piece of the puzzle. If correct, the rest was legwork—find all the products with the infected yeast and get them off the market. Fast. Then, they had to find where the yeast came from. Maybe he and Moshe could infer the yeast source or sources from the bread samples. His RNA analysis would tell the exact virus on a few samples, and Moshe's HFV analysis would check thousands of products, many by the time his package got to Atlanta.

One thing Gunn could do before the bread and pastries arrived from Israel was verify that bread didn't get so hot it would kill the virus. Googling yielded no measurements of interior temperatures for baking breads. He'd have to go home and do some experiments.

As Gunn walked across the lobby on his way home, he whacked his forehead with the heal of his hand. If bread remains cool enough for the virus to survive, then meat or poultry would also, especially if they were not cooked well done. If the virus could survive in a human stomach long enough to be absorbed by the body, it could probably survive in the gut of a lamb, cow or chicken. Rare or expensive meats could be perfect viral harbors and explain their epidemiological data as well as bread. He wondered if steak tartare or sushi was popular in Israel. Damn. He'd already told Ikeya's secretary he was going home to work. Damn. No I mustn't even think those words. I have to clean up my vocabulary for Mele Mele. *And* for myself.

Gunn was committed to testing his thesis at home. He entered the kitchen of their Chastain Park home and reveled in the smells of steamed vegetables from last night and oatmeal that morning. For his experiment, he decided to use a standard recipe and not work from memory. He scrupulously followed the basic sourdough white bread recipe in *Joy of Cooking*.

He worked and stopped thinking about his experiment. He lost himself in thoughts about virus distribution. When he covered the bread to let it rise he studied the whole recipe, something he hadn't done in decades. He noticed that bread is supposed to be baked to an internal temperature of 195°F or about 90°C, pretty hot for any virus but certainly survivable for some. Funny he hadn't found that with Google. And that was a moderate temperature for a thermophilic virus like MEFV. He went ahead with his experiment and called Jeanne Anne. He told her to avoid bakery goods. After he hung up the phone he wondered if he should have warned her about meats or other types of food. What about warning the Daltons in Honolulu?

Before putting his bread in the oven, Gunn inserted a meat thermometer in one loaf. He watched the temperature increase slowly then rise quite rapidly as the baking time approached *Joy's* specification. At the middle of the *Joy* time his loaves nearly passed his usual thump-for-done test. He let them bake five more minutes and removed them from the oven at 200°F internal temperature.

His experiment also showed something he hadn't thought of when he read the baking directions, the time the interior of the bread loaf spent at or above 90°C was very short. The internal temperature rose quickly toward the end of the baking cycle and started down when the loaves came out of the oven. That makes it even easier for a virus to survive.

The bread also tasted good. A short time at 95°C would be a far cry from killing 100% of their thermophilic nemesis.

#

The next day Gunn received an email,

Hello Gunn,

You can't imagine the amount of static I've received from my reimbursement request for purchasing pastries. They **are** on their way. At least you didn't ask for condoms.

BTW, Ian looks better. We're hopeful. Thank God for little favors. And maybe your vaccine and Zmapp.

Moshe

He laughed.

Moshe's mention of condoms reminded Gunn of some graduate school lab work when they needed a way to temporarily seal some flasks even though the gas volume in the flask was changing tremendously. Condoms were the right size, provided enough stretch to accommodate the varying volume, and were sufficiently impermeable for their lab work. Neither of them wanted to ask the matronly departmental secretary to process the purchase order. How do shy young men ask a mother-figure to order a gross of condoms? Uncomfortably.

Gunn's reply email thank you note included, "Let's hope this guess is right. My next one may be pasties. They'll be harder to justify."

The FedEx package from Moshe arrived with a variety of breads, rolls and pastries. Now the hard part, trying to find some viable virus in one of the breads. Or could it be that they would have to look for some trace left by the virus? It's easy to find a needle in a haystack—use a magnet. Here they would be looking for a needle in a needle stack.

At least in this case, Gunn knew to start his looking in the center of each piece of bread. The part that would have spent the least time close to 100°C.

Chapter 24 – Day 38, Friday

Atlanta

With the bread samples in hand, Gunn felt optimistic about the investigation and started the virus search. His own lab could do the HFV test and the DNA lab would start on whatever the quick and inaccurate HFV test pointed to. Because of all the possible food vectors for the hemorrhagic fever virus he worried about the outbreak near his granddaughter. Gunn picked up his ringing phone to hear Ikeya's administrative assistant tell him he was expected in Amhach's office in 15 minutes.

Oh, damn. No. Oh, shoot. If Susan called that means both Amhach and Ikeya will be there. What did I do now? Gunn thought over all the things he'd written and said over the last week. Nothing seemed the least bit contentious.

\#

At Amhach's office, his worries were confirmed. Ikeya was there. Amhach wore his usual dark gray suit with a yellow power tie, this one had a paisley pattern formed by blue and red fractal-like shapes. Ikeya was dressed in his usual dark suit with a red and blue regimental tie. The red and blue stripes of the silk tie were separated by thin gold lines.

Amhach seemed to be wearing some sort of floral aftershave. It permeated his office giving a vague impression of a field of lilacs and lavender.

The only reason for them both would be here is they want to fire Gunn. More accurately, Amhach was after his butt and wanted Ikeya on his side in case Gunn brought a legal challenge against him or CDC. He wondered if Amhach really dared go that far. Gunn greeted the two men, neither of whom smiled, and sat down on the indicated chair.

Amhach put an email in front of him. "Can you imagine any better way to incite panic than to tell a foreign national that you think his bread may be the source of the hemorrhagic fever outbreak?" He was a glowering black vulture. A bald, red faced bird-brain circling its carrion meal.

Gunn was not dead yet. He looked at the paper. Or was he? The paper was a copy of his request to Moshe for samples of yeast-leavened baked goods. "That was a private email to a friend I've known for more than three decades, a former roommate." Someone who's ten times as smart and politically aware as you are, asshole. No! No. I mean as you are, idiot.

Gunn broke his pause. "I know he can be trusted with the information. He will do nothing with the email or its contents that could start a panic." Gunn frowned at the message, but didn't read it. "He would not show it to anyone. Everyone in the Mideast is far more politically astute than we are." He put his hand to his mouth, his fingers curved into an open fist. His index finger touched his chin.

"And, just as no one else in Israel will see your email, nobody but you will see it here at Clifton Road." Amhach was a great Harpie, ready to pounce and defile Gunn. "I suppose you think I never saw it?" Amhach's scowl matched his words.

Ikeya's face was inscrutable. Gunn wondered whose side he was on. Something about him made it hard or impossible for Gunn to guess his thoughts.

Gunn sulked. They were right. He hadn't been as cautious as the situation required. He had to be able to communicate to others, but how. "I didn't know it was that easy to spy on email. I made a mistake." Gunn shook his head. "Because there are no other HFVs transmitted by food, I wanted to get some samples to check my off-the-wall theory." Gunn wondered about the possibility of panic and the certainty of fatalities from the MEFV. He looked at Amhach who morphed into a leopard. "It's so extraordinary for a filovirus to survive cooking or in the stomach, I needed to test my hypothesis."

"There are suitable ways to do that." The leopard across the desk crouched. About to spring on its prey. "Everyone at CDC must be tactful and circumspect."

"Yes, sir," Gunn said. "There are cases, and this may be one of them, where a panic would save lives. It might allow cremation of bodies. You are aware, sir, aren't you, that cremation is prohibited. Both Judaism and Islam explicitly prohibit it." The figure across the desk turned back into a harpie.

"It is not the CDC's job to incite anything. If a panic is needed, then that is a job for the politicians. We cannot ask people to be anti-religious. That's not for us." Amhach seemed to be just getting started.

"You realize, sir, that the Anti-American and Anti-Israeli sentiment probably depends on the number of fatalities. If we do little or nothing or if we act slowly, we are virtually guaranteed millions of fatalities." The harpie turned into a vulture, but on its heels.

Gunn looked at the email on the table and read it. "There's actually nothing in that email that ties my request to MEFV or to any HFV. No eavesdropper, or even any reporter, could tie my request to the outbreak." Gunn suppressed the smile he felt. Was now the time to pretend being contrite? Or should he kick the man while he was down. This might be okay yet. "No one could tell I wasn't testing my hypothesis about improving, uh, the, uh, transmission of H5N1 flu in bread and mistyped the flu's name?"

"We all know what your topic was." Amhach was still belligerent, but less so than a few minutes ago. He morphed from a lurking vulture to a bald-headed Chihuahua. Yip, yap, nip yap.

Gunn checked his inquisitors. Ikeya had a slight smirk. Amhach's frown was gone. "Even if you figured out my actual topic, no one else could. You're the only person with your wealth of background knowledge on my work schedule and insight into CDC's priorities. No one else knows that's all I've been working on. No reporter, or any other person for that matter, who wanted to embarrass you or the CDC, *could* know that I haven't been working on H5N1. This email can't be used against the Center by anyone but you." Gunn wondered if he should press on.

Might as well kick the ass, I mean the donkey, while he's down. Might help next time. "Someone might guess that this is related to the HFV cases, but he's much more likely to think it's related to the flu pandemic they predicted last fall or possibly the AIDS pandemic." Amhach's Chihuahua developed a questioning expression as it looked up at Gunn. It morphed into a cockroach. Indestructible, indecipherable.

"And last month our cover story for the trip to Tel Aviv was attending the flu convention, which would discourage any further prying by reporters or spies. Even that assumes they actually have the email. And another thing that just occurred to me. If someone does manage to access that email, it means they broke into our server. In other words, your center's security was not adequate."

Chapter 25 – Day 38, Friday, Afternoon

Atlanta

Gunn had a trace on the virus. The steps on the RNA molecule, like the rungs on the DNA double-helix ladder, are described by the word it spells in its GAUC alphabet, like the DNA word with its GATC code letters. In other words, RNA is defined by its sequence of the guanine, adenine, uracil and cytosine nucleotide sugars in its molecule. It wasn't really official yet, but at the CDC it was now Mideast filo virus, MEFV. Gunn's name had stuck.

Mideast filovirus had one long string of GAUC letters that matched Reston ebolavirus and another sequence that matched a unique part of Zaire ebolavirus. To a certainty of two nines, 99% as the press would report it, the matches were too good and over too long a part of the sequence for it to be a coincidence. It was not accidental. Gunn printed out all the information he had. He felt guilty wasting trees, but like most of his generation, he did not like reading extensively on a computer screen. He looked at the analysis and at the molecule's *name,* spelled in GAUC, and banged his pencil on the papers. If some animal had both viruses, it could conceivably create the MEFV virus internally. One or the other was fatal to almost any primate, so the *factory* animal would have to be something like a bat or pig, two of the non-primates that have been accused of being reservoirs of Zaire ebolavirus, ones that might harbor and live with both. If pigs are ZEBOV carriers, it ought to occur more widely than it does and it should have started in non-Jewish, non-Islamic areas. But something's the culprit.

Anyway, if the carrier lived with both diseases, then the viruses would have little reason to mutate and combine. Also, the presence of iron and tungsten didn't fit that hypothesis very well. And nothing natural could explain the folded structure Ian had found. No, this Mideast filovirus must be the work of a very skilled group of people, not cells.

But why start with a virus that didn't infect people? There had never been transmission of Reston ebolavirus to people from cynomolgus macaques, the crab eating monkeys that brought it to Reston, Virginia, and other places, and died from it. Maybe it was to improve transmission. Lab workers in Reston had antibodies to fight Reston ebolavirus, so it seemed likely there was at least some viral transmission. The workers were probably very lucky that REBOV hadn't developed a taste for human cells.

God, that was a scary thought. Could the guys who made this superebola know more about hemorrhagic fevers than I do? Gunn shuddered.

The right thing to do now is to turn all the information over to the FBI. This should be straight police work—checking everyone who had access to these two strains of virus. Check out everyone who was on both lists.

The problem with doing the right thing—it may be the wrong thing. Can the FBI be trusted? They botched the Los Alamos leak investigation, prematurely accusing Dr. Lee, and focusing so intently on him they lost all possibility of determining what happened. They hid exculpatory evidence and doctored crime samples to make evidence look more convincing in some capital trials. They botched the search for the perpetrator who caused the anthrax scare and for lots of other less visible cases. Hey, maybe they should get a job working in the Mideast. FBI managers, the Agents in Charge, all the way up to The Director must be yes-men. The boot-licking culture was probably a holdover from the Hoover era.

A bunch of shit-brained toadies. No, no, no. I mustn't even think those words. Gunn pondered how to obtain the access list for REBOV and ZEBOV. Wait, damn it, the original ZEBOV was so much more widespread, its access list wouldn't narrow the first one in any significant way. Darn. He had to think of Mele Mele. No more four-letter words in his thoughts. He had to clean up his act for her, for Pauline, for himself.

There had been Reston outbreaks at several primate centers in the U.S. and one in Italy. Oh, damn, one in Italy. They are close to the Mideast. Where could he learn who received samples from one of those episodes? The last was a decade ago. Then Gunn pounded his desk and cursed. All of those cases were in monkeys from the Philippines. The Philippines, where there was a strong Islamic movement and Al-Qa'ida was supposed to have some terrorist cells. More important than Al-Qa'ida was the Governmental sieve. What a great headline, "Terrorist Cell Creates Deadly Virus Cell."

Anyone could obtain virus samples from the damn Filipinos. No, no. From the darn Filipinos.

\#

"Okay, Shoreham, what do you have this time?" Amhach's attitude was as gruff as his words.

"I thought you'd like to be briefed on my ideas and have a chance to veto anything before it becomes public." Gunn could see Mele Mele sticking her tongue out at Amhach and half-wished he had the courage to do it. "Oh, by the way, I have not even notified Moshe of my findings. It is many hours into their sabbath, but I think I should call Moshe and warn him. All bread from some bakeries will have to be pulled from the shelves and destroyed. He should have verified the HFV presence and may have started on removal. I have not checked with him today."

"Thank you for coming to me first. That's why we're here." Amhach's posture indicated some relenting.

Ikeya had the same sort of smirk he had the day before when Gunn caught Amhach over-reaching and over-reacting.

"It looks to me like boutique breads are the MEFV transmission vehicle." Gunn considered the jargon and decided Amhach might not realize he had named it the Mideast *Filoviridae* virus. "MEFV is our working name for the virus since it was first found in the Mideast. Some of the small bakery samples contained a HFV, a few did not. We're still working on correlating its presence with ingredients." Gunn sat at attention, or at least at his best 55-ish interpretation of it. Be deferential and polite no matter how big an asshole he is. No, no, make that a big jackass. No Mele Mele would call that swearing too. Make it a big jerk. He *is* a big jerk. God damn is he ever a big jerk.

"That's good. What's important about that work?"

Gunn explained his thought about locating the source of the virus by tracking the simian Reston ebolavirus. "It will not be easy to get records of everyone who's had access to the macaques in Italy and the Philippines, but it may be doable. We certainly ought to be able to find out from the American labs who has gotten samples of their viruses."

Amhach looked lost in thought. Too bad he doesn't think about finding the vector. He's only worried about his political ass and who may learn of the investigation.

"We should be able to distinguish strains from different labs, but we haven't yet found a differentiator that is also on the new MEFV." Gunn shook his head. It would be days before the RNA analysis was complete. "We *are* working on it. It provides a good analysis testbed for us."

"Yeah, and it provides some political cover for requesting info from elsewhere." Josh Ikeya nodded in understanding.

"Good point, Josh," Gunn said. "I think the proximity of Al-Qa'ida to the sources of monkeys in northern Luzon, and of the entire Mideast to Sienna, Italy, means that those are more likely to be the source, but our labs should provide a way to test and improve our search."

"Okay. Then what you want is permission to ask for REBOV samples and lists of who's accessed it from the American macaque users, right?" Even though he was generally in the dark about his own center, Amhach looked like he actually understood the discussion, a new high for him.

"Actually, sir, all we need are the access lists. We have virus samples on file." He really has no clue what his agency does.

"Okay, that sounds proper. Let's see what we can learn from our own resources and the access lists. And be sure the work is kept confidential. Very top secret."

"Yes, sir. My plan, with your approval of course, is to use private channels for all requests. A formal request will demand more scrutiny and be visible to many more people."

"You're saying you have friends who can get the information for you?"

"No. But I thought a quiet request to an acquaintance would be less apt to be noticed by anyone." Gunn looked back and forth between Billy Bob Amhach and Josh Ikeya. "If one of you has a friend at Hazelton whom you know we can trust, I would prefer to start with him or her. We need contacts at the Hazelton's Primate Quarantine Unit in Reston and its Primate Center in Texas."

Ikeya shrugged and looked at Amhach.

"I think you're on your own, there," Amhach said. "Be sure you keep it low-key and confidential."

\#

Gunn contemplated the virus and how it could have been designed. Who could do this work? Where could they do it? Not many answers for either. A phone call interrupted his concentration. He answered and found Robinson Winter on the line.

"As you know, Dr. Shoreham, oh, excuse me, Gunn, I'm still trying to understand the virus and how you do your detective work. I hope I can talk you into a beer or some wine and pick your brain again. This time around, I'll understand more of it and the more sessions you're willing to spend with me, the better I'll do. I hope."

"Sounds like a good idea." Gunn tried to recall his schedule for the next few days.

"I have family commitments over the weekend, but wondered in you're free Monday?" Robinson was impeccably dressed in Gunn's image.

"Monday evening sounds good to me." There is so much to figure out about this virus, I can't take off during the day. "Is evening what you have in mind?"

"Perfect. There's a pub I like on Lenox Road. Want to meet there?"

"I know the place you mean." It's not bad, but I've been away too much. "Actually, why don't you come to our house. It's not far from Lenox, near Chastain Park. I have better wine and beer." The agreed on a drink at 7:00.

Gunn thought about enlisting Robinson's help in his search. He's a professional snoop so he may have techniques or avenues that never occurred to me.

Chapter 26 – Day 21, Tuesday

Darrel Li in Herndon, Virginia

At the time Gunn was preparing to go to Tel Aviv, Darrel Li was trying to help his company stay afloat. He had developed methods for inserting genes into fungi. He would modify a virus to include the gene's specific strand of DNA and use the virus to carry the gene into the cells of the fungus and splice them into the fungus's own DNA. The technique was not new and was patterned on the hypothetical way some viruses cause cancer by modifying the genetic structure of their host's cells.

One of the breakthroughs he and CM had achieved, was very fast virus detection, which had greatly increased the speed of their gene splicing development. This should be useful for any situation where someone needs to isolate or characterize viruses. Darrel had known for some time that this fast test ought to be marketable, but CM had not seemed interested and he handled all the sales type work for the company.

Most of Darrel's news came from Chinese language newspapers and they were slow to report certain types of information from inside or outside China. He did not learn about the Ebola cases in the Mideast until two weeks after the initial case. It was another couple of days before he realized that their fast virus tests might help stop the epidemic by speeding proof that a sick person had Ebolavirus, not flu. The fast virus test was unknown except to the two of them. Their tests should help fight viral infection because EBOLA medicines would not be wasted on flu sufferers.

It could also help track the spread of a virus by determining the individuals who do not have any virus in their system.

Darrel walked to his desk. He thought about the private office he had when the company was doing well. Now his desk was in a corner of the lab. He could not get away from the tissue samples and the smell of alcohol. CM had gone from a nice large office and a large oak desk to an office smaller than Darrel's old one and a steel desk. The candy dish of red and black Twizzlers on his boss's desk was the only indication of the better time.

CM was away working on raising venture capital. He'd told Darrel they should try to sell any service or accept any research support. Darrel called the Israeli embassy, from his own desk this time. He had no reason to hide his offer to sell a humanitarian product to the Israelis, not even from his boss, who seemed even less interested in selling to Middle-Eastern countries than any others. The company was in desperate need of cash, whether from investment, research contracts, or sales. The company needed financial help. He and CM would take support in any form they could get it.

When the receptionist answered the phone, Darrel did not recognize her voice. She wasn't the person he spoke with the last time. "Is Herb Rosenthal there please?"

"Not right now. He's out for a week."

Darrel felt a chill and wondered what he should do. "This is Dr. Darrel Li with urgent message for your Center for Disease Control. My company has virus detection system that is much faster than any other. I think you would like to have it to diagnose and track the Ebola cases in Israel. Is there someone else I can speak to who can relay the message to your CDC."

"Thank you, Dr. Li. I will relay the message."

"Okay." Darrel decided he needed to give more information about their technology. "We use viruses to introduce new genes in the DNA of our target. This means we have to know what the viruses do in their host. We have developed a quick viral detection capability that is fastest test in world for RNA viruses."

"Really?" The phone-answerer seemed more interested.

"Yes, so our technology should be useful in combating viral disease outbreaks, especially Ebolavirus. That is something you want to be sure your CDC to know. It can very quickly tell doctors patient has no Ebola. Might be flu or some other viral disease, but if test is negative, it cannot be Ebola.”

“That is interesting right now. I will pass the information along and try to impress on people its important application.” She sounded sincere and interested.

Darrel was surprised. Who should I ask for? Perhaps she is the person to relay the message. He had no further ideas. “Thank you. Herb Rosenthal is person I talked to before. When he returns, please be sure he knows.”

Chapter 27 – Day 38, Friday, Afternoon

Atlanta

Gunn looked at the map of outbreaks another time. The one thing he could see was that no connections were obvious. If people were responsible, then he, she? they? must have spread the virus in a number of places. Probably easier to get travel data from Mossad than the FBI. International travel records can't be secret. They scan every passport at airports, so somewhere a computer knows all.

Gunn prepared an email for Moshe. No, better not send that. Amhach seems to find out about all of them. If he knows anything about my request, he'll have a cow. I'll call Moshe tonight.

On his way home he drove by the Chastain Park Dairy Queen, his favorite DQ. He parked beside it and called the pay phone nearby. Even if he had been followed, a tail would be hard-pressed to realize what was going on. He heard the pay phone ring, and ring again. Can't do any more or someone could know what I'm doing.

He got out of his car, went into the DQ and ordered a small cone and a Peanut Buster Parfait. He took them home and rushed them to the freezer.

After dinner, at ten o'clock, Gunn called Moshe from the phone in his home office. He heard a sleepy and grumpy "Shalom." "Hello, Moshe, this is Gunn. I need to talk to you. Can you call me in 30 minutes?"

Various grumbling and waking noises were all Gunn could discern.

"Look, Moshe, wake up. This is really important. I need you to write a number down."

"Okay, go ahead. Give me the details." Still very sleepy, but at least awake.

Gunn read the number of the pay phone from his cell. "Look, call me in half an hour. Got that? That's 5:30 your time, right?" Gunn saw a Moshe who had become a cross between Andy Rooney and Harpo Marx. He sounded more curmudgeonly than Rooney.

"Shit. This better be good, Dr. Shoreham."

Gunn walked into their bedroom where Pauline watched the start of the news. "Hello, Beautiful. Care to cover my back while I take a phone call?"

"What are you up to now. It's pretty darn late, isn't it?" She looked at him, studied his face.

"Here, maybe. In Tel Aviv it's first thing in the morning. Moshe should call me at the DQ pay phone in about 25 minutes. NSA may monitor the call, but I don't think Amhach will know about it."

"*May* monitor it? *Will* monitor it. So. Okay. Where do I fit in? Some eye candy to distract the fuzz?"

"I like that idea. I also figure you'll be more likely to see anyone following or listening in."

"Maybe. You're pretty good at this spook stuff. Like when you shot that burglar."

"Probably more stupid and hasty than careful." Gunn recalled returning from a trip and thinking someone was in the house. While Pauline called 911, he took his pistol from its safe in their car and went to investigate. Pretty dumb. He was lucky it worked that time. "Muscle isn't my problem, it's caution and watching behind me. Didn't you recently say I was a lousy spook."

"Okay, on a CIA scale, you're lousy because you aren't good at self-preservation. You need more eyes in the back of your head."

This time they drove to the Dairy Queen and parked where Gunn could easily hear the pay phone ring. When it rang, he answered and exchanged a few pleasantries. "I hope you continue to have good news about Ian."

"Yes," Moshe said. "The doctors think his prognosis is excellent and we've actually begun thinking about how soon he and Wild Bill can return on public transportation."

"Thank you."

Moshe cut in before Gunn could continue. "Okay, but none of this stuff is what you called about. You wouldn't get me up only to ask for a status update. What's your real issue?"

"Okay, let's get to the important stuff." Gunn lowered his voice and looked around. He didn't see anyone and Pauline did not indicate anything to worry about. "What's involved in finding out who's visited Israel from the U.S. and maybe from other Mideast countries? Whoever spread the virus probably got some parts of it from here or Italy. More likely here. Almost certainly here."

"Well, if Iraq's included, that visit is probably first. An Israeli visa will keep you out of Iraq, unless you know to get the visa put in a document separate from your passport."

"Oh, yeah. I remember John said Ian should go on a military flight to avoid Iraqi bureaucracy. I didn't understand all the political implications when Ian went to Baghdad. We followed directions and took the free flight. But the MEFV showed up in Tel Aviv first, so our perp probably went to Israel from his home, then on to the Arab countries."

"Well, if he went from here to Baghdad, he had to have planned carefully to avoid having his passport stamped here. Either that or go by a military flight."

"So, either way he made a documented visit to Israel."

"Yep. Mossad or Shinbet must have that info, but I have no idea how to get it. I'll have to ask around to see what I can learn. I can't imagine I'll get anything fast."

"Damnable bureaucracy. If ever time was important it's now."

"I'll do what I can."

Okay, and one other thing, if we need to communicate in writing, use Word to encrypt whatever you're writing and send it attached to the email. Let's use your wife's full name, first, maiden and last, with normal capitalization and no spaces. You can use the same encryption key or password or whatever they call it if you send data in a spreadsheet. I hear Office's protection is very secure.

Gunn wondered what other approaches he could use to find the

MEFV distributor. Damn, maybe it's some disgruntled soldier like Bradley Manning. But if that's the case, he's only an accomplice. No way some soldier could have developed this beasty. Nobody in the military has the sort of training he'd need to develop it. Possibly developed in a government lab and distributed by the scientist? I guess he would be likely to have ties to the military, so he could find his own Private Manning to distribute it.

Sounds like a team bio-terror effort.

Chapter 28 – Day 38, Friday Afternoon

Atlanta

Back to the Rolodex. Gunn looked for acquaintances working at Hazelton's Primate Quarantine Unit in Reston, Virginia, and at their Primate Center in Alice, Texas. One saloon in Alice Springs, Australia, but nothing in Alice, Texas. Ah yes, here's one at Reston, good old Nougat. He's probably retired now, but he should be a good first contact. He dialed the number of Xavier O'Rourke. Hmm. I haven't talked to him in years. I wonder if he still goes by Nougat. Wonder if he ever did. Maybe that was only a name we used behind his back.

"Hello. This is Dr. Gunn Shoreham at the Center for Disease Control and Prevention in Atlanta." Gunn thought about what message he wanted to leave. "Dr. O'Rourke gave some interesting lectures at Harvard Medical School when I was there and has given a number of talks at conferences over the years. I would like to talk to him about some work we are heavily involved in here." Gunn left contact information. He also emailed a similar message to the researcher, or at least to the perhaps-out-of-date email address he had for Nougat.

Maybe staring at the table of outbreaks would help. EBOV outbreaks had mortality rates of 50% to 90% and it looked like MEFV was about 50% in Israel. Probably higher in Iraq and Egypt.

The chances of surviving Ebola the disease had not improved much over time. Even hospitalization didn't help much in Africa. The recent west Africa outbreak data showed almost three quarters of non-hospitalized patents died versus almost 60% in the hospitals. Damn that's horrible mortality. Oh shit, the data look bad even in western hospitals—very few cases but half seem to have died—and all of that was for Ebola, not MEFV.

The outbreaks were all in Africa, though a few isolated cases had occurred elsewhere, so the Israeli mortality experience should be better. Would they beat American and European hospitals? The Israelis were certainly going to extremes in terms of isolation and sterilization when we visited Ian. And the other countries seemed to be going to extremes in terms of denial.

Gunn stared at the table of outbreaks. He made up a time line of events and stared at that. He checked the maps of the outbreaks, hoping some pattern would be visible. With one dead-end after another, he pounded his hand on his desk and on his head. Gone was the euphoric feeling of the morning when he thought he'd found the transmission mechanism. Nothing suggested any insights. He stalked around his office.

He stood and looked out his office window. He imagined the jammed I-85 Freeway, the Northeast Expressway. How lucky those people are, stuck in their cars. If the Ebola gets here, their lives will be far more interesting, like the Confucian curse. The drivers only think they're suffering now. His phone rang. He grabbed it without looking, identified himself and heard O'Rourke tell him his call was returned.

After a few pleasantries, Gunn said, "I'm chasing the Ebola outbreaks in the Mideast. The virus seems to include RESTV." Gunn stopped and realized he should not use his jargon. "I mean it has some characteristics of Reston ebolavirus and probably was taken from your virus about, I don't know, maybe in '05. I hoped that you could direct me to a list of everyone who's had access to any infected tissue from your Hazelton facility."

"You probably reached the right person, Gunn, but I don't think I can or should give you the list."

"What?" Gunn's interjection interrupted Xavier's measured denial. "What's the problem?" Gunn tried to recall Nougat's appearance. He saw a balking mule.

"Actually, there are two problems. First is that we need to protect ourselves. This certainly involves a potential felony, so it's legally serious. Second, if you determine that we are innocent but that we are the source of the outbreak in Israel, you'll want to satisfy all the law's requirements so you can use your information in court."

"It sounds like you're not denying me your information, only telling me I have hoops to jump through, right?" Gunn nodded in thought. "Ones that are likely to be important down the road?"

"Right. If you get a subpoena for our customer list, no lawyer will be able to throw out your information at trial. At least I think that's correct. Like everyone else, courts assume their own omniscience. And if I respond to your subpoena, no one at Hazelton can say I acted inappropriately."

Gunn saw the Supreme Court making some pronouncement on Ebolavirus. Opining on things none of them understood. "I get your point. Just that I hate the thought of dealing with lawyers." *And I sleep with one.* Maybe she'll help me. No, can't ask Pauline, this has to use CDC's legal bagels.

"You may be right and I'm probably reacting to what I've seen on *CSI.* I admit I haven't had any lawyer tell me what I have to do."

"Ugh. Yeah. I hadn't thought about convicting the bastard, I mean terrorist." Gunn told himself to think of his granddaughter. "I only thought about stopping him and the disease and doing that as fast as possible. Conviction is a whole 'nother matter."

He hung up. "Damn." He yelled at the window. "Now I've got to deal with the—no don't say it—scumbag Amhach and the damn lawyers. At least if they do all the preparation, Amhach can't rag on me about it."

He sat down and turned toward his computer. What did he need in a memo to Amhach to get the subpoena? The lawyers will have a field day slowing us down with a pile of paperwork. While he tried to think of the things he needed for the lawyers, he checked his email. A message from Jeanne Anne. He opened it.

John's sick. Gone to Kaneohe Bay Hospital.

"Eyze chara baleben." Gunn thought for a moment about the epithet. At least he had not thought anything that would offend Mele Mele, and he doubted either Jeanne Anne or Pauline would be bothered by the Hebrew lament. He tried to convince himself that a visit to the hospital in Honolulu when a Marine got back from a tour in Baghdad would not be unusual. Why hadn't Jeanne Anne said something about it. Why such a terse note?

He clicked on Reply and wrote, "Why did he go to the hospital? What sort of symptoms did he show?" It was just over a week ago that Ian checked himself into Sourasky. A week variation in incubation time would be normal. Oh, crap. God, don't even think it. Need more info.

Gunn collected the information he'd need for the subpoena.

Chapter 29 – Day 41, Monday Evening

Atlanta

Gunn got home from work, exhausted and bewildered. How could a person get along so well with one lawyer and suffer so with others? The day had been like a month trying to localize a virus, all condensed into one day. No doubt the lawyers barricades were all important, but damn they're a pain. He collapsed on the sofa in the living room and looked at the blank television. He felt neither the inclination nor the energy to turn it on.

Pauline came in a few minutes later and turned on the TV, which was tuned to CNN, as usual. She wore a light brown pantsuit with a yellow scarf that showed off her color and figure and had some envelope in her hand, probably homework. "You look spent. Want a glass of wine?"

"Can you pour it in?" He turned toward the ceiling and opened his mouth. In a moment Pauline handed him a long-stem glass filled with... He smelled the wine. Swirled it and smelled again and took a sip. With Bordeaux, probably a mix of Cabernet Sauvignon, Merlot, and Cabernet Franc. He closed his eyes for a second. "I love you." Gunn looked at his beautiful wife.

"Me? Or the wine?" She had a matching glass of Bordeaux in her right hand and a brown business-letter size envelope in her left. She handed him the envelope. "This was in the mail."

The top three lines on the envelope read.

Personal and Confidential

Dr. Gunn Shoreham

Personal and Confidential

The priority mail envelope had been addressed by hand and felt rather thin but with a bulge in the middle. It had a Washington, D.C., postmark. No other source identification.

Gunn opened it and found a second envelope inside. A standard #10 business envelope that repeated the hand-printed notation

Personal and Confidential

Dr. Gunn Shoreham

Personal and Confidential

but nothing more on the front. The back had "Personal and Confidential" written across the flap. All handwritten in what appeared to be the same hand as the outside envelope. It felt like it contained quite a few sheets of paper.

The second envelope did contain a dozen or so pages that appeared to be copied from an engineer's notebook. The first page showed some heavily redacted information that he studied for a moment and realized it was probably the cover page for the access log to a secure facility. The other pages, which appeared to come from later in the log book, contained a list of people, organizations and dates. The dates ranged over a couple of years. Several years on each page. Nothing looked very interesting. He went to the first page and scanned it.

He studied the paper, but the identifying information in the top half was blacked out. One redaction had "antine Unit" at the end of a line. Another ended in "A" or maybe "/A." The obscuring mark had missed the end of those two lines. Nothing hinted at the identification. The bottom of the page was similar to the second page, but the dates were quite old, late '80s and early '90s. He looked at the bottom of the page and saw his own name, and above it was a line that showed USAMRIID in the column labeled "Organization."

"antine Unit" could be Hazelton's Primate Quarantine Unit. The "/A" might be VA as in Reston, VA. Somebody up there likes me. He turned to the next page, where the dates ranged over the period over the first half of 2003. The dates on the third were were the rest of '03 and so it continued on the other sheets. He read the handwritten organizational entries. Most were "CDC" or "USAMRIID," but a few had mixed case names that were hard to read. He tried to parse those undecipherable ones from late 2008. Two looked like a check mark followed by *ir* and some more junk. He had no clue about the last letters. The associated names were as hard to read as the organization, but it looked like it began with "GA," had an "i" in the middle, at least there was a dot above whatever was there, and ended with some inscrutable scrawl that could be almost any number of letters.

"What is that stuff?" Pauline seemed to pay more attention to the news than anything else.

"Not sure. Heavily redacted." He took another sip of wine. "I think I have conflicting legal and ethical issues and need some education on the law. When you have some time we need to talk."

"Can we do it late or tomorrow? I've got another reception for Botkin tonight." She turned off the TV.

"I'm tired. I'll probably collapse before you get home." Gunn squinted hard to increase the tears to his dry eyes. "Let's aim for after work tomorrow." Gunn scratched his chin. "Damn. Just remembered. Robinson Winter should stop by soon. Maybe I'll still be awake when you get home." They kissed and Pauline left for her reception.

Gunn took the papers into his office. One of the few sources for the Reston Ebola part of the MEFV virus is the Reston Primate Research lab in Virginia. Nougat wouldn't let Gunn see their paperwork because of lawsuits. Maybe he's worried about his job. On the other hand, if this is a criminal matter, the courts might throw everything out unless we get a subpoena. Meh. Maybe, and maybe he's only guessing. "CSI" or whatever it was, isn't world-class legal training. Damn, he wished Pauline were there.

The rear doorbell chimed. Gunn asked Robinson in and offered him a drink. Robinson accepted a glass of Bordeaux and they went into Gunn's office. Robinson asked about MEFV and EBOV, concentrating on the differences. He worked on learning the correct usage for both terms.

After twenty minutes of questions, answers and discussion, Robinson said, "At the highest level there seems to be a lot of similarity between investigating a crime and searching for a virus."

"Hadn't thought of that." Gunn considered searching for connections between disconnected events, probably about like looking for connections between viruses and sources. "Maybe I should get your help on deciphering some heavily redacted information. Some angel must intend to help me find the bastard behind the MEFV." Gunn had to stop talking like that, even when only men are present. "Correct that, I need help finding the terrorist behind it."

Gunn filled him in on what he'd received. They both studied the pages from Reston. "Maybe Nougat agrees that speed is essential," Gunn said. "So he sends me the info I need, but in a form that is hard to trace, difficult for anyone but me to decipher." Gunn studied Robinson to get his impression.

"You're a doctor, not an officer of the court or a cop. The rules should be less stringent for you." Robinson acted comfortable with his answer.

"Let's say he hopes I can do something with it. What do you think of the Fourth Amendment? You think it doesn't actually apply here?"

"No. Not that at all," Robinson said. "I think you obtained the info in a way that the courts would allow you to use it."

"Okay. So I seem to have been anonymously sent the access list." Gunn looked at the papers and picked up his wine for another sip. "If I can identify someone on the list, what's the chance I'll ruin part of a prosecutor's case against the guy?"

"More important, if you can do it, but don't, and more people die, what are your legal and ethical liabilities?"

"Sounds like one of those friggin' artificial cases that give law school students fits." Gunn stared at the sheets.

"Yeah, but this one seems heavily weighted toward you."

"Sounds good. So, if the organization is ProteinGen, which that "√ir*" scrawl might be, then..." Gunn looked blankly across the room. "*GA*--, hmm. That must be George Austin. That bastard. He develops the virus then offers to help us detect it so he can be sure to subvert any data we find that could be used against him."

"We need to find out about him." Robinson started typing on his laptop. "I'll google him."

Gunn held up a finger. "Let me give you my WiFi password. It should be faster than whatever you have."

"Thanks." Robinson logged onto the CDCdocsNet, as Gunn had named it.

"He tried to friend me on Facebook so we should be able to check on him there, too. Wonder if he's incriminated himself. Probably not, he's not as dumb as those teenage idiots. But now may be the time to take him up on Facebook and see what's there, too."

Robinson looked over Gunn's shoulder at Austin's Facebook page. "He seems to post stuff several times a day. With that volume of messages, we'll quickly have a good handle on Dr. George Austin. Much better than the stuff Google found."

"Yeah, look at all this." Gunn scrolled through pages, many with family pictures.

They both read and looked at the postings. "Those messages show a man in love with his work and people around him." Robinson shook his head. "What's going on? I can't imagine anyone like that being a mass murderer."

"Yeah. Maybe he's not our guy." Gunn frowned as they continued looking through the messages. "Doesn't eat very well, does he? Look at all the posts about fast food."

"Hmm. He talks a lot about his wife and children." Robinson pointed to posting after posting. "Let me look at those."

Gunn got up and Robinson took his chair and pointed to the posting times.

Robinson started systematically going through the messages, running his finger to the posting dates and times. "He certainly could fake all this stuff, but it looks like he's never more than a day or two from his family. If it isn't faked, he couldn't have made a trip to the Middle East. Wasn't gone long enough."

"So. Who the hell is the fucking murderer? How do I find the bastard?" Gunn picked up the papers from Nougat and stared at them. He studied the name on the register. "Y' know, handwritten *CM* resembles *GA*. Poor writing makes it especially easy to misread. Any doctor worthy of his bad handwriting could make C Maçon look like *C Mxxxixx* or *G Hxxxixx*. And both ProteinGen and Virein, could look like $\sqrt{ir}$xxx."

"Who is this Maçon? Have you friended him?" Robinson looked at Gunn.

"Yeah I think I did. Go back to my homepage and see if you find some posts from Charles Maçon." Gunn spelled the name.

Robinson clicked away and started scrolling through pages and pages of posts, looking for Maçon's name. "Aha. Got it. He clicked on Maçon and started scrolling through the postings.

"He does seem angry at not keeping his company further in the black. Nothing very concrete but he only posts every couple of weeks."

"No alibi doesn't make him guilty." Gunn frowned and looked back and forth between the Facebook postings and the register pages from Nougat. "Doesn't make sense. Why would Charles have even gotten a sample of the virus?" Gunn pronounced his name in a pseudo-French manner, as though it were Sharle in English.

"What do I really know about him?" Gunn shook his head. "Not much. He has complained about bankers screwing him and some people equate bankers with Jews."

Gunn tried to recall all the discussions he'd had with Charles Maçon. "Could he have unleashed this virus in Israel as some kind of demented attempt at revenge against bankers?" I think he has the equipment to handle the disease. Not as good as Austin's, but adequate. "When I tried to reach him a week or so before the EBOV appeared, he was on travel. Seems he was gone for ten days or so, plenty of time to go to Israel, Iraq and Egypt."

"Wonder what Google will tell us about Dr. Charles Maçon." Robinson found lots of information about a St. Charles Maçon in Voges, France, as well as some about Dr. Charles Maçon. Several articles on Virein's financial woes and their technology also turned up. "Doesn't look like much more. Can't believe anything here would push a doctor over the edge to mass murderer."

Gunn watched over Robinson's shoulder while he scrolled down through Google's hits. "What's that one?" Gunn pointed to an old reference to Charles's family. "See what's there."

"Looks like he has a sister Françoise Maçon." Robinson's search turned up a reference to her at the World Trade Center. She had been killed in the collapse on 9/11. "That might provide enough incentive for a madman to target some of the Arabs anyway. What do you think?"

Gunn pounded his desk. "What if my actions prevent a conviction? What if my inaction lets more people die?" The FBI will worry about legality. He supposed cops were held to a higher legal standard than he. Courts and public opinion expect doctors to save lives. "Don't I have to stop him?" Gunn tightened his fist and pounded his desk so hard the bottle of shells from Mele Mele tipped over and some small cowries spilled onto his desk.

Robinson stared Gunn in the eyes. "You seem to know him pretty well. Could your personal relationship be coloring your analysis?"

"If he's our man, I obviously don't know him well enough. Damn, what do I do? What do we do? Is he even our terrorist?"

"I'd say you're under much stronger obligation to stop him than get a conviction."

Gunn hung his head. "I doubt this unintelligible and circumstantial crap would convince the courts or even the Feds to do anything. What do you think?"

Robinson made a non-committal shrug. He scrunched up his face but said nothing.

"No visible danger to Americans. And I can't believe that all of this together rises to the point where anyone would grant a search warrant." Gunn studied Robinson. He seemed to agree. "Can't imagine a judge or the police would do anything." Gunn rubbed his forehead. "Oh, God. You're right. If he's guilty, *I* have to stop him."

Robinson rolled his eyes and shook his head.

"You going to come with me?" Gunn studied the reporter. "I could sure use some muscle if I'm going to confront a terrorist."

"I can't." Robinson shook his head. "My kids and my paper both expect me around this week."

#

Gunn took a small digital recorder and his computer. He opened his gun safe and removed his Dan Wesson RZ-45. "Hello Ball Buster," he said to the empty room as he checked the clip. In five minutes he'd packed enough for a couple of nights and he walked back through the living room.

He wrote a note on a piece of his wife's stationery.

My love Pauline, I have to go on a short trip to Washington. I have an idea who may be behind this—too vague to expect help from any law enforcement agency. As usual I'll carry my .45, and I'll call to fill you in.

I hope to meet Dr. Charles Maçon tomorrow afternoon and get him to confess or convince me he had nothing to do with it. If I call and start my conversation with anything other than *I love you*, call the police to rescue me. I know I'm only being paranoid, but it's a nice way to start my call anyway.

All my love to you,

Gunn

He copied the note and put one on the television in their bedroom and one on her pillow. Hmm. She knew how tired he was. He went to each note and wrote,

P.S., I'm wide awake because of so much adrenaline. I'll take a thermos of coffee and stop and call as soon as I get sleepy. Hope to go part way, maybe to Charlotte or Greensboro. I'll spend the rest of the night in whatever clean-looking motel I can find.

He started the coffee and took his bag to the car. What better protection than a big body guard like Robinson. Too bad he couldn't come along.

Gunn took his quart thermos of caffeine, got into his Mercedes, and headed for Herndon, Virginia.

Chapter 30 – Day 41, Monday, Night

Atlanta

After Gunn left his home he drove slowly to the Northeast Expressway, hoping he'd be awake and alert enough to drive a hundred miles, to be in South Carolina for the night. On the freeway he set his cruise control at 5 mph over the speed limit, working from 60 up to 75 as he left the metro area. He had such a long drive, he decided to take a chance on speeding despite the late hour. Everyone else seemed to get away with it.

A couple of hours later Gunn passed Spartanburg and Charlotte. This was incredible. He never thought he'd make it so far. Amazing what a ton of adrenaline will do. During the long drive he thought about the information and equipment he had. This gun was so heavy. He wished he had a small, easy to hide weapon. At least this one had lots of stopping power.

He made a couple of pit stops and drank most of the quart of coffee. At ten he still felt wide awake. He said "Call Pauline" distinctly and waited while his Galaxy called home. "I love you. I'm continuing. I'm still wide awake and alert. I'll keep you posted."

"Thanks for calling. Be careful." Her voice was slightly slurred.

"I'll try to get him to confess. I have some strong, but all circumstantial, evidence. I've changed my plan during the drive. I'll try to make my phone call you while I'm talking to Charles so you can corroborate my story, if it comes to that." She didn't seem to follow his conversation. They signed off with repeated *I Love You*s.

Finally, about one AM he stopped at a Holiday Inn in Blacksburg, Virginia. He checked in with Pauline. "I love you. I can't believe this. I haven't driven this far so late at night in 20 years." They chatted for a few minutes. After the phone call he turned its volume down and put the ringer on vibrate. Now neither voices nor the ringer could be heard on the phone. He went to bed and was asleep in seconds.

Early in the morning he put on his holster, and secured the pistol in it under his left arm. He turned the recorder on and put it in his right jacket pocket. He spoke at conversational levels and turned on the television, with the volume low, like a quiet conversation. After a couple of minutes, he turned off the TV, and took out his recorder. The playback showed it worked well enough. He put his Galaxy in his left jacket pocket where it barely cleared his pistol. He left for Virein in Herndon.

As he passed Roanoke, Gunn called Charles Maçon at Virein. "I'm in Washington today and wondered if I could take you to lunch?"

"Sounds okay to me. A break will probably do me good." He sounded relaxed.

"I'll be there about 12:30 or 1:00. Want me to pick you up at your office?" They agreed. Gunn reset his cruise control to 72, two miles per hour over the speed limit. He'd heard Virginia had unmarked state patrol cars.

He voice-dialed Pauline to tell her he loved her and give her some modifications to the details of his plans, things his subconscious produced overnight.

"You sure you want to do this?" She sounded like she was asking him to reconsider and come home, not asking a question.

"This guy may be the most despicable person I know. But maybe he's innocent. I hope to resolve that at least. I've got my Dan Wesson, so I'm well protected. There's also the revolver in the car's safe."

"You know you're scaring me." Her voice pleaded.

"I'll be careful."

She groaned.

\#

When Gunn got out of his car in Herndon, he turned his recorder on. A gong sounded when he opened the door into Virein's office. It had a vacant reception area. He started to look at some glossy but very old product brochures framed on the wall. Must be the last time they split with that much money for brochures.

Charles Maçon appeared. "Hey, Gunn. Glad to see you." He held out his hand.

Sure seems nice. Darn. He hoped he hadn't made some horrible mistake. Well, he knew he'd never seen any indication Charles was a terrorist. "I hope you picked out a place to eat. I'm starved." Gunn shook his hand. "I don't know this area at all."

"Perfect. Got a good place. Not great, but good. I thought you'd be ready to go. Let's do it." They headed out the door into the parking lot chatting about the weather and the fact it was late enough in the day and early enough in the week that it would be easy to get a table.

Gunn motioned toward his black S63 in a visitor slot next to the front door. "I can drive."

"You drove all the way up here?"

Charles's skepticism made Gunn wonder if he'd made a mistake not to rent a car for the day. "Yeah. I had some time to kill and hate the way TSA treats everyone. It wasn't as bad as I expected. The Blue Ridge is beautiful."

During lunch Gunn asked about Virein's finances and its relationship with banks. The answers confirmed his fear that Charles blamed the banks for a major part of Virein's troubles. But nothing he said indicated any particular hostility toward any group.

They finished the main course. "In the midst of researching some background on Virein products I stumbled across a Françoise Maçon who was killed on 9-11. Is she any relation to you?" Gunn put his utensils on his plate and pushed it slightly toward the center of the table. It was time to start testing his theory.

"Yeah. She was my little sister. Mom was so busy, I raised her like a daughter. My single-mom had to work, so I was more her father than Mom was a mother. The God damned Arab terrorists killed her." Charles had finished his meal, but occasionally poked at the remnants of his salad.

"Oh, God. I had no idea. I didn't mean to open an old wound." Gunn studied Charles.

"Fucking Arabs." Charles was mumbling so low it was hard to hear.

Gunn doubted the recorder would pick that up. Even if it did, it only confirmed what he already knew. "Wow. That makes a tough life for a kid. I mean, having to raise siblings seems much harder than anything I think kids should have to worry about." Gunn knew that many children were forced to raise children, especially now with so many single parents.

Charles ordered a piece of apple pie à la mode for dessert. His face reddened. "It's not even an old wound." Charles's teeth clenched and his jaw muscles flexed. "Hardly a day passes when I don't miss her. Her death was more like losing a daughter than a sister. We had sibling love, not rivalry. His voice was still low. "She'd just been offered an off-Broadway lead. Her dream of being an actress was finally becoming real and the bastard Arabs killed her days before her first starring role."

Gunn would not lean forward. It might improve the audio recording quality, but it might allow Charles to see his holster. Not worth the chance. He was already too nerdy with his jacket buttoned. "No one can be prepared for losing a child. Or a kid sister. That has to be the most horrible thing possible. I can barely imagine what you must be going through."

Should he try to lower Charles's anger level? Anger might push him to reveal something, but polemics against a group would not be enough to prove anything. "What are *your* non-work activities?"

"For an entrepreneur there isn't any *non-work*. I work and I'm married to it. Eat, live and sleep Virein." Charles talked normally. "It is my family now." The ice cream and filling for his pie were gone.

"Can you tell me about your sister? Is the play she was going to be in one I might know?" Gunn motioned to the waiter to bring the check.

"No. It wasn't any big name play. I can't even recall the name right now. Something about boating or something. But it was important to Françoise and to her acting career." Charles's face color returned to normal.

"I suppose she must also have had a job in the Twin Towers?" Gunn puzzled over Françoise's fate. The attacks were in the morning, not a common time for aspiring actors' jobs as waiters.

"Yeah. She was a paralegal at a small company on the twelfth floor of WT2. She must have been helping others escape. Nearly everyone else in the firm and on that floor made it out." Charles put his hand to his eyes, probably to hide the tears.

"Wow. That's an impressive back-up job for an actor." Gunn looked at the ceiling. "I thought they all supported themselves as waiters. You had an extraordinary sister."

"Yeah. She was really smart."

"You said she was like a daughter to you. I have some idea of what losing a child is like." Gunn closed his eyes for a second as he shook his head. "My son went into the hospital last week and was diagnosed with a hemorrhagic virus two days ago. He must have picked it up in Baghdad, part of the outbreak in the Mideast." Calling John a *son* instead of a *son-in-law* should elicit more sympathy. "We're terrified for John and for our granddaughter, who may lose her father." The waiter brought the check. Gunn looked at it for about a second and handed the waiter his American Express card.

"Oh. What was he doing in Baghdad?" Charles's tone was conversational. Only his words showed any concern that his *friend* might lose a son. Charles started to extract his wallet from his back pocket.

Gunn motioned for Charles to put his money away. He realized he'd said no one could prepare for losing a child, then he'd told Charles he was preparing. Gunn hoped Charles didn't pick up on his mistakes. "He was stationed there. Doing what one marine can. Trying to keep the terrorists at bay." Gunn added a tip and signed the credit card ticket for their lunch.

At Virein Charles led Gunn into his office. "Come on in. Let me tell you about some of our latest work." The tiny office had a window behind the desk with a beautiful view of the parking lot. No pictures adorned the walls or desk of the tiny office. A few papers were on Charles's metal desk. He motioned for Gunn to sit in the side chair and went behind his desk. As he sat, Charles pointed to a dish of red and black Twizzlers. "Help yourself if you'd like some more dessert."

So far the only negative comments Gunn had heard were vague racist remarks. He needed to lure Charles into talking more about his virology work, perhaps he would reveal something that tied him to the outbreaks. The technical smarts and equipment to create MEFV are almost as distinctive as a fingerprint. Maybe Gunn could elicit information about work Charles had done with viruses and yeast.

"Your web site says you're modifying fungi to increase their protein content. It sounded like you expect to have a GM mushroom that has as complete protein as a hamburger?" Gunn tried to recall what he'd seen about Virein. He leaned back in his chair and looked out the window at the sky.

"That *is* what we're doing. We're pretty sure we can make mushrooms that are nutritionally a substitute for meat."

"Nutritionally equivalent?" Gunn stared blankly at Charles.

"Uh-huh. As complete a protein. We're working on trace constituents to improve taste, texture and nutritional balance."

"Wow. That is impressive." He glanced out the window. "Are you using viruses to modify the genes?" Gunn looked back at Charles Maçon.

"That's it."

"Do you have time to give a quick tour of your lab here?"

"Yeah. It won't take long. We don't have much." Charles rose and motioned for Gunn to walk toward the lab. Like any proud entrepreneur, Charles showed Gunn the facilities from outside the room that housed their lab. He talked about their work on MeatRooms.

There was very little equipment for handling dangerous agents, nothing approaching BSL-3, let alone the level four biosafety hazard that the CDC required for Ebola. Didn't mean they couldn't have Ebola here, but it seemed unlikely. Gunn kept his hands in his pockets and touched nothing.

"I have some work I have to get done right away, so I'll let Dr. Darrel Li tell you more about our work." Charles pointed to the person sitting next to the lab door. He introduced them and said a few words about each person's work before excusing himself.

Darrel described the work they were doing, viral detection and gene modification, and how it showed promise for increasing the world's food supply and quickly isolating viruses such as the EBOV in the Middle East.

"Oh, are you working on MEFV, the Middle East HFV?" Gunn studied Darrel.

"No. Not working on it." Darrel shook his head. "Trying to sell fast virus detector to Israelis to fight epidemic there. We need money so I talked to them."

"How do you know it'll work? Have you tried your test on any RNA viruses? You don't really have any facilities here, do you?"

"We have a few. We have RESTV because it's safe for us to use."

While that may not have been a smoking gun, it was damn close. No make that darn close. If it was eight years ago they got their RESTV from Hazelton, Gunn should be able to find some distinctive sequences in it. If any of them appeared in MEFV, it would pretty well nail the coffin. "Yeah, I remember some work quite a few years ago. How long have you had the RESTV?"

"About ten years."

Bingo. But that still didn't explain how they could have developed MEFV. "You used to have a much bigger lab. Did you have more equipment then?"

"We had much better and more equipment." Darrel nodded. "Don't know what happened to it. Maybe stored away somewhere."

Chapter 31 – Day 42, Tuesday

Herndon, Virginia

Darrel took Gunn to Charles's office so he could say goodbye. Darrel closed the door as he left. Charles pointed to his chair and mouthed that he'd be off the phone in a few seconds.

Charles returned the phone to its cradle. "Not much of the old Virein left anymore. You can see why we weren't able to help you a month ago."

Gunn nodded. He might as well go for the throat. "Yeah. You must have more equipment someplace. I can see why you were so mad at the Arabs, as you call them, after 9-11, but why the Israelis? Or was that just an accidental release?" Gunn spoke in a slow staccato and mumbled some words, but spoke *one-one* for *eleven*. He moved his gaze to the window for a second to avoid Charles glare. Charles motion refocused his attention.

He had a 38 revolver leveled at Gunn. "And now give me that pistol under your jacket. Do it slowly." He held the pistol out at arm's length. The muzzle was only about a yard from Gunn's chest.

Gunn was unsure of how to react. He bolted upright in his seat. "I don't have a gun." He could feel his eyes dilate and a questioning expression appear on his face.

Then he remembered it was there. "Oh. I do have one" He raised his right hand in the air and slowly unbuttoned his jacket with his left hand. "What's the problem. I carry it for traveling. I always take it on long drives."

"Go ahead. Take it out slowly and put it on my desk." Charles now had two hands on his revolver.

Gunn pulled the lapel of his jacket so the holster was clearly visible, though the 45 was not where Charles could see it because of the desk. "I'm right handed. I'll take it out with my left hand, is that okay?"

"Yes. That's good. And keep it pointing at yourself."

"I'm reaching down to get it from the holster and set it on your desk." Gunn did as he described and ended with the 45 on the edge of Charles's desk, pointing more or less in his direction.

"Thank you, now back away from the desk so you can't reach it."

Gunn put his hands on the arms of the chair and pushed it back. "Can you tell me what's going on? Why are you doing this?" He hit the wall and put his hands up again. He was less than three feet from the desk. He tried to think of ways to get out of the mess. His gun was no longer of any use, at least not to him.

"You're questions are too pointed. You know too much."

Gunn sat at attention with his hands in the air.

"Anyway, to answer your question, my father was killed by police in Jerusalem when he was in the Holy Land on a pilgrimage. Those fucking Israelis never even apologized."

"Oh my God. What extraordinary losses."

"It may have been unintentional, but he was still killed. You may be next." Charles leaned over his desk and pulled the Dan Wesson farther from Gunn's reach.

"What, you mean because of," Gunn paused, "my concern for your *nine-one-one* loss? Of course I'm distressed that you lost your sister. Your company is struggling and I was trying to help you."

"Be quiet. I've got to figure out what to do." Charles looked distracted. He moved Gunn's pistol into the desk's top right drawer.

Gunn was quiet for about 10 seconds. "How am I supposed to be quiet when you're pointing a gun at me?" He spoke loudly and tried to sound as agitated as possible.

"Shut up, damn it." Charles held his pistol up. He waved it as though it were the handle of a whip. He was flailing Gunn with his imaginary lash. He stopped with the pistol pointed toward Gunn's mouth. "I can always permanently shut you up."

"What the hell." Gunn paused a few seconds. He hoped his phone had dialed. Only way to check required reaching in his pocket to unmute the smart phone. Something he couldn't do. "Do you need money?"

"Shut up."

Gunn was quiet for about five seconds. "Would you please not point that gun at me?" As before he spoke loudly and tried to sound in a panic. He looked at Charles with the largest eyes he could manage. He must look terrified and obedient. It seemed like it had been a half hour since he carefully pronounced *call 9-1-1*. He hoped his Galaxy had called for help. If it had been that long, the call didn't work. What should he do? Try to mollify him?

"Do you want to call *Pauline*? She'll confirm that I'm no threat to you." If the Phone hasn't called 9-1-1, maybe it would call some one else who can help. Will Pauline even recognize the problem? Oh, yeah, of course she will. She knows what I'm up to and where I am.

Maybe I can get him talking about Françoise. "Can you tell me about your sister? Or the play? Was it Broadway or Off-Broadway?" What questions could he ask to take Charles's mind off whatever he was planning. "Had she actually started her starring role before *nine-one-one*?"

"Quiet."

"May I call Pauline." Gunn paused for a fraction of a second longer than normal. "She played one of the nurses in South Pacific in high school. Did Françoise's role include any singing?"

"No. No singing. Musicals are passé now, at least in legitimate theater. Nobody but high schools do them anymore." For the first time in minutes he looked at Gunn as he spoke.

"I had rotator cuff surgery about six months ago and my shoulder really hurts. May I put my hands down?"

"Yeah, okay. But keep your hands on the chair arms and don't do anything fast."

"Of course. I won't do anything to make you nervous. When you point your gun at me it scares the devil out of me." The last sentence Gunn spoke quite loud. He hoped someone was listening.

Gunn looked around the office. Nothing looked like it would help him calm the situation or allow him to take charge. Through the window behind Charles he saw three police cars pull into the parking lot. The police ran from their cars, but he couldn't see them after that. He heard the faint sound of a gong. Complete change of tactics. It would be nice to get a confession on tape, preferably the 9-1-1 tape. But if the call went to Pauline, then there is no 9-1-1 tape. Hope my recorder is working.

"Did you distribute the Ebolavirus in the Mideast? Is that why you pulled the gun on me?" Gunn's attention was fixed on Maçon and his pistol.

"Shut up. I need to think. You were too heavily armed. And you're too fucking inquisitive." Charles seemed deep in thought, but he never took his eyes off Gunn.

No chance to move safely. "Do you think killing Americans will get you off the hook? A jury here would probably acquit for the murders in Baghdad, but not if you go on killing.

Charles stared at Gunn. He wore the expression of the hardened killers in 1930's Cagney or Bogart movies. No remorse. No care about another's life. After a long pause he nodded.

"Does your nod mean 'yes?' You might as well say it out loud so the recorder picks it up." Gunn watched him carefully.

Charles screwed up his face. "What recorder?" His snarl said more than words.

"Well there are several. The one at 9-1-1 and the one in my pocket. And, of course, the police are probably outside your door listening right now. Don't you want to be clear for posterity?"

Charles glowered. "The Arabs killed Françoise and the Jews killed Dad and Virein."

"What Jews killed your father?" Gunn tried to sound as skeptical as possible. "Was that what your quiet muttering said?"

"Shut up, Gunn. Let me think. Dad was an innocent bystander killed by Israeli police. They may not have meant to kill him, but they've never even said it was an accident."

"It's all over, Charles. Look outside." Gunn pointed toward the window behind him.

"Yeah, sure." Charles rolled his chair to a slight angle so he could see out and still watch Gunn.

The door burst open. Gunn dove for the floor. He hoped the desk would be between him and Charles's revolver. He heard it go off. His ears rung.

In a few seconds, minutes or hours to Gunn, the police had both men against the wall. Gunn saw Charles revolver in the corner. He must have dropped it and as it discharged. "The phone that called you is in my pocket," Gunn said. He nodded toward his jacket pocket.

The officer patted Gunn's pants and jacket and extracted the Sony recorder and the smart phone. He held the phone to his ear. "Hello?" Another policeman put cuffs on Charles.

"I turned the volume all the way down, officer." Gunn's hands were still against the wall. "You'll have to turn it up to hear whoever's on the line."

The cop looked at the phone. He pushed the volume button several times. "Hello, officer?" the Galaxy spoke.

Gunn relaxed. Pauline's voice. "I'm okay," he said in a loud voice. So, his attempts to call 9-1-1 had failed, but one of the ones to Pauline worked.

The police finished securing everything from both Charles and Gunn. Recorders, phones, wallets. They had not yet checked the desk.

"I have a Dan Wesson 45 automatic, which is in the top right desk drawer. Dr. Maçon took it from me."

Gunn was still in handcuffs. That was incredibly stupid. Now I have some idea how smart people can do such idiotic things. My job is take care of my family, not hunt mass murderers. I try to do the best thing for people and nearly get myself killed. Idiot.

Chapter 32 – Day 44, Thursday

Darrel Li in Herndon, Virginia

Darrel still felt confused by the arrest of his boss, the company president, the Candy Man, Dr. Charles Maçon. He did not understand what happened Tuesday when they led Dr. Maçon off in handcuffs. The police asked him a few questions about Ebola. He knew nothing about it. He did not ask; they did not tell. One of the basic survival rules in China was, "never say anything to police unless you have to."

He had not been allowed into their lab yesterday but decided to try again today. He went in the building entrance and saw everything was still closed. A man in a generic suit saw Darrel walk in and greeted him.

"Are you Dr. Darrel Li?" The attitude did not seem particularly friendly.

"Yes." Darrel studied the man. Another cop?

"I'm Special Agent Foyd." He held out his badge.

Darrel studied the brass badge. It had an eagle atop a bulbous shield. Is it a real badge? How would I know? Better assume it is. "Hi Mr. Floyd."

"Foyd, not Floyd." He spoke mechanically. "We are investigating the activities of Charles Maçon and Virein. Do you or did you work for Virein?"

"Yes." He seemed to know the answer before he asked the question. For 18 minutes Darrel answered questions about his background, and what he did at Virein. No questions related to his contacts with MSS Agent

Chen or Mossad Agent Rosenthal, or whoever the Chinese and Israeli agents really were. Only answer questions asked. Never volunteer any information. The FBI may be less dangerous than the MSS, but the rule still seemed correct. Answer with monosyllables whenever possible.

Chapter 33 – Day 44, Thursday

Honolulu

Jeanne Anne picked up Gunn and Pauline at Honolulu airport. "I didn't know whether to take Mele Mele out of school or not. Hope you don't mind she's not here, Dad."

"Good choice, Honey. This MEFV is so dangerous, I don't want her anywhere near it. I'm glad John went to the hospital from his flight back. Good thing you didn't get close to him." They headed for Kaneohe Bay Hospital.

Gunn identified himself to the receptionist as they signed in. The head nurse of the isolation ward met them and introduced Gunn to John's nurse in his anteroom.

"At least we'll get in and see him this time," Jeanne Anne said.

"He's still very sick," the nurse said. "If your father weren't here, we wouldn't let you into his room." Ms. Rianna Whitfield according to her name tag. She turned to Gunn. "We've given him a general antiviral, Relenza."

"No Zmapp?"

"No," the nurse answered. "We're trying to get some, but it hasn't gotten here yet. Too much Ebola, not enough Zmapp to go around."

"What? What the Hell's going on?" Gunn clenched his eyes and his fists. His whole body trembled. "Oh." Gunn swallowed his damnation. "Excuse me, I know you had nothing to do with the Zmapp shortage, I was yelling at the system, not you. Please forgive me. I've been trying to stop all this sailor talk for Jeanne Anne's sake and my own." Gunn pointed to their daughter. "It actually sounds like you're doing the best you can."

"He's also on Vancomycin to prevent opportunistic infections, sir." She held out John's chart for Gunn.

"Thank you, Ms. Whitfield." Gunn looked through the window in the inner door at the *margarita* drip on John's IV stand and wished the vanc was as nice as a real margarita. He looked at the chart for a couple of minutes. The three visitors put on light red bunny suits and covers over their shoes. Pauline started to take off her heels, but was stopped by Gunn. "Leave your shoes on. They provide much more protection than the booties. We have to make sure everything is covered, including your shoes. When we're done they'll burn the shoe-covers and everything else."

"Dad, you said Ian has completely recovered?" Jeanne Anne watched her father.

Gunn stopped. He held the mask in his hand. "Yes. He says he feels fine now, not 100%, but getting better every day. His lingering weakness is what you'd have the day after a bad case of flu. Right now his biggest problem is he lost most of his hair." Gunn looked at his daughter. "Actually, because Colleen is at the end her chemo, she may prefer him bald."

"Colleen's his wife?"

"Yeah. And in Africa the only common lasting effect of Ebolavirus has been ostracism. Friends and relations are afraid of recovered EBOV patients. Many rof them had to move from their villages, because of fear of the people around them. Unjustified fear. When people survive, recovery is complete." Damn, why'd I say that? Darn it, I must not scare her.

"Unjustified ostracism, like the way AIDS patients were treated in the '90s?" Jeanne Anne's expression was a mixture of fear and questioning.

"Yes."

"And you told me I can't touch him except through all this stuff? I have to keep my double gloves on?" Jeanne Anne had the questioning expression Gunn remembered from years of her growing-up interrogations.

"Yes. Touching isn't safe. This is a horrible virus. Very infectious. It may be able to go right through your skin. We have to stay completely covered. I think the normal protocol is to allow no visitors. Remember, they only let you in because I'm here. It's that bad."

"Thanks, Dad. It *will* be my first time in his room." Jeanne Anne touched her father's arm.

They finished dressing in hair covers, surgical gloves, masks for their mouths and eyes. Their reddish astronaut suits covered everything, even their faces. The same procedure Gunn, Wild Bill and Moshe had used in Tel Aviv when visiting Ian, only the color had changed.

"Let me apologize before we go in, Jeanne Anne. I have to ask John some questions. I have to try to puzzle out how he contracted this horrible virus."

"Yeah, I understand, Dad. I know your job."

When all three were completely covered in their hazmat suits, the nurse let them into John's room. Gunn despaired. John's arms looked gangrenous. Did he need treatment for that too? Gunn started planning his MEFV questions. He had to make sure there was not some new transmission mechanism in John's case.

Marine Major and son-in-law John Dalton showed the classic end-game symptoms of hemorrhagic fever. He had a severe rash that resembled the one Ian displayed the day Gunn left to return to the U.S. His arms were almost completely covered by red-purple pimples and blisters. Some of his skin was black. Gunn pulled the sheet over some of the worst sores. "Have they fixed you so you don't hurt too much?"

John's nod was barely perceptible, as though even nodding hurt. Headache and joint pain. Typical, unfortunately.

Ian had recovered. Gunn knew John's prognosis was worse, the military had not received the EBOV vaccine.

Jeanne Anne went to John's bedside and took his hand. "How do you feel today, Darling?" Gunn wished they could touch each other, skin to skin. Too dangerous.

John smiled. His mouth moved but no sound came out.

"I love you." Jeanne Anne bent down so her ear was closer to his mouth.

John closed his eyes and squeezed Jeanne Anne's hand.

Pauline walked around to the other side of his bed, next to all the hookups.

"Oh, God. How I love you." Jeanne Anne studied her husband's disfigured face.

The monitor beside his bed stopped beeping. Just a tone.

"Oh my God." Gunn put his arm around his daughter. "He stayed in this world long enough to say *I love you.* He struggled to stay alive, so he could tell you."

Jeanne Anne turned and buried her head on Gunn's shoulder. "Oh. Dad. ...."

Pauline started around the bed, back to where Gunn and Jeanne Anne were. One step and the heart monitor started to follow her. "Oh God. I'm caught." Pauline disentangled herself, moved to her daughter and hugged her.

"Oh, dear God." Gunn squeezed Jeanne Anne, hoping to comfort her a little. "This has to be even worse than seeing two marines at your door."

Jeanne Anne sobbed and pounded on her father's chest. "No. No. No."

"Oh, dear." Gunn realized he used a mild word and thanked his subconscious for being cleaner than in years. "How can we tell Mele Mele? Maybe remind her about the passing of her pet cat, Raoul." Dear Lord, a ten year old shouldn't learn so much about death.

"No. Wait, maybe it's not the end," Pauline said. "Check the monitor, Gunn. Maybe I pulled some wire loose."

Gunn ran around the bed, picked up a cable from the floor and plugged it into the monitor. Its beautiful beeping restarted.

\#

The next day Gunn returned from some errands for Jeanne Anne. When he walked in
the door, Pauline called to him. "They're interviewing Amhach about the MEFV outbreak,
containment and the arrest of Charles Maçon. The news people seem to be making your
director the hero."

"Life's a bitch and then you die." Gunn hugged Pauline.

Chapter 34 – Day 71, Wednesday, 4:30

Atlanta

The FBI agent came into Gunn's office, right on time. After introductions he fumbled with the package he held. "We found a journal in Maçon's apartment. Most of it shows the deranged person who unleashed the Ebola. We'd like you to look through some parts of it and see if there's anything more you think we should be concerned about, or information we might need to prosecute Charles Maçon. Special Agent Foyd held out the large envelope.

"Will do." Gunn took the thick brown envelope.

"It is a partial copy of what we think is Charles Maçon's handwritten diary. This part should include all the information we have about his Ebola development. A few redactions have been made, but it is mostly intact and legible. His handwriting is unusually good for a doctor." Agent Foyd pointed to the sealed brown envelope with his card stapled to the front.

"Anything special you want from me on this?" Gunn glanced at the envelope. It was labeled "Confidential."

"Best for us? If you could mark it up to make it more accessible to a typical investigator or lawyer. If you can translate any medical jargon, it will help us. You can write your translations right on this copy. Most important is explaining any parts we might need to get a conviction."

"Okay. Sounds easy enough."

"We've also included some parts of the diary we thought you might want to see. Things of minor legal importance, but ones that may impact you personally."

"Ooh. Thank you, sir." Gunn stood. "I didn't realize you knew about my personal involvement?" Gunn looked at Foyd.

"Yes, sir. We're glad your son-in-law finally recovered. The least we can do at this point is give you a little background and closure. Please call us as soon as you're done."

"Of course I will and I'll get to it right away. I see it's labeled *confidential*. How do I treat it?"

"Ideally it should be locked up and shown to no one." Foyd pointed at the big red stamp on the envelope. "We don't expect you to have training in handling sensitive information, but your normal medical confidentiallity and keeping this locked up the best you can is all we expect. *Confidential* is primarily a classification level meaning little more than *keep it from the press*."

"We have all sorts of safes here, I can lock it in one of them if you like."

"That would be good. Thank you."

Gunn nodded and studied Agent Foyd.

"We hope you don't mind. We'll probably want to depose you on the diary. You know, to make sure we understand it."

"Do you think I'll be called to testify at his trial?"

"No way to know." Foyd looked deep in thought for a few seconds. "He may not go to trial. Might even be extradited and tried in Israel or somewhere. I have no idea how this will play out."

"If you're allowed to talk about it. I have one question."

Foyd nodded. "Ask away. I'll see if I can answer."

"Charles had one employee at the end, a Chinese researcher, Darrel Li." Gunn studied Special Agent Foyd. "He seemed so painfully shy, is he implicated in this mess?"

"You hit one of the interesting sidebars. A lot of that is classified. As far as we can tell, Dr. Li was only trying to get money for the company. We've nothing so far indicating he knew anything about the spread of the germs. At this time we have no reason to believe he was involved in causing the outbreaks." Foyd described the FBI's best explanations for Darrel Li's contacts with foreign governments.

After Agent Foyd left, Gunn took a red pen from his top desk drawer, and sat down at his desk with the facsimile of Charles Maçon's diary. He annotated Charles's technical jargon and put in some remarks of his own.

Toward the end of the diary section he found complete confirmation of his work:

> I have a lot more respect for Julie, now. Selling was a lot harder than I realized. In Israel I discovered that salesmen really earn their commissions. How can they stand the constant rejection? I'd always thought they made tons on sales, and some may, but boy you have to take a lot of "get lost" to make a sale.

> I got into three small bakeries with no trouble but couldn't get close to the yeast store for any large bakeries. I figured it was time for me to get out of there before it hit the fan. Same treatment in Baghdad. By now I'm beginning to look and feel like a pastry importer. Did I miss my real calling?

> I asked for a tour of the bakeries I got into and spread a little finely ground Maçon yeast in the air near their yeast or sourdough starter. I suggested I import their breads into the U.S. and their greed did the rest.

\#

"I've just been going over Charles Maçon's diary for the FBI. You want to know the worst part I found?"

Pauline nodded.

"DARPA, I mean the Defense Research Projects Agency, knew about this bug and how it had been developed but said nothing. They didn't tell anyone. I don't know, maybe they think it's a national security issue or possibly they never connected the dots, but in a very real sense they're responsible for John's MEFV."

"Our government seems to do a good job of alienating." Pauline rolled her eyes and shook her head. "Or maybe it's our form of government. We try to rescue countries from despots, and instead, or at least in addition, we create Al-Qa'ida, Khorasan, ISIS/Daish and I wonder how many other terrorist groups. And it sounds like DARPA's concentration on a poorly conceived mission almost killed our granddaughter's father."

Maybe they should try getting rid of Defense from DARPA's name. Go back to just ARPA again. Gunn thought about the wide variety of good and questionable research they'd supported. The continuing rumors of non-lethal weapons for police sounds like a good, maybe even great, cause. Ignoring possible threats to Americans from their weaponization of biologicals, is pretty awful. He rubbed his nape.

She nodded. "I think we deserve a vacation. Can you get away so we can go to Hawaii?"

"Yeah. Let's do it." He bit his lip. And no more damn swearing.

– THE END –

Author's Note on Science and Acronyms

Science

A scientist reviewed parts of this manuscript and basically said it's not possible. Some of the specific problems this virologist noted are listed below. This novel plays on the real and truthful desire for revenge and the near-universal fear of uncontrollable forces, like terrifying diseases. Hopefully my readers will not be offended by the implausibility of the virology. After all it may be possible for Melioidosis, PEDv (Porcine Epidemic Diarrhea Virus), or rabies, if not Ebola.

The virologist said:
1. Probably impossible for a mammalian virus to replicate in yeast. Only possible for individual proteins, not whole viruses.
2. CDC would be able to identify a hybrid of Ebola viruses.
3. PCR results can be delivered in 24 hrs.
4. All evidence suggests that a direct blood-blood or virus-to-blood pathway is required for initial dissemination. Even in outbreak areas, those who adopted safe practices were not infected.
5. If contaminated flour was the (successful) culprit, contamination should have been in all bread from any given bakery, which implies outbreaks would be more clustered.

In retrospect, given our experience here in the U.S. with EBOV, we should no longer be so afraid of this virus. If you get it, the disease is terrible. But no casual contact of the man in New York, nor of the very sick Texan, contracted the disease. Only the nurses, who dealt with the Texan's bodily fluids, got sick. Otherwise healthy patients generally survive with routine ICU maintenance, even without vaccines, antibodies, or other drugs. [Author's note: this doesn't take into account mis-diagnosis, which has often happened with the first cases of almost any disease appear in one area, like the Texan's virus mentioned above. The CDC requires a level four Bio Safety Lab for handling Ebola and similar agents. They are rare: none are in Middle East and even in the United States there are less than fifteen.]

Many governments have experimented with the weaponization of diseases, including some of those in the *Filoviridae* family such as Ebolavirus and Marburgvirus. The Soviet Union and Russia have admitted several laboratory cases of Ebola and Marburg hemorrhagic fevers. At least this novel should provide some fodder for conspiracy theorists who don't pay attention to likelihood, veracity or plausibility.

Acronyms

Most acronyms or initialisms that are invented, unusual or specific to the CDC or U.S. Government are listed here. Eliminating them would make the dialog, even internal dialog, unrealistic. Some government employees, especially those like Dr. Amhach in the fact-free faction, hide behind the acronyms because they don't know what they're talking about.

Acronym Pronunciation Meaning

Acronym	Pronunciation	Meaning
BSL	Bee sil	Bio-safety level (BSL-4 is best)
BtEA	Bee teay	Biotechnology Entrepreneurs Association [*]
BTW		By the way (texting shorthand)
CDC	See dee see	Center for Disease Control and Prevention
CM	See em	Candy Man or Charles Maçon
DARPA	Darpa	Defense Research Projects Agency

---

[*] Author's invention. The H5-- are Gunn and Moshe's code words

Acronym	**Pronunciation**	**Meaning**
DNA	Dee en ay	Deoxyribonucleic acid
EBOV	Ee bov	Ebola virus
H5D1	Ache five dee one	Dengue hemorrhagic fever[*]
H5E1	Ache five ee one	Ebola hemorrhagic fever[*]
H5L1	Ache five el one	Lassa hemorrhagic fever[*]
HFV	Huff vee	Hemorrhagic fever virus
MEFV	Mef vee	Middle-east Filoviridae virus or Filovirus (Ebola's family)
MoH	Em oh ache	Ministry of Health, an Israeli ministry
MSS	Em ess ess	Ministry of State Security (Chinese agency)
RESTV	Rest vee	Reston (ebola) virus
RNA	Are en ay	Ribonucleic acid
SBIR	Sibber	Small Business Innovative Research Program
WT2		World Trade Center tower two

Maps

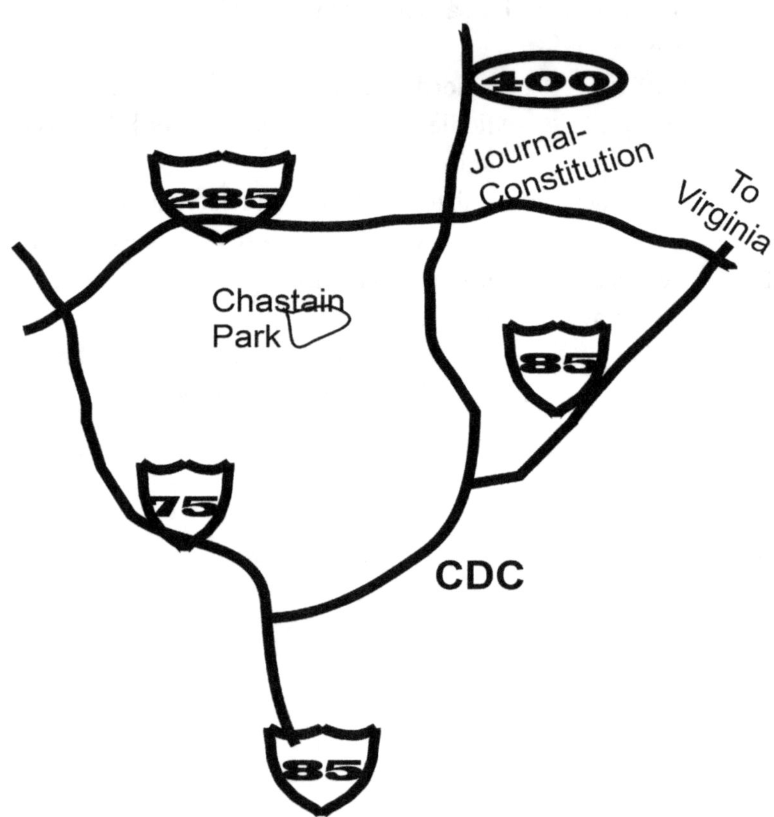

Gunn Shoreham's Atlanta

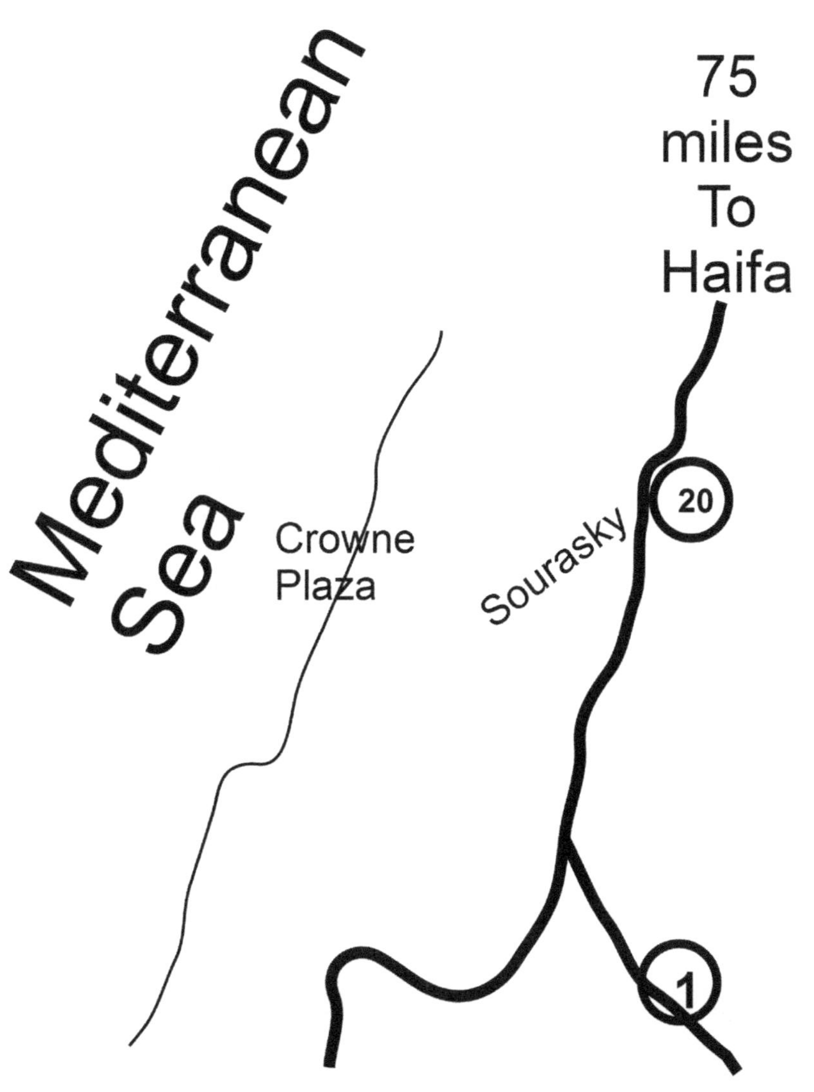

Gunn Shoreham's Tel Aviv